TO MARRY A LORD

Reformed Rakes Series: Book IV

JENN LANGSTON

SOUL MATE PUBLISHING
New York

TO MARRY A LORD

JENN LANGSTON

Cover Design by Rae Monet, Inc.

Published in the United States of America by
Soul Mate Publishing
P.O. Box 24
Macedon, New York, 14502

ISBN: 978-1-64716-009-8

ebook ISBN: 978-1-68291-912-5

www.SoulMatePublishing.com

BY JENN LANGSTON

THE PERFECT SERIES

His Perfect Bride
His Perfect Game
His Perfect Lady

PERFECT SERIES COMPANIONS

Catching the Baron
Winning The Duke
Redeeming The Earl

TOUCHED BY FIRE SERIES

Embracing The Knight
Enslaving The Day
Ensnaring Lord Starsen
Enchanting The Duke Of Demoon

REFORMED RAKE SERIES

To Love A Marquis
To Tame A Viscount
To Teach A Gentleman
To Marry A Lord

To my three, sweet Angels.

I love you more than I can say.

Thank you so much for giving Mommy time to write.

I enjoy every second we spend together,

and I hope none of you grow up to be too cool for me.

Hugs and kisses!

FATHERS, MOTHERS, AND GUARDIANS, do you have unwed children or charges that need to stand apart in the marriage mart? Or, perhaps you have a bad habit you wish to break or a skill you wish to master? Here at *Lady Constance's House of Reform* we specialize in turning pesky problems into vague memories. We offer a range of services that are tailored to your specific needs.

Those who suffer from shyness, lack of social graces, or problematic dancing skills have no reason to fear after seeking our assistance. Our lessons promote confidence when dealing with the opposite gender. Our individualized plans will put anyone at ease.

In addition, we offer schooling in a range of languages. If you are looking to learn Latin, French, Spanish or Italian, we are your best option. We will cater to your needs and set up tutoring that will fit with your lifestyle.

Don't delay! Help is available, now!

For employment opportunities, bring your direct inquiries to the head mistress on Cannon Street. We are seeking strong, capable women. Thank you.

Chapter 1

"Damn it!" Hannah Dobson, Countess of Rivers, exclaimed as she hit her slippered toe on the ill-placed piece of furniture, for what had to be the twelfth time.

Ever since she'd been helping at the House of Reform, she'd commented on the placement of the hall table, but no one listened to her. She supposed it didn't help that she was always in a hurry. A languid pace was not for her.

"Did you hit your toe again," Regina laughed as Hannah limped into the classroom in which they had agreed to meet.

"That bloody table shall be the death of me," Hannah grumbled. "I just don't understand why it needs to be there."

Hannah set her jaw as Lady Regina Serra shook her head. Considering the woman had founded the House of Reform with Lady Constance and the newly married Viscountess Washburne, Hannah firmly believed some of the blame belonged to the young woman. However, she knew it truly wasn't the table that was bothering her. Ever since her friend, Genevieve, married and rushed off to the country, she'd lost another reason to be in London. The trouble was, she didn't exactly belong in the country either.

"If I moved the table, I daresay you would locate it just to stub your toe in its new location. *I* believe it would be better for the two of you to work out your differences."

As Regina burst out laughing at her jest, Hannah rolled her eyes. "I can see nothing amusing here and therefore suggest we move from this topic."

Once the lady composed herself, she straightened her back. "Of course. Did you finish checking in on the classes?"

Hannah nodded, then gave her report regarding which clients appeared distressed and which ones were pleased. Luckily, she hadn't walked in on any gentlemen getting too friendly with their instructors. It didn't happen often, but considering they'd seen several marriages between clients and employees, they needed to be vigilant.

Overall the House of Reform provided good services, and Hannah was pleased to have been a part of it, but she didn't truly belong here either. Since her husband had died, she thought her life would improve, and although it had, she still felt displaced. For ten years, she'd never belonged anywhere, and she suspected that feeling wasn't going to go away anytime soon.

"Very good." Regina leaned back in her chair. "Tonight we shall be celebrating Miss Raycela's betrothal. I've been working with that girl for far too long. Do you plan on remaining for our tradition?"

Shaking her head, Hannah forced a smile. The ladies who seemed against marriage for themselves only gathered together to celebrate the union. Never had they toasted when one of their clients mastered a language or became proficient at the pianoforte. Only for the interminable torment of marriage. It just didn't make sense to Hannah.

"No, I can't stay. That's actually another matter I wanted to discuss with you today. I shall be leaving London soon, and therefore, will be unable to offer my assistance with the classes any longer."

"Leaving? But, why?" Regina seemed truly appalled at the idea.

Hannah laughed at the horror on the woman's face. "Ever since I married all those years ago, I've spent the season in London and the remainder of the time in the country. Even though my husband is gone, I see no reason to end this custom."

"I've spent my whole life in London and can't imagine ever wanting to leave. Is there anything to do in the country? It seems like it would be rather boring."

"Why don't you arrange your schedule to pay me a visit? It would be a wonderful opportunity for you to see, and I would dearly love to have a friendly face and some news of London."

After Regina gave a cautious, yet noncommittal reply, Hannah took her leave. In truth, she had no other manner of answering the question. After all, the estate where she would be spending the winter would be very different than the one where she'd spent the previous winters. For the first time in years, she planned to return to the earl's estate.

In the past, her brother, Anson Greenleaf, Marquis of Melbourne, was kind enough to take her in when her husband had exiled her to the country. However, she would not rely on him any longer. With his new wife and child, it wasn't fair to infringe upon their time. Not to mention, with her husband's death, she now felt slightly more comfortable spending time at the house that had been her prison for her first year of marriage.

A fortnight later, she stepped foot onto her late husband's estate. As she breezed through the doors, she took in a deep breath. It smelled different. She smiled, not sure if it was reality or if it was the knowledge her husband was gone that gave the place a more refreshing aroma. Regardless, she liked it.

"My lady," Mr. Rawlings, the butler, gave a deep bow. "It's wonderful to see you after all this time."

"Thank you. I decided it was past time for my return."

"Of course. I shall have Mrs. Rawlings prepare a room for you."

Knowing she would have a little bit of a challenge with the new Lord Rivers, Hannah put her shoulders back. "The countess's chambers will do nicely. Seeing as my designation hasn't been altered, I see no reason to change my quarters."

"Very good, my lady." The man's face gave no indication to his thoughts.

As she supervised the moving of her trunks, she debated paying a visit to the new lord, but decided against it. She'd been informed that he had taken up residence here a month or so after title had passed on to him. Being the nephew of the late earl and next in line, he'd known this would be his future, so she didn't imagine he'd been surprised. And, considering the man had never approved of her, she didn't intend to remain in his company long. As a matter of fact, she planned to encourage him to spend some time in London.

Considering his past reception of her, she didn't expect he would want to share a household with her. She also understood he needed to examine all of his holdings, not just the country estate. They would be able to manage well together if he spent his winters in London and seasons in the country—the exact opposite of her.

She smiled. This would work out. A few months of this, and she would finally find her place and the feeling of displacement would dissipate. Her future would be simple, she just needed to rid herself of the new earl first.

~ ~ ~

"She's doing what?" Lucius Dobson, Earl of Rivers, slammed his hands on his desk as anger rushed through his body. This was unacceptable, and he suspected the woman knew it. His late uncle's wife always had her own way of doing things, as she was quite spirited.

He groaned. If he couldn't find a way to make her leave, she was only going to make everything more difficult for him. That was not what he needed right now.

"Mr. Rawlings, please show the countess to my study at once."

The man bowed and left the room. Lucius let out a sigh. He'd known remaining away from the estate all those years would make taking over the earldom more difficult, but he couldn't go back and change that fact now. His uncle had left the books in a fine puzzle and Lucius had wasted too much time before moving here to see to his duty. It didn't matter now. He'd accepted his fate as there was no avoiding it in any case.

"You wished to see me . . . Umm, my lord?" His late uncle's wife gave a small smile. "It seems so strange to address you as such."

He fought off the urge to return her smile as he stood. The woman was even more beautiful than the last time he'd seen her. However, he kept his scowl firmly in place, not wanting to be affected by her. He hated how quickly he noticed everything about her. She had no right to come in here with her blond hairstyle so meticulously perfect framing her high cheekbones and pert nose. Then, there were those brown eyes. Those soulful things had gazed upon him years ago as if he should be the one to save her, but, he could not. He wasn't her husband.

"And, how would you like to address me?" He lifted a condescending eyebrow, needing to bring himself back to the present. "Shall we be Lucius and Aunt Hannah?"

The disgust on her face struck him. "Heavens, no. That would be highly inappropriate. I've never been an aunt to you, and I don't intend to begin now."

"Then, as the Earl of Rivers, you may address me as Lord Rivers."

Her face paled. Interesting.

"I don't believe I'm ready to hear that name again. I suppose we are stuck with my lord and my lady."

Nodding, he held out his hand toward the chair placed before his desk. "Tedious, but serviceable. Please have a seat, my lady."

Again, she smiled and the sparkle in her eyes hit him in the stomach. Why was it she could always do that to him? He turned away, not wanting to notice her beauty any longer. He'd seen his share of attractive women, but none of them had ever compared to her.

She settled in the chair as he took his own seat. "I was rather busy unpacking my belongings, so if this is to be a social visit, I'd dearly love to reschedule for another time."

Clearing his throat, he forced his mind to focus on what he needed to say. "Not simply a visit. Your arrival was a surprise to me, and I don't appreciate being left out of the decisions."

Her lips pinched tight. "I can understand, but my movements don't need to be monitored by you or anyone else. However, I will be happy to inform you that I always spend the season in London and the winter in the country."

It was difficult to stifle his reaction. "You intend to remain here through the winter?"

She nodded. "I understand it's a long time, but I believe it will be a good time for you to use this opportunity. You see, with me being away from London, it's an ideal time to check out the townhouse. I'm certain there is much in the city requiring your attention as the earl spent the majority of his time there."

This time Lucius couldn't keep his jaw from going slack. This woman was dismissing him from his own home? It was true he only recently inherited, but how dare she believe she had a right? This was much worse than he'd originally believed. He crossed his arms.

"I'm not going anywhere. And, if you intend to stay, there needs to be an adjustment to your choice of quarters."

Her eyes narrowed. "My choice of quarters? You mean the countess's chambers? If you hadn't noticed, I'm still the countess."

"That is true, but I'm the new earl, and those rooms are reserved for *my* countess, not my uncle's."

"I will happily vacate as soon as she is found and awarded the title."

They stared at each other, neither one of them flinching. Lucius wondered how his uncle could have put up with this unmalleable creature. From his memory, he didn't recall this difficult side of her. She'd been sweet and carefree. He imagined it was good that . . . No. He wouldn't think along those lines. Moving down that path never served him.

"Think of the talk that would generate. Besides, you can't be comfortable having your room connected to a man who is not your husband."

She tossed her head back. "There will be no talk, considering I'm your aunt. That being the case, I'm not sure we can classify you as a man."

The defiance in her eyes made him clench his fists. She was deliberately goading him. As if she believed doing so would make him change his mind and leave for London. Well, she had it completely wrong. He would not be manipulated.

"Although your assessment of me and the situation is quite incorrect, I'll not remain here arguing with you. If you insist, you may remain in the countess's quarters, but I will also be remaining in mine."

She nodded. "Good. Then, I have no reason to believe that you would use that door. Therefore, I have nothing to fear from you. As I said—not a threat."

The defiant tilt of her head ignited him. He wanted to tell her how she was wrong. To give her reason to be afraid. To warn her that he had every right to use that door. But, he couldn't force himself to do such a thing. No matter how furious she made him, she deserved to feel safety of her own—albeit temporary—quarters.

"Now that we have the rooms established, I want you to know that this will be nothing like London. I'm not here to socialize or to attend parties. Don't expect anything from me, because you will not receive it." Her eyes widened, but he ignored her surprise. "I'm certain you have matters you would like to attend, so you may leave."

With her mouth slightly agape, she woodenly stood and left his study with her back straight. Once she was gone, Lucius let out a sigh of relief. Her being here was not ideal, but he would manage. Likely she was accustomed to an active social life and would hope to connect with the nearby families.

The winter months would be long, but if she spent the majority of her time elsewhere, he wouldn't be bothered by her presence. Yes. That was the solution. The manor was large, and he saw no reason to stand on ceremony.

He simply needed to keep his mind focused on his lengthy task ahead and ignore any distractions. That being the case, before long she would be returning to London. Then, once he deciphered all of his uncle's ramblings, the books would be in working condition, and he would finally be able to find his own bride and move on with his own life.

~ ~ ~

Hannah shoved the needle in the fabric, listening to the hum of the thread as it pulled through. Normally, she adored embroidering. It was her little secret that had kept her sane all these years, but today the activity couldn't hold her interest. She'd been living at her late husband's country estate for a week now, and she was growing restless.

Letting out a sigh, she tossed the offending fabric aside, wishing she had someone she could talk to or a worthwhile task to occupy her time. The out-of-doors were no longer something she enjoyed, and the lack of another human made the long hours tedious. The staff was minimal since no one had been informed the lord and lady would both be in residence, so talking to them took them from their duties.

And, they were most certainly worried after their positions since the earl had passed. She certainly didn't want to be the reason why someone was released.

Her mind drifted to her wretched *nephew*. From their last conversation it was clear the man loathed her, and she had to admit the feeling was quite mutual. Every time she'd seen him, which was minimal over the years, he had seemed perpetually miserable. Never once had she seen him smile. Had he not been such a horrid person, she might have felt inclined to take it upon herself to coax a grin or two out of him, but how could she when he was so decidedly unpleasant? Not to mention the fact he seemed to be ignoring her. He went as far as to take his meals in his quarters.

As she collected her embroidery and put everything away in her basket, she realized her desperation for interaction with another person was so great, she would overlook her prior dealings with the new Lord Rivers at this moment. She shook her head at the sad truth as she made her way to his cave of a study and lightly knocked on the door. The anticipation welling inside her was embarrassing.

The gruff voice inside immediately granted entrance. She smiled. Clearly he wasn't expecting it to be her. Otherwise, she knew he would have put up more of a fight.

"Good afternoon, my lord," she sweetly greeted, ignoring the wide-eyed shock that he quickly masked under a scowl as he got to his feet. "I hope I'm not interrupting something important."

"What can I do for you?" His blue eyes watched her warily.

Clicking her tongue, she leisurely walked around the room, taking in the dark paneling, shelving, and furniture. It was worse than a cave. More like a dark hole in the ground. This room held no happy memories for her, but she wouldn't let them intrude now. After making a circle, she put her hands on the back of the tall chair placed before the great desk. Her husband loved the power he felt from sitting at the larger piece of furniture as she helplessly stood before him.

"I always hated this room. I don't know how you stand it. The decor is dreary and demands a person be in a constant state of distress."

He lifted an eyebrow. "No one is requiring you to be here. So, why have you come?"

Discomforted, she lightly ran her fingers along the fine leather of the chair. His eyes zeroed in on her movement, and his jaw locked. What was she doing wrong? Did he dislike her so much he didn't want her to touch his belongings? She narrowed her eyes.

"When you said you weren't here to socialize, I didn't realize you meant to lock yourself in this room without having the decency to join me at dinner."

His eyes slowly moved back to meet hers, his haughty eyebrow still lifted. "If you wanted to keep up your active social life, you never should have left London."

"Don't pretend to know anything about me. I'm not asking for much, besides, from your lack of social skills, I'd venture to say you would benefit from engaging in an occasional conversation."

The long stare he gave her portrayed nothing of his feelings. "Are you trying to get me to join you for dinner by insulting me? If that's the so-called manners I'm lacking, I'm not sure I wish to sit in on that lesson."

Irritated, she blew out a breath. "I'm merely stating a fact as your manner of speaking to me has never been polite."

"Now I'm impolite? Keep going, this is just getting better and better."

"Never mind. As a matter fact, you can just forget I even came in here. I just thought it would be pleasant for the two of us to spend a marginal amount of time in each other's company. Clearly, I was wrong."

She was frustrated with him and herself. She spun on her heel and marched from the room, slamming the door behind her. That man was horrible, and she never should have lowered herself to resort to speaking to him. Embarrassment stung the backs of her eyes as she stomped through the halls with no particular destination in mind.

"I don't recall you having such a temper."

At the sound of his voice, she jumped. How had he moved so fast? The dimly lit hallway didn't give her much aid in trying to discern his thoughts. However, the fact he followed her meant he felt something. Remorse, perhaps?

"With the infrequency and limited visits, I must reiterate that you know almost nothing of me."

He tilted his head back as if to study her better. "In recent years, I have to agree, but I thought we got along fairly well, perhaps, eleven years ago."

Blinking, she tried to recall the time when he hadn't outright hated her. "I'm sorry, my lord, but not only was that a long time ago, and therefore not an adequate portrayal of my current self, but I can't recall the time you are referring to."

His gaze dropped before meeting hers again. "I suppose our interactions were not as memorable as I thought. Besides, I suspect you've met a significant amount of people since then."

Guilt swamped her. She could remember when her husband had presented her to his nephew soon after they'd wed. At the time, she recalled having known him previously, but she couldn't remember why. Over the difficult years of her marriage, she had blocked out some of the lighter memories of her childhood as they had seemed so far away. It was likely she also had forgotten meeting him as well.

"It's not that, I just feel as though I've always known you."

He nodded. "I suppose I'll accept that. Now, I've come because I'm prepared to offer you a compromise."

Surprised with such a drastic change from the man who normally held no emotion toward her but contempt, she swallowed. "I would be pleased with a compromise as long as the expectations are reasonable."

"Of course. And, this is your opportunity to negotiate your terms. I gather you are wanting to make dinner a more formal affair. I will be amenable to arrange my schedule. Next, you are lacking a companion. I have no objection to visits from your friends or—"

"I thank you for this. Truly, I'm touched, but I also am a little confused." She still couldn't read his expression and that fact irritated her to no end. "Why are you doing this for me? You made it clear you want nothing to do with me and after kicking me from the study you are now offering me anything I want to ensure my happiness?"

He cleared his throat and shifted his feet, clearly uncomfortable. "I understand your confusion. It's true, I haven't exactly welcomed your presence here, and I'm apologizing for my abrupt attitude."

Her mouth dropped open. "Although I'd like to believe this is all true, after years of your demeanor toward me, I don't see you're capable of changing so quickly. From my experience, I would venture to say you want something from me."

"I can't argue with that. As I mentioned, I'm offering a compromise. Traditionally, both parties benefit in some way. However, my apology is sincere. My behavior as of late has been uncalled for due to the circumstances, but I'm hoping you can help with that."

Tired of this game, she crossed her arms. "Just tell me what you want from me, and we can sort out the rest afterward."

He let out a sigh. "Uncle Herman wasn't pleased his estate and title would be passed to his brother's son, not to mention the fact he was quite fond of teaching lessons. To that end, he decided to keep everything about his finances written in code to make my life as difficult as possible. As his wife, I believe you are the key I've been missing. I need you to help me decipher his books."

A cold sweat broke out over Hannah's face. How could she explain that she would never have been used for something so important to her late husband? That he had never loved her? It was humiliating. The thought put fire in her stomach and she refused to allow that horrid excuse for a husband to put her through the torment of admitting such right now. He was dead. She wouldn't allow him to hurt her again.

She straightened her back. "Now that I know what you want, we can return to negotiating my terms."

Chapter 2

Lucius couldn't stop his eyes from straying to the countess as she poured over his uncle's notes. With her head bent down and biting her lip in concentration, she didn't seem to notice him at all. The truth of that stung. He loathed how he was so very aware of her every breath when she didn't notice he remained in the room.

To further complicate matters, she had it right that he didn't like her. He had never approved of her marriage to his uncle, and she hadn't even had the decency to provide the man with an heir. Ten years she'd been given. Surely that was plenty of time. Then, Lucius would have been saved all of this.

He clenched his fists at the familiar bitterness. "Have you found anything yet? I would hate to think I made a compromise for no reason."

As she lifted her head, she glared at him. "How long have you been working on this? Months? And, you expect me to snap my fingers and have the answer? You must be daft if you think it to be so simple."

Leaning back against the cool leather, Lucius crossed his arms. "You were his wife and knew him better than most. One would think you would have better luck deciphering his words."

Her laughter was bitter. "When are you going to stop with all of these assumptions? Why don't you try asking me things instead of telling me what I know? I daresay you will get much farther that way."

With a heavy sigh, he acquiesced. "Tell me, my lady, did you know anything of his intention to code his books in this manner?"

"No." Her defiant chin was lifted as if she expected his challenge, which he would not disappoint.

"I find that difficult to believe seeing as he mentioned you in his letter."

"What letter?"

Her eyes widened, and he silently cursed. He hadn't meant to give so much away. His overwhelming need to beat her always overrode his better judgment. Now, he had to choose his wording carefully lest he reveal too much of himself. From what he'd recently seen of her, he certainly didn't want to offer her any more power than she already possessed.

"Apparently, Uncle Herman wrote me a letter to be sent upon his death. Your name was mentioned."

A pallor washed across her face as she stilled. "What did he say? May I see it?"

Her reaction puzzled him. "I did not bring it with me. Besides, he only mentioned my duty to care for his widow."

Shock registered on her features. Again, he wondered after her reaction. Would she ever make any sense to him, or was he condemned to never understanding her? He wished he knew the answer to that.

"I see."

Although she clearly did not, he stood and moved about the room, needing to distract himself from asking her any additional questions. "After that rather unpleasant letter, I took my time in coming to the estate. I did my duty, but in my own time, not his."

"In a strange way, I believe that would have made him proud."

He spun around to look at her. "Proud? That's not exactly what I was searching for."

Her laughter was music, particularly after the discomfort of their conversation. "I know, but Lord Rivers was quite an unusual man. He didn't act in the manner you would expect from a typical gentleman. I'd expect he would appreciate a little defiance in his heir."

"What about in his wife?" he couldn't help but ask.

The merriment drained from her face. "No. Of course not. In respect to me, he was as typical as they come."

Nodding, Lucius finally felt as though he understood the motivations driving her. After years of obedience to her husband, she was now exercising independence. As the head of this household, he would allow her some, but he had his limits.

"Getting back to the ledger sheets, how long do you suspect it will take to glean anything from them?"

Her sigh was telling. "Honestly, I can't say. It's as if he's written everything in a riddle with no key for us to decipher the clues behind his meeting. There has to be something more."

Lucius swallowed. The woman was smart, as there was something more, but it wasn't something he wanted to share. However, he knew he had no choice if he wanted her full help.

"Turn to the first page," he instructed stiffly. "There's an inscription."

He silently waited as she followed his instructions, then grit his teeth at her audible gasp. So, he hadn't been reading into something from his uncle that didn't exist. She clearly saw it, too.

"He's laughing at you." She sounded shocked. "How could he treat his own heir like this? I would think he would want his estate to be tended to properly."

"Well, since I didn't remain by his side to learn his lessons, I suppose he saw the need to ensure I earn my position now."

She stood and crossed the room to stand before him. "How can you do that? Stand there and defend a man's action we both know is wrong? I may not know you, but I can't believe you've done anything so heinous as to deserve this."

The burning passion on her face resonated with him. He couldn't be sure if it was the sight of her fervor or her defense of him, but he'd never wanted to kiss her more. Remaining motionless cost him dearly. She was glorious and the way her brown eyes smoldered made it clear she saw him now.

He ached for her. So badly, he couldn't stand it. However, she barely knew he existed. And, the part of him she did know, she didn't like. Forcing his body to take in a breath, he attempted to calm his reaction.

Clearing his throat, he looked away. "The man is dead, and there is nothing we can do to change what he has done. Therefore, I don't see a point in defaming the man over it."

"Then, you're not upset by all this?" Her brows furrowed.

He shook his head. "Simply because I won't speak ill of my uncle doesn't mean I'm not upset. I'm bloody furious. You are absolutely right, I don't deserve this. Nor did I deserve the other so-called lessons he imposed upon me. I've been angry with that man for far too long. And, I don't imagine I will ever let go of that."

As his anger at his uncle reignited, Lucius had trouble catching his breath. He hadn't wanted to say so much, but he had bottled up his emotions for far too long. Her own apparent issues with the man only helped to open a tidal wave of troubles he had kept guarded.

She grabbed his arm, and Lucius went completely still as shock rooted him to the spot. "Come with me. I have a perfect solution for you."

~~~
~~~

Hannah questioned her own sanity as she walked out the door with the new Lord Rivers by her side. The compulsion to fix his pain had come to her naturally just as it had to touch his arm. A shiver ran through her. She'd actually touched him. Her breathing increased at the memory. She could still feel the tips of her fingertips as they'd curled around his arm. The tingle from his shock as it seeped into her bones. It was both curious and enticing.

When they made their way toward the stables and she called for two horses to be readied, he made no sound and didn't question her. Once she climbed the mounting stairs and settled on her mare, she turned to see him on his stallion and looking at her expectantly.

Nerves engulfed her. She hadn't ridden a horse in years. Her late husband had taken the joy out of the pastime when he'd sold her favorite mare as a punishment for spending too much time on horseback. Determined not to embarrass herself, she began slow. However, everything came back to her. Including the joy.

The urge to send the beast tearing off at a run assaulted her, but she was conscious of the man following behind her. She still had no idea what to make of him. She knew he was struggling with his new position and the betrayal from his beloved uncle, so she knew she had to award him a little more patience than she preferred.

Sweat broke out across her forehead. His reaction after she'd questioned him about defending his uncle was distressing. The look on his face had been, almost, one of fondness. She couldn't reconcile that to what she'd known of the man. Brushing the thought aside, she realized she was thinking into the matter much too far.

Once they arrived at the old hunting cabin, she sent up a silent prayer that it remained standing. He dismounted, then offered his hand up to her. Heat flushed her cheeks at the thought of touching him again. This reaction was unlike her. It was true he was powerfully attractive, but so were a number of men out there, none of which made her so much as blink twice.

She swallowed, then took his hand and tried to dismount, but she hadn't done it in so long her foot became tangled in the stirrup. Before she realized what was happening, she unceremoniously fell forward, arms flailing.

His hands clamped around her like a vice as he stumbled backward before steadying them. The feeling of safety and security and enveloped her, and she got the strange sense that with him she would never have to fear falling again. Her eyes met his. The intensity of his gaze as his hard body pressed against hers brought a disquieting trembling in her stomach.

"I'm sorry," she breathed.

"Are you now?" An unexpected sparkle lit in his eyes. "Not two seconds out here and you are already in my arms. I fear I've been set up."

Horrified that he would believe her capable of such a thing, she pushed against his chest. "My lord, I would never--"

"Calm down." He laughed. "I'm merely jesting."

He smiled at her, and her heart skipped a beat. The sight was so striking she wondered why he hadn't done it more often. Perhaps he had, just not at her. She shook off the thought. That's not why they were out here.

"Thank you for catching me."

"You are very welcome. Now, can you tell me why you thought I needed a visit to the hunting cabin? Although it's been years, I've been here before."

She turned toward the cabin. It had been years for her as well, but it appeared the place had been well taken care of. She only hoped what she sought still remained. Otherwise, this would be quite an embarrassing trip.

"Follow me," she instructed. "I have a spare key hidden to allow us entrance."

After locating the key, he took it from her and let them inside. The fact that nothing much had changed struck her. Moving to the window, she pushed the draperies aside to allow the light to flood in as the earl lit a few candles. The place was cozy, and warmth and security surrounded her in these walls. She smiled.

"You seem rather pleased," he observed.

"This place doesn't seem to have been affected by time." She moved toward the bedroom. "I simply hope looks aren't deceiving."

She stood before the bed, then bent down to reach under the straw mattress. Reaching as far under it as she could, she let out a sigh of relief when her fingertip touched the solid piece of wood. Drawing out the framed canvas, she propped it up so they both could see it. He joined her in front of the painting.

"What in God's name is that?" Horror echoed in his voice.

Hannah surveyed the horrid painting of her late husband and tried not to laugh at the lack of talent of the painter, combined with the unflattering position he'd been staged in.

"Whenever my late husband would act a certain way with me or show me how his decisions were always right and mine wrong, I'd escape here. This was my little secret. And, when I look upon this unfortunate picture that I'd salvaged from the rubbish pile, I realize he was wrong. How could he always be right when it was his decision to hire this painter and have this atrocity commissioned?"

He faced her, his expression completely unreadable. His lack of reaction brought heat to her cheeks. Perhaps she shouldn't have brought him here. She'd kept the secret for so long maybe it should have remained that way.

Clearing her throat, she tried to hide her embarrassment. "When I was eighteen, it didn't seem so silly. I'm sorry I made you come all the way out here."

Her shoulders sagged as her head bent to look at the floor, but to her surprise, his long finger slid under her chin and lifted her to look back at him. "You brought me out here to try to make me feel better? To ease my anger?"

"Yes," she whispered, her body shaking at his light touch.

"Thank you." His voice was thick. "I . . ."

His gaze dropped to her lips, and he slowly leaned forward as he brought her chin up higher. Time stopped as fear enveloped her. She wanted to run and hide for she knew what an agonizing thing kissing was, but she also knew the punishment for turning away.

Instead, she waited as his face slowly came toward her. Keeping immobile, she hoped it would end soon. Then, his lips touched hers. They were soft and gentle, not hard and demanding as she'd expected. He moved his mouth over hers, and she had to admit the sensation was rather pleasant. Then, he pulled back and gazed upon her rather curiously.

"I'm sorry. I shouldn't have done that." His raspy voice held no remorse.

Discomforted by the confusing experience, she took a step back. "Then, why did you?"

He ran a hand along the back of his neck as guilt flashed across his face. "I really can't say. I'm just touched by your gesture, and I became overwhelmed by it. Don't be afraid of me. It won't happen again."

Searching his face, she saw nothing but honesty. "Very well. I suppose we can throw out the painting now."

He shook his head. "No. Let's put it back. I may need to use it again."

Thrilled that he hadn't seen her idea as ridiculous, she grinned. "Then, help me hide it under the mattress."

Once everything had been returned to its place, they made their way back to the horses. As she allowed him to help her mount her mare, she tried to ignore the spark she felt at his touch. Something had happened when he'd kissed her. Something bad. For the first time, she wondered if she'd made a huge mistake by returning to the estate.

~ ~ ~

Lucius tossed his shirt onto the bank and dove into the frigid water. The biting cold seeped into his flesh, but it did nothing to assuage the burning need inside him. He was dearly paying for the horrible mistake of kissing the countess yesterday, and he wasn't sure how he would be able to survive that event.

Their light touching of lips had been minimal, but it was enough to tease him and make him want more. But, dear God, she didn't. Although she hadn't shied away, he'd felt her revulsion. He pulled his head above the water as memories of her disgust threatened to drown him. The worst part of it being that he couldn't even blame her.

Hauling himself out of the water after his useless swim, he wrung out his breeches, then dressed, ignoring how the now wet material clung to him. Dwelling on his mistake was getting him nowhere. He needed to return to the estate books.

The short trip back to the manor put him in no better of a mood. Part of him wanted to send for the countess and insist she work with him, seeing as he had joined her for a very uncomfortable dinner last night. However, the other part of him recognized that for the terrible idea it was. He wasn't ready to see her, let alone be in a room with only the two of them.

As he entered the manor and made his way toward the stairs, he realized fate had her own plan. The countess moved toward him, light in her eyes. The sight took his breath away.

He wished her excitement stemmed from a desire to see him. However, the thought disgruntled him. Since when had he become this person who spent every second pining after a woman? He'd had his share of ladies. Prided himself on that fact over the years. So, why did this have to come up now?

"My lord, I have some exciting . . . You're wet?" Her voice held a question.

"Yes." He forced amusement in his voice. "That is typically the state one is in after a swim."

She tilted her head. "A swim? The water must have been freezing out there. Why would you do such a thing?" She shook her head and held up her hand. "I'm sorry. Forget I asked."

"Well, then, if that is all. Please, excuse me." He turned to go.

"Wait. I have something to tell you." She glanced down at his soaked shirt that clung to his chest. He shifted, uncomfortable under her gaze.

He waited a heartbeat for her eyes to return to his, when they did not, he couldn't help his grin. Perhaps she was slightly more affected by him than she wanted him to believe. Either that or it had been a good long while since she'd seen a man in such a state of undress. Regardless, he liked her preoccupation.

"If you give me but a moment, I would be happy to meet you in my study."

She blinked and looked up at him, her cheeks bright pink. "Of course."

Chuckling to himself, he watched her scurry off toward the study. Perhaps the cold water had helped him. As she'd said before, she didn't see him as a man. It was likely he only needed to remind her of that fact and . . . and, what? He stopped himself. He couldn't gain anything from this. The past was the past, and he needed to look to the future.

That thought utmost in his mind, he dressed, then made his way to the study. Once there, he paused in the doorway and took a deep breath. He needed to find the person he'd been before. The untouchable bastard he'd acted for years. Stepping into the room, he shut the door and she jumped.

"Do you think it's such a good idea to close the door?" Her eyes watched him warily as he moved toward his desk.

"I don't want my business spread about the house. And, I don't understand why it would be a problem."

She raised an eyebrow as he sat. "Well, last time we were alone you kissed me."

At her open acknowledgment of that moment, he gripped the arms of his chair as his body reacted. "I told you it wouldn't happen again."

"How can I be so sure?"

The fact she was so concerned over it sent fury through him. His earlier hope had vanished. Her clear distaste for him was enough to ensure he not touch her a second time. He hated himself for having such a weakness for this woman.

"Not only have I given you my word, but you are not the type of woman I am typically attracted to."

Her mouth fell open. "Are you saying I'm unattractive?"

Surprised she would translate his words in that manner, he coughed. "That's not it at all. I'm merely saying I usually go after women with black hair. And, short. Yes. I prefer my women small. That's what I'm looking for."

"I see." She shifted in her chair. "So, you won't kiss me again because of my blond hair, and I'm too tall?"

"Among other things," he hastened to add, feeling like a fool. "Are you disappointed that I'm not going to kiss you again?"

Her eyes widened. "Wherever would you get that idea?"

Leaning back in his chair, he shrugged. "Your line of questioning is sounding that way. Although, I do hate to disappoint a lady, I wouldn't advise kissing between us."

"Neither would I." Her chest rose and fell rapidly. "Now, I think it would be better to get back to the reason why I came to see you."

"Of course. You have something to tell me?"

She nodded as the sparkle entered her eyes once again. "I was looking over the paper left in the ledger book and I believe—"

"Wait a minute. You are going through the books without me? That's not part of the arrangement." He certainly didn't like the idea of her finding any reference to anything his uncle had written about her. No. He would provide her the information when he was there.

"I'm sorry, my lord. I had only thought to help." The luster had drained from her expression. "In the future, I'll refrain from looking over anything without you."

"Good. In the future, we shall do this together. Now, tell me what you have discovered."

"The entire page isn't meant to be cohesive. Each line is unrelated to the others. That's why none of it makes any sense."

"It still doesn't make sense, but why do you believe is not related?"

She scooted to the edge of her seat and put her hands on his desk. "The sentences on each of the twelve lines go together. Take the first one for example. 'The key is locked. Now, unlock the floor under the child I never had.' Both talk about the same thing whereas the next line mentions flowers."

"What are you saying?"

"This took him years to write. You can tell by the deterioration of his handwriting toward the end. I think each line is another clue, totaling twelve in all. You have to follow them individually."

The ridiculousness of the idea had him scratching his head. "Are you saying this is some kind of coded treasure hunt? With each line bringing me another properly written ledger sheet until I understand what it is I inherited?"

She shrugged. "That is very possible. The earl enjoyed having people put up a good fight for his entertainment."

"Then, I suppose there is only one thing for us to do now. We need to solve that clue and see what we are up against."

A wide grin stretched across her face. "I'll have you know that I believe I have solved the first one."

Chapter 3

Hannah winced as Lisa, the maid, pulled a tangle out of her long blond hair while styling it for the day. Unlike the previous three mornings, Hannah hadn't awoken with excitement today. Although she and the earl had followed the first clue and found an old coffer affixed under loose floorboards in the nursery, they still had yet to find the key. She knew the missing piece was locked away in her late husband's possessions, but his heir couldn't seem to locate it.

Regardless, she had to admit matters between them had greatly improved. Although he had forbidden them from talking about their search outside of the study, their dinner conversations had been pleasant. She could tell his lack of progress with the key had been wearing on him, but he tried not to let it show.

Their kiss had never been brought up again, but it was something that was never far from her mind. She'd never experienced anything quite like it and each time his face moved closer to hers, she secretly hoped he would kiss her again. The fact she knew he'd never do so didn't stop the hope. It was disgraceful, she knew it, but she couldn't erase the feeling.

"Lisa, tell me what you think of the new Lord Rivers." Hannah couldn't stop herself from wanting to know more about him.

"What do you mean, my lady?"

"Just that you've been working for him for a few months now, and I thought you might have some insight into the type of man he is. Having not been here long, I don't know him well."

Watching the woman's face in the looking glass, Hannah tried to discern her every thought. She knew the earl spent much of his time alone in the study, but she desperately wanted to get a better sense of the man. She didn't want to dwell on why.

"I haven't had any contact with him, personally, but the talk among the staff is he appears to be a fine man." Lisa met her eyes in the mirror and gave her a wink. "He's also not bad to look at."

Hannah laughed. "I've noticed he doesn't smile much, though. And, when he does, it's quite a sight to behold."

"Then, I will have to be around the next time he does it." Lisa gathered Hannah's hair on top of her head and began pinning it in place.

A knock sounded at the door. Not expecting anyone this early, she imagined it must be a staff member delivering a message. Considering she was dressed, she called out to grant entrance. To her surprise, Lord Rivers opened the door.

His eyes moved to Lisa and then back to her sitting at her dressing table. "I'm sorry. I didn't mean to interrupt. I thought you'd be ready for the day."

"It's quite all right, my lord," she responded, confused by his presence at her bedchamber door. "What is it I can do for you?"

A small smile spread across his face and her heart stopped. Then, he held out his hand and a small key dangled from his fingers. Her eyes widened as she realized what this meant. Excitement filled her and she jumped up, ignoring Lisa's attentions as her hair fell free of the pins and spread over her shoulders.

"My lady!" Lisa's voice held horror but Hannah didn't care.

"You found it. Where?"

The merriment drained from his features, replaced by something dark and intense. “It’s of no consequence. I merely wanted you to know I located my missing key. I will leave you to prepare yourself for the day.”

Shocked, she watched him swiftly leave the room. If he thought to go to the nursery without her, she’d be furious. Why had he shown her the key if that had been his intention? As she sat back in the chair and submitted to Lisa’s styling, the woman muttering under her breath, Hannah realized her blunder. Likely, he didn’t want Lisa to know of the key. And, the fact he disliked women with blond hair was surely off putting with that blatant display of hers.

As soon as she finished her breakfast, she hastened to his study. Luckily, he was inside and rose as soon as he saw her, anticipation on his face. She took that to mean he hadn’t gone without her.

“I’d begun to believe you were never going to make it here,” he complained as he walked around his desk. “Are you ready to go see what my uncle thought was so important to make it near impossible to find?”

She wanted to argue that it was his departure this morning that had delayed them finding out, but she was too impatient to wait any longer. “Let’s go.”

As she took his offered arm, that familiar shot of awareness pricked at her, only to be compounded when he smiled at her. Completely oblivious to her thoughts, he pulled her along toward the nursery. She tried to concentrate on the excitement of what would lie ahead, but all her thoughts centered on the man beside her. It was unnatural.

“You are very quiet today,” he observed when they reached the nursery. “I would have thought you would be as excited as I am.”

Releasing his arm, she allowed herself a much needed breath. “I am. I hope you will find everything you are searching for. Most importantly, the answer as to why he would do this."

He snorted. "Understanding how that man's mind works isn't something anyone can handle. I'll settle for ledger sheets."

"Very practical of you. Now, open it."

With a heart stopping grin, he pushed the key in the lock and wrenched open the lid of the old coffer, which gave off an audible squeak. Inside, he drew out a handful of coins and a few pound notes along with a sheet of paper. His brow furrowed as he unfolded the aged paper and silently read.

"Bloody hell. That bastard," he muttered under his breath, looking as if he would crumble the paper up, but instead he handed it to her as he marched across the room.

Her hands shook as she glanced down at her husband's scrawl.

Well, my boy, this is it. You're earl, and I'm dead. We both knew this would happen, so I'm not surprised. I'm writing this to you now because you just rushed off in your fit of rebellion. If you don't return to learn from me, you'll be reading this note when I'm dead, which I suppose is right now.

I imagine you would like to know my plan, so pay close attention. What you have found is the first part of your inheritance. The minimal funds my wife and I have been living off of will run out shortly. And, all additional income from the estate has been instructed to be set aside, not to be accessible by you. If you wish to see another shilling, you must decipher the clues in order and find it on your own. Once all has been found, the keys and notes can be turned in according to the last instructions in order to receive further income off the estate.

In the event that you fail, and I expect you will, all funds shall remain where they are, while the obligations are still yours. And, if you think to sire an heir before your inheritance has fully been claimed, that child shall not be recognized by the estate. Take heed, if you can't keep it in your trousers, your nine-month clock shall begin ticking.

Stunned, Hannah stared at the note as her cheeks heated from the crude comment. Although she knew her husband capable of something so horrible, the fact he would do this to his own heir sickened her. And, to not only take away his ability to support himself, but to deny him the chance of having a child. It was unthinkable. Fury and hurt welled inside her.

"Are you all right?" She pitched her voice low as to not set him off.

"All right?" he barked. "How can I possibly be? The man has ruined me. You saw how long it took to find that clue, and I didn't even solve it. This is a damned mess. Now, I have nothing."

He ran his hands through his short hair and the ends stuck up. His mussed hair combined with the frustration on his face made him appear so vulnerable. She walked up to him, desperate to help.

"Not nothing, my lord. You have me."

~ ~ ~

The words spoken from her lips made Lucius freeze as all traces of his anger melted away. *You have me.* Oh, how he wanted that to be true. However, the countess didn't belong to him, and she never would.

Images of her free hair cascading around her shoulders that morning assaulted him, and he had to bite back a groan. The sight had nearly killed him. And, to see her in such a state while standing only a few feet from her bed had sent his mind into a frenzy. He'd fled from her as quickly as he could, but the damage to him had been done.

"It's Lucius." He tried not to wince at his gruff voice.

"What?" Her eyes grew wide.

"My name is Lucius. If we're going to continue this together, I'll not have you call me by my title. Besides, at this moment, I have no desire to hear the reminder."

"Don't do that." She shook her head. "You are the Earl of Rivers now. Be proud and be better than him. Simply because he misused his power doesn't mean you can't take this title and turn it into a name we both can stand to hear. Do it for the two of us. I challenge you, Lucius. Make the name something you and I want to say."

The strength in her words called out to him, but the sound of his name on her lips drove the point home. For her, he would do it. He would accept both her challenge and that of his uncle's. Before he died, he would ensure she smiled when she heard that name. She deserved as much.

"Challenge accepted, my lady." He bowed his head in acknowledgment.

Red streaked up her cheeks. "I suppose you should call me Hannah. However, if you dare add 'aunt' to it, I swear I'll box your ears."

He grinned. "I'd love to see you try."

She put her hands on her hips. "Then, say it."

This playful side of her was both intriguing and endearing. However, he could feel himself being dragged further under her spell. This wasn't good. The woman was naturally vivacious, but it meant nothing. She still didn't truly see him, and he knew it.

"I would, but I believe it would be better for us to get back to the study. Now that we know his intention, I'd like another look at the paper to see exactly what we have to do."

She was shaking her head before he was done talking. "Absolutely not. That's not what we need right now. Nothing will be solved with frustration. I think you need to step aside first. Take some time to get away from everything."

"What are you suggesting?" He lifted an eyebrow. "The hunting cabin again?"

Her laughter washed over him. "I don't believe you need that just yet. Perhaps a simple ride or go for a walk?"

"It sounds as though you are suggesting I need the break and not you. However, you appeared to be just as upset as I was a moment ago."

She opened her mouth, then closed it. "That's not the same thing."

"I don't agree with that." This was a bad idea, but he was powerless to stop the words from flowing. "We should take a break together. You seemed to enjoy riding. I would be agreeable to a daily ride before the winter sets in."

Her lips pressed to a thin line. "I suppose an occasional ride would be acceptable."

He frowned, not liking her forced tone. "Is it an aversion to me or to riding?"

"I don't have an aversion to either," she hastened to assure him. "It's just that . . . Never mind. I should very much like to join you."

Not appeased, he crossed his arms. "I'm not going to let you leave until you tell me what the trouble is. I intend to fix it for you."

The smile she gave him was genuine, and he felt a stab directly into his chest. This woman always got under his skin, and he didn't know why. He wanted to protect her from the world. To erase all the pain he had caused her, which he was beginning to believe was much more than he'd originally thought.

"Now, I'm the one who is touched by your gesture." She reached out and lightly touched his arm. "As you had done, am I to give you a kiss to bestow my gratitude?"

He blinked, wondering when he had fallen asleep. This was not supposed to happen, and certainly not something he expected. But, bloody hell, he wanted her to kiss him more than he wanted his next breath. How could he deny himself or deny her request?

"I promised you I wouldn't kiss you again," he reluctantly forced out.

Her face fell as she removed her hand. "Yes, you're right. I'm sorry."

"You made no such promise, though." He held his body rigid, wishing he could take the words back, but silently praising himself for encouraging her. He needed her to kiss him before he himself broke the promise.

A sexy smile lifted the corners of her mouth, and he was sunk. "Do you want me to make that promise?"

He shook his head. "Absolutely not."

"Then, it would be acceptable for me to show you my gratitude?"

He nodded and then held his breath as she moved closer to him. A mixture of anticipation and fear danced behind her eyes. He wondered why she was afraid, but couldn't ask now. Everything inside him focused on her and keeping his body motionless.

Her eyes fell to his lips, and he thought he would expire from his desire for her. So little space separated them, but it could've been miles for what it felt like. Suddenly, she bit her lip and backed away.

"I'm sorry. I can't."

Confused, he took a step toward her, closing the distance between them once again. "Why not? It's simple. I can help you."

She shook her head and retreated again, her eyes wild. "No. I just can't. Please, excuse me."

Without wasting another second, she spun around and fled the room, leaving him to stare after her, dumbfounded. He felt like such a fool. Anger rushed through his body. He'd promised not to kiss her and then practically begged her for it. Never again. He was done with this. Done with pining over her.

Grabbing up the little bit of inheritance he had collected, he made his way to his study. Although he couldn't produce an heir yet, that didn't mean he couldn't make arrangements to obtain a wife. For months he and Lady Bernadette had developed a rapport, and he had promised her he would write once he had inherited the title. Well, he imagined it was time to send her a message.

~ ~ ~

Hannah wandered through the kitchen, ignoring the questioning glances from the staff members passing through. She knew her behavior was cowardly, but she didn't care, for this was definitely better than accidentally running into Lucius. Even thinking his name sent a shudder through her body and embarrassment stinging her cheeks.

Although she'd been avoiding him for the past three days, he still kept his word and joined her for dinner every night. However, she hadn't been able to force herself to look at him and their conversations had been minimal. Still, he returned to the dining room each and every evening. A man of his word, exactly like he'd said.

To make matters worse, she still wanted to kiss him. In fact, she regretted not taking the chance. However, in that instant, all she could think about was how her husband used to grind his mouth against hers, nearly choking her with his tongue, and upon occasion, forcing his lips to hers so hard her teeth cut the inside of her mouth. She couldn't be sure that it wouldn't be the same with Lucius. Perhaps his first kiss had been a mistake. Did she truly want to take that chance?

A small boy darted from behind a table and ran in front of her, nearly tripping her. She gasped, then met a set of wide green eyes of a child that couldn't have been more than eight.

"I'm so sorry, my lady. Please don't punish me."

She tilted her head to the side. "And, what have you done that needs punishing?"

"My mum said we had to stay away from the lord and lady of the house. I didn't mean to—"

"Now, I'm going to . . . my lady!"—Hannah turned to see a girl of perhaps ten moving toward them.—"We're so sorry. Let me get rid of him for you. Please don't blame my mother for this."

Frowning, Hannah looked at the two children. Why were they so afraid? "I have no intention of bringing harm to you or your mother. Why don't the two of you have a seat at the table, and I'll see to it you get something to eat while we find your mother."

The boy's eyes widened in excitement while the girl appeared horrified. "Don't do that. I mean, we can just go."

Suspicion narrowed Hannah's eyes, and she opened her mouth to speak when Lisa rushed up. "Alex, Daisy, what are you doing here? I told you to keep out of the way."

Surprised, Hannah looked at Lisa with new eyes. Although she appeared to be the right age to have children, considering they had never talked about it before, Hannah had never known the woman had a family. The truth made her feel bad.

"Are these your children? I had no idea you were even married."

A blush ran up Lisa's cheeks. "Norman works in the stables. I'm so sorry, my lady. My mother has fallen ill, and I thought the children would—"

Hannah raised her hand. "Don't apologize. They are fine."

"Normally when I have to bring them, Cook puts them to work on something, but she's been too busy to look after them."

"Again, they are fine. And, as it turns out, I'm doing nothing at the moment and wouldn't mind spending a little time with them."

"Oh, no, my lady. I could never ask you."

"You're not. I'm offering. I've always wanted to have children. How about I entertain them for just two hours a day until your mother is well? That should give the staff a break and you will have no need to worry."

Lisa bit her lip as she looked between Hannah and the children. "If you truly don't mind, I would be much relieved."

"Then, it is settled." Hannah smiled, brightened at the thought of being able to play at being a mother, if only for a short while. Her husband had blamed her constantly for her inability to be good enough to supply him with an heir, so she knew motherhood was a joy she would never experience.

"Norman will be able to take them soon, but if you'd like to begin tomorrow, I'm certain they would enjoy seeing something other than the kitchen."

"That's the truth," Alex muttered.

"Alex!" Daisy scolded. "Mind your manners."

"Come along you two." Lisa guided her children away. "Don't show Lady Rivers you have no manners, then she will certainly change her mind."

Watching the trio walk away, Hannah felt an ache inside her chest. When she'd been young and naïve, that's how she had envisioned her life. A husband and children. Now, she had nothing. And, if Lucius didn't claim his inheritance, she would lose the comfortable life she had now as well. She suspected her husband had secretly enjoyed that fact when he'd made the arrangements for his heir.

She knew what she had to do. With her shoulders back, she made her way to Lucius's study. She would help him solve the puzzle, not just to help herself, but because she'd promised him, and he'd been wronged by the earl just as she had.

Her knock at the door was greeted by silence. She tried again, but still no answer. Not to be deterred, she pushed open the door and stepped inside, seeing him bent over studying papers on his desk. She silently shut the door behind her.

"Go away," he said, not looking up. "I don't wish to be disturbed."

She crossed her arms. "Whatever happened to us doing this together?"

His eyes shot to hers. "Hannah? What are you doing here?"

"I came to apologize." She looked down at her linked hands. "I never should have acted in such a manner."

"And, what exactly are you referring to? Running from the room? Avoiding me for the past few days?"

Heat rushed up her cheeks. "Both. And, before that when I spoke so boldly about things for which I had no right."

He let out a sigh. "We can sit here and argue about how you have every right to kiss whomever you want, especially if he is willing, but I'm onto something with this next clue."

Excitement tore through her at the possibility. However, the knowledge that he admitted to being willing to kiss her reverberated through her entire being. Again, she wondered if he would be gentle like she'd caught her brother kissing his wife, or if Lucius would be rough like his uncle. Shaking off the thought, she moved toward the desk and drew her chair closer to see what he was looking at.

"Show me." Her voice was thick, but she cleared her throat, hoping he didn't notice.

He handed her the paper. "Again, I know where to find the box. It's buried in the garden, but I don't know where the key is. I see all the little clues he left in these pages for me. The bastard was trying to test me. To see if I was listening to his teachings."

Glancing down at the paper, she read the clue. '*You can find what you seek under the expensive piece that has aged better than I.*' She smiled. Not every clue would be quite as easy, especially with a list of twelve, but she knew this one.

"I can tell you one thing. Your uncle certainly didn't count on one aspect. When he wrote this clue all those years ago, he had no idea you would have me to help you. Nor did he realize how many times he would use this exact phrase to describe a particular ancient vase that his mother purchased and he hated more than anything."

Lucius's mouth dropped open. "You are telling me that you solved this clue in less than one second whereas I have spent days on it."

With a shrug, she pushed the paper back to him. "Well, we can't be sure I would have known the first part. Let's just say we make a good team."

He grinned. "If we're doing this as a team, I certainly hope you don't have a problem getting dirty."

As he stood and rounded the desk, she wrinkled her nose. "You can do that part. I think I'll just remain here."

To her surprise, he reached down and took her hand, pulling her to her feet. A zing of fire shot up her arm. "I don't think so. You're coming with me. Otherwise, I won't tell you what I find."

He hadn't let go of her hand, and his touch and proximity made her feel odd. She didn't understand it. After years of torment at a man's hand she couldn't fathom how she could even tolerate the touch of another. However, again the desire to kiss him overwhelmed. Before she could act on it, she quickly let go of his hand. She needed to get hold of herself.

"Very well, I shall join you, but only so far. You can't expect me to go out in the garden with you. As a lady and your aunt, you should respect my right to abstain."

He grinned. "I suppose I shall give you that. We *will* find it. I promised. All of it. You don't need to worry about that."

She nodded, trusting him. If she believed nothing else about him, she knew his determination to be true. Then, he would move on to the other property and she would finally be able to live free of any man and any obligation. In London for the season and back here for the winter.

However, the thought didn't bring her the relief she had expected. As a matter of fact, she actually felt more at home here at the estate than she'd felt in a long time. She didn't want to give that up. Nor was she ready to live a lonely existence again. She'd found something she'd been missing this past week or so. She just needed to decide if it was something worth fighting for.

Chapter 4

Lucius pushed his stallion harder, loving the feel of the speed and the freedom gained on the back of the horse. The weather was overcast and cool, but nothing could have stopped him from getting out of the manor. Although Hannah had never joined him for his rides, he agreed with her assessment that they both needed to escape from the pressure of his uncle's puzzle.

Two days ago, he'd unearthed the second box exactly where he'd expected under the bench where Uncle Herman had caught him getting overly friendly with one of the maids. He'd taught him a valuable lesson that day. And, one he knew he should heed.

Taking in a deep breath, Lucius slowed the horse and set him on the path back to the stables. The garden coffer had given him a better outlook on this situation. Not only had it been filled with enough funds to sustain him for the time being if he were careful, but the simple note from his uncle helped.

'*Remember what I taught you. Each lesson, even this one, has a purpose. Heed them and you will certainly succeed.*'

The thought that his uncle did care for him and didn't simply wish to see him fail made everything easier. Although some of the things the man had done over the years had been unforgivable, Lucius would like to believe they'd been done with at least a thought as to what was best for him.

When Lucius made it back to the manor, he wasn't ready to return to his work in the study. He wished for the opportunity to see Hannah without the formality of dinner or the obligation of the clues between them. Although nothing permanent would come out of it, he truly enjoyed being with her. He longed for her to be herself around him as she had been years ago.

As he moved through the halls, the sound of someone playing the pianoforte drew his attention. Could it be Hannah? He'd never heard her play before, so he wasn't sure as to her talent. Pulled to the perfectly executed piece of music, he made his way to the ballroom. When the song drew to a close, her musical laughter filled the silence, and he froze outside of the door.

"You are such a wonderful dancer. You don't know how happy you've made me."

The following silence shot searing jealousy through him. Had her dance partner kissed her in reply? Lucius clenched his fists and turned to go, then he stopped. This couldn't go on. Her husband may be dead, but she couldn't carry on like this with a staff member in plain sight and with the possibility of being caught from anyone who walked by.

With his head held high and his anger in check, well mostly, he marched through the doors only to come to a dead halt at the scene before him. Hannah stood with a little boy before her while a young girl remained off to the side. A glance to the pianoforte revealed one of his staff members. He gained a new appreciation of the man as he hadn't realized he possessed such talent.

"My lord, I hope we haven't disturbed you." Hannah glanced at him guiltily as she tucked a stray lock of her hair behind her ear.

"Not at all. I heard the music and was drawn here."

The young girl sighed. "It's a sign, my lady. He's the one you should be dancing with. Not Alex."

"No, Daisy." Hannah's eyes nervously shot to the child. "His Lordship has more important things to do than to play our game."

"Why don't you let him be the judge of that," Lucius suggested, loving the idea of holding her in his arms for a dance. "What game?"

Hannah's back straightened as she lifted her chin in defiance. "I'm entertaining the children. We are dancing."

"Yes," Daisy exclaimed with an exuberance only a child could possess. "Lady Rivers told us how she loves to dance, but no one will dance with her."

"That's enough, Daisy." Hannah's cheeks turned bright red.

"Probably because she steps on gentlemen's toes." Lucius winked at Daisy, smiling when she giggled, then he faced Alex. "Good Sir, would you mind if I borrowed your dance partner?"

The boy's eyes were filled with awe as he looked up at Lucius and shook his head. He inclined his head at the boy, clearly he wasn't accustomed to speaking to lords. It made Lucius wonder what the young lad thought about having the honor of dancing with the countess. That was one privilege which he himself couldn't wait to partake.

"Lord Rivers, this is unnecessary." Hannah bit her lip, looking at him as if he were a snake posed to strike.

"I see why you lack partners. When one arrives, you do your best to make him leave." Then, he turned toward the pianist. "A waltz, if you please."

He moved toward her.

"Lucius," she warned.

"Don't complain. Please, just dance with me, Hannah."

The pleading in his voice must have been convincing enough, for she stepped forward and lifted her arms. Joy rushed him as he took her hand and put his other on her tiny waist, pulling her in as closely as he could without turning obscene.

As the music began, he led her into the steps. The fact that he had waited for eleven years to dance with her wasn't lost on him. She'd been seventeen not yet in society the last time he'd seen her before she'd wed his uncle. He had dreamed of dancing with her like this. Then, it had been too late.

His entire body burned at the feel of her in his arms. He wanted to be closer still, but this was much more than he should have done. For someone who supposedly lacked partners, she danced like she was born to do it, which only compounded his enjoyment.

"Tell me, how is it that someone such as yourself lacks partners?"

She let out a heavy sigh. "No man wants to dance with a married woman, and especially not one with a possessive husband. Not to mention, the men who did want to dance with me weren't ones I would accept, lest I find trouble."

Although he didn't like the sound of that, he didn't wish to ruin their dance. "Well, anytime you want to dance, come to me. I enjoy dancing with you, and I mean you no harm."

When she looked up at him, there was vulnerability in her eyes. "You mean no harm or you cause no harm?"

He furrowed his brow. "What do you mean?"

Her eyes fell to his lips. "Just tell me. I have to know."

Unable to concentrate, he stopped their dance. She looked like she wanted to kiss him, and he'd be damned if he would miss this opportunity. Either he would pull her away or send everyone out and close the doors. But, harm? What was she talking about?

"Hannah, what—"

"My lord?" Mr. Rawlings said loudly from the doorway, drawing his attention. "You have guests awaiting you in the drawing room."

He cursed, having a sickening feeling he knew exactly who had come to see him. "This isn't over. We will finish this discussion."

As he left her standing there, he had a sinking suspicion that any progress he'd made with her during the dance was lost with each step that he moved away from her.

~ ~ ~

The very first thing Hannah noticed about the visitor was she was blond. And, tall. She just couldn't reconcile this person to someone Lucius would choose for himself. The fact he would be attracted to this lady, yet not her, was confounding and maddening.

Both Lady Bernadette and her mother, Lady Winslow, looked around the room disdainfully as if they were already making plans to redecorate. That, too, irritated Hannah. She had never been awarded even the slightest allowance for so much as a curtain, yet these ladies already thought they had a right to make such changes.

"So, tell me, Lady Rivers, how long do you plan on remaining here with your nephew?" Lady Winslow asked.

Forcing a smile, Hannah faced the woman. "My plan is to remain on the estate through the winter. Whatever the earl plans has no bearing on my living arrangements."

The lady lifted an unconvinced eyebrow. "I see."

"What about you, Lady Bernadette?" Hannah picked up her cup of tea, wishing she had a splash of whisky to flavor the beverage. "How long do you plan to remain for your visit?"

"Presently, I don't know. You see, Lucius, I mean, Lord Rivers, has been after me for months. Following me at every event and visiting me often. The last time he'd begged me to marry him, I told him to write to me as soon as he inherited." Lady Bernadette chuckled. "That naughty boy waited months, but he did write to me."

The girl was lying. Not only could Hannah not see Lucius acting in such a manner, but she saw the calculating glint in the young girl's eyes. Hannah couldn't help the enjoyment she received from being seen as a threat. Not that Lucius thought of her in such a way, but it felt good to be seen as competition nonetheless.

"Then, you are betrothed? I'm sorry, I hadn't heard. I offer my belated congratulations." Hannah infused her voice with excitement.

Red crept up Lady Bernadette's neck. "Well, it's not official at this moment. I never said yes, and so I'm awaiting him to offer again now that he has taken on the title. It's only a matter of time."

"And, he *will* offer for my daughter," Lady Winslow assured.

Hannah nodded. "Of course. Men move rather slowly, but if he wrote to you, I'd imagine you'll have what you are looking for before long."

The girl beamed a smile at her. "I think the two of us will get along rather well."

With a nod, Hannah tried to make herself like this girl who would become her niece. After all, this woman, along with Lucius, would control her future. As a widow, she had no rights and would have to rely on her husband's nephew and his wife for charity. Again, she was struck with the wrongness of Lucius and this girl, but she cast the thought aside. Clearly, he'd been so anxious for her to come he'd requested her presence immediately.

That being the case, where was he? The question assaulted her out of nowhere. He had remained long enough to offer her an introduction, then escaped, claiming estate matters. The idea had received a smile from Lady Bernadette, but had only raised Hannah's suspicions.

After enduring a few more minutes of uncomfortable small talk, Hannah excused herself to allow the pair time to settle in. Then, she made her way to the study in order to face

Lucius. Although, she couldn't claim to know him well, his behavior was odd for someone who had supposedly decided this was the woman he would marry.

Lucius looked up from his papers when she walked in the study and closed the door.

"I'm coming from the drawing room where I spent a good deal of time with Lady Bernadette and her mother," she informed him.

"And?" His closed face gave away none of his feelings.

"She seems very blond—I mean nice," she quickly corrected as heat flashed up her cheeks.

Lucius chuckled. "She is blond."

"I thought you didn't like blondes." Hannah eyed him suspiciously, having expected more of a response from him considering he intended to marry the girl.

A sparkle danced in his eyes. "I only told you that so you wouldn't feel uncomfortable around me."

"Because you find me attractive?" She held her breath, desperate to hear him say yes.

The corners of his mouth twitched as if he held back a smile. "Are you here now asking this because you are jealous? You didn't seem too concerned before Lady Bernadette arrived."

She gasped, surprised he would come to that conclusion. "I can't believe you would think such a thing."

"It's not hard to see really. You come in here and ask me if I find you attractive only minutes after the appearance of a lady to whom I had written. You don't have to deny it or play games with me." The light in his eyes and his tone of voice betrayed his teasing, but discomfort slithered through her. In truth, she feared he was right.

He let out a laugh. "Calm yourself, Hannah. I'm only jesting. Not that I would mind your jealousy, but I know you don't feel it."

Forcing a weak smile, she sat in a chair as he reclaimed his seat. "I see. Were you also jesting about lying regarding your preferences?"

As he drew his fingers through his hair, the teasing light left his eyes. "Do you truly want an answer? I honestly don't think you do. There is too much between us for such discussions."

"I disagree. With so much between us, honesty is even more important."

The torn look on his face almost made her take it back. But, she had to know. Her emotions around him ran rampant and to know he found her attractive would mean quite a bit to her. She desperately wanted to hear him say it.

As he stood and paced the room, a look of distress covered his face. She couldn't understand his reaction. If he found her beautiful, surely he could tell her. Reality sent cold dancing up her neck. He didn't find her attractive in the least. That was the only explanation for his reluctance.

Searing heat replaced the cold as she stood. "Forget I asked. You are right. I would have preferred not to know. I fear I've thoroughly embarrassed myself, so I'll leave."

As she moved past him, he reached out and touched her arm. She froze. The heat of the contact spiraled through her. It only embarrassed her further. How could her body react to him as it had to no other, and he not find her the slightest bit attractive?

"If you already know the truth, then you shouldn't mind hearing it from my lips." He gazed into her eyes, and she couldn't look away. "Of course, I was lying about my preferences. No man with blood in his veins can look at you and not be attracted. You are the most beautiful woman I've ever seen, and I'm not immune to your charm."

"W-what?" Her heart stopped, and she couldn't breathe. He was close. Much too close and she never expected such a confession from him. Her eyes fell to his lips. She didn't know if he would be gentle like before or harsh like her husband, but she didn't care. Suddenly it no longer mattered. She just needed him to kiss her.

"Don't look at me like that," he breathed, his voice barely audible.

"Like what?" Her voice emerged in no better shape than his.

"Like you want me to kiss you."

Hearing him voice the very thing she wanted, a thrill ran through her entire body. In that moment, she couldn't think of a good reason not to kiss him. However, she also couldn't do it. This had to come from him.

"What's so wrong with that?"

She chanced a look into his eyes, and gasped to see the midnight sky reflected in their depths. His passion both excited and frightened her. However, her husband had never looked at her in such a manner. There was always an edge of anger in his face. She saw nothing of the sort reflected in Lucius's eyes.

"I promised not to kiss you," he stated, a note of steel in his tone. "I don't break my word."

She bit her lip, drawing his attention. Determination filled her as did a boldness she was unaccustomed to when dealing with such a situation. "Then, how do I get you to kiss me?"

~ ~ ~

The floor could have disappeared from under Lucius's feet, and he would have been less surprised. Hannah was the most confounding, frustrating woman he'd ever encountered, and at this moment she was killing him. There was no simple answer to her question as he could see fear in her eyes lurking behind her desire.

When he'd asked Lady Bernadette to join him at the estate, he'd never imagined it would have such an effect on

Hannah. Although he quite enjoyed her response, it worried him as well. She was an experienced woman, but everything in her stance right now told him something was not quite right with her. The last thing he wanted to do was rush her or push her into something she was uncomfortable with.

"Lucius? I want you to kiss me. Please." The desperation in her breathless voice did him in. There was nothing left of his reluctance.

His fingers curled around her upper arm as he moved in closer to her, using his other hand to cup her cheek. He moved slowly, giving her every opportunity to escape, although knowing he wouldn't be able to handle her withdrawal at this point. His body burned for her from years of yearning.

The feel of her body pressing against his had him stifling a groan as he lowered his lips to hers. The first touch was lightning, exactly like that day in the cabin, but he intended for this to last much longer. Although she was just as still as before, her hand lightly touched his arm.

Encouraged, he moved his mouth over hers, rejoicing when she mirrored his movements. Desire pumped through his veins, demanding he deepen the kiss, but he resisted. She needed this time to accustom herself to him. Instead, he used this opportunity to memorize the feel of her against him. The scent of her. The touch of her lips. So much he had longed to experience for so long.

When she melted against him, he knew he had won. Taking the small victory, he tried to cool his ardor and although his body wanted so much more, he pulled back from her. The wonderment in her eyes followed by her slow smile as she looked up at him made him want to puff up his chest in pride.

"That was . . . I mean . . . Is it always like that?"

He chuckled and ran a hand down her cheek, relishing her shudder. "Oh, no. I've got so much more I can show you. But, I think that's enough for today."

Her breathing was heavy, and her eyes rounded at his words. "What if I don't want more?"

Head jerking back, he dropped his hand from her. Had she not enjoyed his kiss? Impossible. It had been very obvious she had taken as much pleasure from it as he. Perhaps she only wanted to experiment with him, and now she'd had her fill.

"My promise is still intact. You can be assured I shall not kiss you unless you ask me to."

The smile she bestowed upon him took his breath away. "Then, I shall ask again, but I don't need more. Just keep them all like that."

All. Never before he had he heard a better word. Although he wasn't sure about his ability to not want more, he would do whatever it took in order to be able to have as many kisses from her as possible for as long as he could. He knew this was only a temporary arrangement, so he would take every bit of pleasure he could while it lasted.

"I shall do my best." The strain in his voice made it unrecognizable, even to him.

"Then, you can kiss me again." She stepped closer to him.

Everything inside him rejoiced at the opportunity to hold her in his arms again, but he moved back, taking a deep breath. At present, he wanted her too badly to give in. However, the hurt in her eyes almost made him change his mind.

"As I said, that's enough for today. I can only take so much. If you are not looking for more, then don't push me."

A mischievous glint entered her eyes but it quickly disappeared as she took a step back. "I can already tell that's going to be a problem. I already want to kiss you again."

He groaned, as his body immediately hardened at her words. Dear God. The idea she wanted him in any way was more potent than anything he could ever imagine.

"Careful," he warned.

She bit the side of her lip and slid her hand up his chest. He froze and bit back a curse. What was wrong with her? Did she not understand she was playing with fire? He didn't think so.

"How much more?" Her voice was a whisper. "Will it hurt much?"

Jerking back as if he'd been struck, his ardor was extinguished. Immediately, her question from the ballroom returned to him. Her preoccupation with being hurt bothered him more than he cared to admit. The natural assumption wasn't something he wanted to believe.

"Why do you ask?" He had to force the question from his throat.

She swallowed and lowered her gaze. "The way you kiss me, it's . . . different from when my husband would kiss me."

Clenching his fists, Lucius willed himself to speak the words. "Did he hurt you?"

Her eyes didn't meet his. "That's not what I said. I merely stated it was different. With my inexperience, it's likely I simply don't know what I'm talking about. Either one of you could very well have no skill whatsoever, hence the difference I'm noticing."

"If I accept that challenge, you will get more than you are bargaining for, but, be assured, pain will be the last thing on your mind." He practically growled. "You'll feel so much pleasure you'll be unable to walk afterward."

His threat bit out in anger had a different effect on her than he'd anticipated. The sight of her lips parting while she clutched onto the lapels of his jacket, as if her legs already were weak drove him mad. He wanted this woman with a fierceness he'd never known. Kissing her had been a mistake for it had only wetted his appetite for her.

"Show me," she whispered.

A war waged within him. She clung to his jacket, pulling him closer, as her eyes beckoned him, but the last rational thread in his mind told him it was much too soon. She needed more time to accustom herself.

When she raised her face up to look at him and touched her lips to his, the thread snapped. His arms came around her, crushing her to him. The feel of her firmly against him was unlike anything he could have imagined. His body was in a painful state and he knew she could feel it, but he didn't care. She wasn't an innocent who didn't understand the effects she would have on a man.

In an effort to conform to her wishes, he kept a tight rein on his control, but the second her hands wound around his neck, pulling him against her tighter, he gave up. Running his tongue along the seam of her lips, he begged for entrance.

A knock sounded at the door, and reverberated through his overheated body. Immediately, he broke away from Hannah and turned to lessen his labored breathing. Her eyes were wild and filled with shame. This would never do.

Walking to the door, he cracked it open and listened as Mr. Rawlings told him of Lady Bernadette's desire to see him. Then, he closed the door and ran a hand through his hair. In truth, he had forgotten about the lady, and he had no idea what to do about her.

"I should be going," Hannah said in a false cheery voice.

"Yes," he replied, not knowing how else to respond.

As she left, he fell into his chair. This was a fine mess he'd gotten himself into. One woman could fill his dreams, but only temporary, whereas the other could be his future wife. He simply needed to decide which was more important.

He sagged, cradling his head in his hands. In so many ways this was much harder than the challenge his uncle had set up for him.

Chapter 5

"He's going to bite you." Daisy looked at the mare disdainfully.

Hannah laughed and patted the mare on her nose. "First of all, this is a she. And, secondly, unless you try to hurt her, she'll do nothing of the sort."

As if in response, the mare nudged Hannah. Loving the bond she'd been developing with animal, despite her past, she nuzzled the horse's neck.

"I want to ride her," Alex pronounced. "One day I'll work out here with my father so I need to be real good with these horses."

"No riding," Norman said as he stepped out of the stables, giving his son a pointed look. "If you want to learn to care for the beasts, that's one thing, but no eight-year-old of mine will be riding one."

Listening to father and son argue the benefits of riding versus not, Hannah couldn't contain her smile. The young family was a welcome distraction, and helped to ease an ache she had felt on the inside at not being able to have children of her own. And, this was exactly what she needed after her kiss with Lucius yesterday.

An unbidden shiver ran up her spine at the memory, and she looked out over the field hoping to dislodge the sensation. Years of unhappiness in her marriage had caused her to turn to alcohol to dull the pain, but she'd worked hard to give up whisky since her husband's death. In recent days, she hadn't as much as thought of the stuff. Until last night.

Lucius had left her body in such a state of turmoil, the temptation to imbibe had been strong. Not to mention, his quick agreement that she leave him. Embarrassment stung her cheeks. He hadn't turned her away, but he hadn't been overenthusiastic about her advances either. She was so ashamed. Kissing him had been a mistake. Not only had she clearly made him uncomfortable to force him into something he didn't want, but regardless of his reaction, she couldn't deny her desire to kiss him again.

Movement from the direction of the garden caught her attention. Her throat clogged. Lucius was walking with Lady Bernadette. The sight of the two of them smiling and enjoying the day was a sharp blade plunged into her chest. She couldn't explain why, but the feeling robbed her of breath. The only explanation she could come up with was the fact she'd never seen him with another woman and having him to herself all these weeks had been pleasant. She nodded. Yes, that was it. Definitely, not jealousy.

"Who is that lady with Lord Rivers?" Daisy's voice was low although her father had returned to his duties.

Ripping her attention off Lucius, Hannah focused on the children. She was supposed to be watching them, after all. "That is Lady Bernadette. She has come with her mother for a visit."

Daisy narrowed her eyes. "But, what is she doing with the earl?"

With a swallow, Hannah tried to force her voice to sound cheery. From the young girl's comments over the past days, it was clear she had decided Hannah would be a good match for Lucius. The idea was preposterous. Not only was Lucius her nephew, but she would never subject herself to marriage again.

"I believe they are enjoying the garden, but that's none of our concern."

Shocked eyes shot to her. "None of our concern? You mean you don't care? But, what about your dance?"

Hannah forced out a laugh. "I danced with your brother as well. One dance with a gentleman means nothing."

The girl didn't look convinced. "I don't believe that, and I think you should ask him. He's on his way over here now, so you'll have an opportunity."

As Hannah chanced a glance in his direction, sweat broke out across her forehead. Facing Lucius would be difficult on his own, but with Lady Bernadette by his side, Hannah wasn't sure she could handle it.

"What have we here?" The lady's face was awash with pleasure, likely from her time with Lucius.

"We're visiting the horses, my lady," Daisy explained as she dropped into a curtsy. "Do you like horses?"

Hannah found her voice at the lady's appalled expression. "Lady Bernadette, allow me to present Daisy Peakes. Daisy, this is Lady Bernadette."

The woman ignored Daisy as she gazed upon the mare with disgust. "I don't know why on earth you would wish to be out here with these creatures. We hire people to tend to these duties."

From her response, Hannah couldn't be sure if she referred to the horses or to the children. "Why pay someone to handle something I enjoy?"

With a laugh, Lady Bernadette clutched Lucius's arm in a possessive manner. "Of course you do. Well, the earl and I were just discussing the merits of attending a ball together tomorrow night. What do you think? Should Lord Rivers escort my mother and I?"

Not reacting to the obvious dismissal was rather difficult. Clearly, Lady Bernadette didn't wish for her to attend. She wondered if the girl saw her as that much of a threat or if she truly didn't think Hannah would want to go to the ball. The question burned in her mind.

"Yes, Lady Rivers, what do you think?" Lucius's deep voice washed over her. "Should I attend the ball? And, if I do, would you accept my escort as well?"

Shocked, Hannah swallowed. "I'm not sure what to say, my lord."

"And, you don't have to say anything," Lady Bernadette assured, her color high as she released Lucius's arm. "What a thing to suggest, Lord Rivers. With her husband recently passed, of course she wouldn't want to attend a ball."

Lucius's eyes never left Hannah's. "I disagree. The lady is no longer in morning, and she hasn't left the manor since she's been here. I believe it would be good for her to attend a gathering."

It was true that Hannah did wish to go, but she also knew she couldn't allow Lucius to jeopardize his relationship with his future wife for her. In addition, it would be too difficult to see the two of them presenting as a happy couple while she was left forgotten.

"I thank you for your consideration, but I'm afraid I must decline."

The smile Lady Bernadette gave her was triumphant. "There, you have it. Now, come, my lord. We must prepare. I need to have that maid laying out my gown."

If Daisy heard the tone directed at her mother, she thankfully didn't comment. Hannah was glad the girl had remained quiet for this uncomfortable encounter. Clearly, Lady Bernadette wasn't fond of children. Hannah wondered if Lucius was aware of that fact.

"Of course. And, she can prepare the countess's gown as well. As the head of this household, I must make the decisions that are best for all members, and I insist you attend, Lady Rivers."

With that, he turned and led Lady Bernadette back to the manor. Hannah stood there with her mouth open. She most certainly did not appreciate his high-handed decision, and she refused to accept it. Death had freed her from one controlling Lord Rivers, and she refused to be subjected to another. As soon as the children were out of her care, she had every intention of telling him so.

~ ~ ~

Lucius sat in his study staring at the next clue, but not really seeing it. No matter how hard he thought, he couldn't decide what had possessed him to insist Hannah attend a ball with him and Lady Bernadette. It was true that the lady's assumption that Hannah wouldn't go had angered him, but it shouldn't have pushed him into this.

Although he wanted Hannah with a fierceness he'd never known, his walk through the garden with Lady Bernadette had helped to clear his mind of the kiss he had shared with Hannah and had set his priorities to right. In the end, he knew his attention would be better served in pursuit of his future wife.

Now, all he could think about was holding Hannah in his arms for another dance. This one not in the company of children and certainly not one where all eyes would be on them. Anticipation lit his skin, and he cursed. Propping his elbows on his desk, he held his head. What was he doing? In an attempt to clear his mind, he tried to picture Lady Bernadette in that position, but he couldn't.

The door swung open, snapping his head up and his mind back to the present. He inwardly groaned to see Hannah. Not trusting himself at the moment, he stood, but kept the desk between them as he warily watched her close the door and approach him.

"Care to explain yourself?" She put her hands on her hips as she glared at him.

Although the fight in him rose at her challenging posture, so did his desire. She couldn't possibly have any idea how desirable she was at this moment. He could almost feel the heat in her molten gaze.

Clearing his throat, he forced his reaction away. "In regard to what?"

"Don't play games with me. You know very well why I'm here. And, you may have his title but you are *not* my husband."

"I am very aware of that fact." He crossed his arms, not liking that she compared him to his uncle.

"Then, don't treat me like he did," she spat the words. "I'm not an item that you can choose what to do with."

At her words all anger left his body, and he rounded the desk, hating that he'd brought out such a response in her. "You know I don't see you like that, and I'm truly sorry you felt that way. In the future, we can have more of a discussion before I make my decisions."

She nodded, visibly calming. "Thank you. I can accept that."

"Then, the matter is settled." He leaned his hip against the desk, knowing she wouldn't like his next statement. "However, my decision regarding the ball still stands."

"Why?" Her hands balled into fists as her eyes narrowed. "You have no right to force me to do this."

He let out a laugh. "Actually, I have every right, and I'm doing this for your own good. You never leave the manor. You insist I ride to escape, yet you don't even walk in the garden. You simply wander through these halls day after day. It isn't good for you."

"Your information is inaccurate. Or, have you already forgotten my trip to the stables today? I'd refrain from making assumptions if I were you."

Her attitude matched her words, but he could see the truth in her eyes. However, his observation hadn't been an assumption. Much as he didn't like it, he was too attuned to her. Too acutely aware of her every move. Seeing her outside today had been a surprise, and it had definitely been the first day she had taken a trip outside.

"Lying to me won't serve you." He softened his voice as he studied her. "Hannah, tell me why you don't wish to go to the ball. I know you love to dance and considering you spend the season in London, I imagine you don't have an aversion to crowds."

Her shoulders fell as if he'd knocked the fight out of her. "I've already told you dance partners are hard to come by. I'm forced to remain there in the background." Her gaze dropped to the floor. "It's the watching I can't stand."

The pain in her voice undid him. He moved to stand before her and lifted her face to meet his gaze, then dropped his hand. "You know I will dance with you. Two dances belong to me, and if I must spend the remainder of the time seeking partners for you, I will."

She pulled her bottom lip between her teeth. "Why? Why would you do that for me? You must secure enjoyment from the night as well."

Mesmerized by her hopeful eyes, he knew he would move the world for her if she wanted it. The guilt carried around with him obligated him to do that at least, but when she looked at him like that, it felt like so much more. Regardless, she would have whatever she needed.

"All I require is a smile on your face at the end of the evening."

She placed her hand on his chest. "Sometimes I wonder if I ever really knew you. All those years . . ."

Her words trailed off as her eyes zeroed in on his mouth, and she slowly moved forward. The world froze that instant. Allowing her to kiss him would be a huge mistake, but he wasn't sure he was capable of denying himself the pleasure. At this moment, he could justify anything, but he knew later would be another matter. He couldn't allow this to happen.

He opened his mouth to put a stop to her movements just as her lips came in contact with his. The result of having her top lip caught between his evaporated his doubts as lightning struck his body. He gathered her into his arms and kissed her.

Although he knew he needed to move slowly with her, everything inside him screamed to deepen the kiss. To take what she would give, but he held himself back. Then, her bold hands slid up his chest and wound around his neck, pressing her further up against him. That was it. He needed more.

Securing his hand in her brilliant hair, he held her to him as he ran his tongue along her lips. The slight parting was what he craved, and he was filled with a joy he hadn't expected. Not wasting any time, he slid his tongue into her hot mouth.

To his surprise, she didn't respond and made no move to kiss him back. Not content, he ran his free hand over her back as he tried to persuade her to react. Nothing.

"Kiss me, Hannah," he whispered against her lips. "You started this. Don't deny me now."

When he tried again, she tentatively met him. He coaxed her and it wasn't long before her desires took over. The result had him aching with a need so strong he contemplated taking her on the sofa. Her hands were in his hair, keeping him in place. He reveled in her passion, but he also knew this had to stop. Otherwise, he would do something they would both regret.

Reluctantly, he drew back. She didn't release him, she merely looked at him with desire and wonderment on her face. The sight combined with her swollen lips and heavy breathing tested his control. Instead of giving in, he pulled further away until her arms left him.

"That was unlike anything I've ever experienced."

He let out a strained chuckle. "Glad to hear it, but you know it can't happen again."

The luster left her face as she nodded. "Of course, but thank you. I suppose you would like me to promise not to kiss you again?"

Swallowing, he knew he could never ask that of her for it wasn't what he wanted. "I don't think that's necessary."

Mischief sparkled in her eyes. "Good. Because I can't make such a promise. Not after that."

With those parting words, she turned and fled from his study. He let out a deep breath as he dropped himself onto the sofa. Everything within him rejoiced at her words, but he knew he shouldn't feel this way. Bloody hell, what was he doing? This was not going to end well for him.

~ ~ ~

Hannah paced her bedchamber as the walls began to shrink before her very eyes. After her glorious kiss with Lucius yesterday, she could hardly think of anything else. To make matters worse, each time she gazed upon him, her heart skipped a beat and she knew her desires were clear on her face. As a result, she'd done her best to avoid looking at him at all through dinner last night, and he'd been suspiciously absent from breakfast.

Sitting on the edge of the bed, she ran a hand over her face. Had that been because of her? She didn't know what was wrong with her. She supposed that after years of suffering attentions from a man without the benefit of the slightest enjoyment from it, she was desperate for any such attention now. The idea was shameful.

She wished she could have discovered this with another man. Clearly, Lucius had no desire to continue with her, and she didn't blame him. Not only had she proven to him her experiences had been difficult, but she'd been married to his uncle. Then, there was Lady Bernadette. If he spent all his time kissing Hannah, she knew he'd lose his chance to marry his chosen bride.

The air in the room suddenly felt stifling as if it would choke her. Crossing the room, she threw open the window and held the curtain back as she glanced out over the garden. At one time she'd known those paths so well, she could have navigated them in the dark. She let out a humorless chuckle. Ten years later, and she was still afraid of being out of doors.

Recalling Lucius's comment about her not leaving the manor, she took a deep breath and stepped out onto the balcony, allowing the curtain to fall down to close her in. Terror clawed her throat to be essentially shut outside, but she knew it was only in her mind. One step back and the curtain would easily brush aside. She needed to do this. It was the key to conquering her fear.

She concentrated on taking deep breaths as she held onto the railing. Seeing movement below, she took in the sight of Lucius. Her nerves calmed as she kept his smiling face in view. Not wanting him to see her, she moved to the corner. Longing hit her in the chest as he bent down and pulled a discarded flower from the path. Then, he turned and offered it to Lady Bernadette who Hannah now saw sitting on a bench.

The good feelings left her as sickness struck her. Backing up, she knew she couldn't watch the happy couple any longer. Another step and her back met up with something solid. Panicked, she spun around to see the window had been closed.

Nausea rolled in her stomach as the edges of her vision blacked out. Memory mixed with reality and she was eighteen again. She couldn't breathe.

"Dear God. No! No! Not again. Help!" She kept screaming as she banged on the glass. "Please, don't. I'm sorry. Don't do this to me."

An eternity of seconds passed before the window opened. Throwing herself inside, she landed unceremoniously on the floor curled into a tight ball.

"I'm so sorry, my lady." Lisa's stunned voice barely registered through the haze of fear still threatening Hannah, but she could do nothing to assure the woman. "I didn't know you were out there. I'm so sorry."

A loud banging made Hannah wince and crawl further into herself.

"What in God's name is going on?" Fury dripped off Lucius's words. More humiliation would come now. She knew it well.

Hannah felt herself being pulled from the floor, but she couldn't make her limbs move. The warmth of being cradled against Lucius's chest seeped into her. He held her close as he knelt on the floor.

"I'm so sorry, my lord." Misery leaked into Lisa's every word. "I came to clean her room. It was empty, but the window was left open. I didn't know she was out there when I closed it. I had no idea."

"Hannah." His voice was gentle. "Are you harmed? Is that what happened?"

Allowing his soothing presence to leach into her, she managed to calm a little bit. Although her heart still hammered in her chest, she tried to sit up. Lucius helped her, but her body wouldn't stop shaking, so she remained on the floor.

"Yes," she responded in an unsteady voice. "Lisa's not at fault."

"You don't look well. Should I fetch the doctor?" Lucius's eyes were full of concern.

Embarrassment burned her cheeks. This was a huge mistake brought out by her memories. "No. I'm well. Please don't let me keep you from—"

"Dear heavens!" Lady Bernadette gasped from the doorway. "What has happened?"

Lucius cleared his voice as he stood. "Lady Rivers has

taken a nasty fall. I believe she simply needs some rest. My lady, would you permit me to assist you to your bed?"

With cheeks so hot, she knew they had to be crimson. Nodding, she lifted her hand, expecting him to pull her to her feet, but he surprised her by scooping her up in his arms and setting her upon the bed.

"Thank you," she squeaked.

He nodded and then turned to Lisa. "Assist her as necessary, then let me know her condition after she has settled."

Once Lucius ushered the onlookers out, Hannah buried her face in her pillow. Her humiliation was complete. How could she have thought Lucius would prefer her kisses over sharing a lifetime with someone who was somewhat normal? She wasn't right. She was broken. Her husband had seen to that. She moved through each day like everyone else, but she knew the truth.

"My lady, are you well?" Lisa's voice was timid. "Had I known you were out there, I never would've closed the door. I swear, I—"

Hannah rolled over to look at the woman she considered a friend. "Stop. I don't blame you. It's me. In the future, I'll make sure the curtain is open."

"And, you can be assured I will never close another window without checking behind it. I can't believe I didn't see you when I moved the curtain aside."

Heat touched Hannah's cheeks again. Had she not been spying on a private moment of Lucius's this never would have happened. She supposed she deserved it. As her husband always told her, she'd brought it upon herself.

"Think nothing of it." Hannah bit her lip as a thought came to her. "Lisa, do you think you could help me with something?"

"Of course, my lady."

Feeling marginally better, Hannah sucked in a deep breath. It was time for her to mend the pieces of herself that were broken. This wasn't going to be an easy road, but she would succeed.

Chapter 6

Lucius took Hannah's dance card and wrote his name down for two of her dances before handing it back. "Are you sure you should be here," he mumbled under his breath.

She rolled her eyes. "What happened to you being the head of the house and demanding my presence at the ball?"

Her words were teasing, but he could still see a weariness in her eyes caused from whatever had happened to her on the balcony earlier today. He had every intention of sneaking up to her bedchamber earlier to talk to her once he'd seen Lady Bernadette downstairs, but the lady hadn't given him a second to dislodge himself from her.

"That was before. How are you feeling?"

The breath she let out was full of irritation. "If you intend to keep asking me that, I'll scratch your name off my dance card. And, I hope you haven't forgotten your promise."

He shook his head. "I haven't. You shall dance your fill tonight."

Her musical laughter was a balm to his soul. "I'm not asking for the impossible. It would be nice to share at least two more dances than the ones I have with you."

As he moved on from Hannah, he glanced around the room. He intended to do far better than two dances for her. At one point, he had spent a lot of his time on the estate with his uncle, so the people were familiar. As Hannah wasn't requiring anything other than a skill on the dance floor, he imagined it shouldn't be too difficult to secure a few partners for her.

"So, the dragon emerges from his cave."

Lucius turned and grinned to see his friend, Ronald. "Dragon? If I recall correctly, it was you who could breathe fire."

The man laughed. "It's good to see you. When you took over as earl, I moved back to my estate, expecting to see you at social events like this. I'd begun to believe your uncle left poisoned food for you."

Pasting on a smile, Lucius shook his head. His uncle definitely had poisoned his life, but not in the way his friend referred. "It's simply been an adjustment. I've been away for ten years after all."

Ronald nodded in mock pity. "Must be a very difficult life if you're arriving with two enchanting creatures. If I had two blond princesses like that, I wouldn't want to share either."

"It isn't what it looks like. One is visiting as a guest with her mother. The other is my uncle's late wife. Actually, since you brought her up, I have a favor to ask of you. The countess has trouble securing dances at events such as these. I wonder if you could be so kind as to claim one of them with her."

His eyes glanced off to the side, and he nodded. "Of course. Not to speak badly about your aunt, but she would have better results if she didn't look at everyone with disdain. It diminishes her beauty."

Anger flashed through Lucius. "The lady has suffered a stumble today. It would better serve you to pass judgment after you've met her."

His friend spread his hands wide. "I meant no insult to your family. It was just an idle observation. Now, I need you to introduce me to your friend. From the looks of it, if I don't get over there soon, her dance card will be full."

Shocked that Lady Bernadette caused such a stir, he sought her out. She stood to the side of the dance floor with her mother. The look on her face read irritation and jealousy.

There were no gentlemen around her requesting dances. A stone settled in Lucius's stomach.

Following his friend's gaze, he found Hannah. Clearly the hostess had decided to offer introductions. Hannah stood with the woman and no less than five men who were puffing out their chests trying to gain her attention. The sight sickened him.

Hannah had never been to a ball before without having the threat of her husband—either dead or alive—hanging over her. These men didn't know that threat. She may not be in her first season, but her beauty outshined everyone in the room. He clenched his fists. Perhaps the men needed to understand that threat.

"Are you going to introduce me or not?" Ronald pressed.

"That's not the visiting friend," Lucius explained through clenched teeth. "She's my aunt and clearly as innocent as a debutante. It seems she's in need of protection tonight."

Ronald grinned. "Leave that up to me."

As they approached Hannah, her eyes met Lucius's, and they were bright. Seeing the pleasure in her chocolate depths, he cooled his anger. As long as none of these men thought to attempt to remove her from the room, there was no harm in her enjoyment. In addition, her dance card would be full.

He pushed his way to her. "My lady." He bowed his head. "Are you well?"

"Did you do this?" She ignored his question. "Thank you."

The fact she didn't consider that her own vibrancy and beauty called out to all these men made him shake his head. How could she not see it? The woman truly was a treasure.

"No. You did this. But, I did bring someone I'd like you to meet."

Her attention moved to Ronald and she smiled. "I see. Please introduce us, I have an open waltz I've been dying for someone to ask for."

Searing jealousy burned through Lucius at her flirtatious manner toward Ronald. And, the man's responding grin and wink didn't help. Perhaps requesting assistance from his friend had been a mistake. Regardless, Lucius had no choice now. He swallowed down his bad decision.

"Please allow me to present Lord Ronald Phelps, Baron Christen." Then, he turned to his friend. "This is Hannah Dobson, Countess of Rivers, and my aunt."

As the pair began their conversation, or rather their flirtation, Lucius realized he once again had become invisible to her. The truth knocked the wind out of him like a punch in the chest. He slowly backed away as the mask of loathing he'd adopted all these years drew back into place. It had taken weeks of her presence to reclaim himself and in one instant, he was back to the bitter rake he'd been for the past ten years.

Panic flashed in Hannah's eyes, and she quickly glanced around. Immediately, his insides came to attention, ready to battle for her. Of their own accord, his feet brought him back to her side. When her eyes settled upon him, she visibly relaxed and didn't break eye contact. She needed him. And, just like that, his world was righted again.

Thankfully, the first notes of his waltz began, and he knew he would have the time with her to fix this without arousing suspicion. One dance. That was all he could give her for now. He couldn't allow himself to be dependent on her. The back of his head burned with the force of Lady Bernadette's gaze. Once he saw to Hannah, he would have to make amends with the other lady as well. It was a delicate balance, but for Hannah, he would manage.

~ ~ ~

Hannah nearly melted into Lucius's embrace as he led her into the waltz. Her heart was beating so furiously, she didn't know how she would survive the night, but she couldn't exactly leave either. He held her up and led her expertly, although her attention kept sliding toward the guests.

"What is wrong?" Lucius's low voice reverberated through her. "If you inch any closer to me, there will certainly be talk. We're pushing propriety as it is."

"I'm sorry." Shame filled her, and she tried to pull back, but he held her tight.

"Don't go anywhere. I said pushing, not pushed. Now, talk to me. Something happened to you today in your bedchamber, and I saw that reflected in your eyes just now. What is it?"

She ducked her head down, focusing on the buttons of his coat. How could she explain? Ever since she'd been locked on the balcony, the lines of present day and memories seemed blurred. Tonight, she'd never expected to have so many gentlemen who wanted to dance with her. It reminded her of her first week in London. Her husband hadn't liked it.

Taking a deep breath, she tried to block out the memories of his anger when other men would talk to her. Eventually, she'd suffered enough of his insults that sustaining more hadn't been worth the dances. She had taken to trailing behind him at such events. The men, it seemed, had taken the hint quickly and she was largely ignored.

"I don't know if I can do this," she whispered.

"Do what? Be the belle of the ball? Outshine every woman here?"

Pleasure washed through her at his words, and she spared a glance at his face. He seemed earnest enough, but he was clearly trying to ease her discomfort. Which he'd already done by his presence.

It had occurred to her that with all the men, she would find one willing to share a kiss with her, but in the end, she wasn't interested. Although she had a good selection tonight, there was only one man she wanted to kiss. And, he was unavailable and didn't want her.

"I'm being serious," she responded to his compliment. "I think this is too soon for me to handle this."

"You didn't attend balls in London during the season?"

"I did, but this is different. There, everyone ignores me like they always did. Here, they see me. He sees me."

Lucius's grip on her tightened. "He? Who is he?"

Biting her lip, she looked to the side at the couples gliding past them. She hadn't meant to say that. In truth, she'd thought she had heard her husband's berating voice. The fear that hit her was instant, and she panicked, however irrational the thought.

"Nobody. I shouldn't have said that."

"Hannah, how do you expect me to protect you if I don't know where the threat is coming from? If I had any idea you were avoiding society to hide from someone, I—"

"That's not it. I'm talking about my husband. It's silly, I know, but I just became awash with memories, and it scared me."

Lucius's Adam's apple bobbed as he swallowed. "I understand he didn't treat you as he should have. I can't tell you how sorry I am for that, but he can't hurt you anymore. We've been unsuccessful in our task lately. Tomorrow, we will begin working together again. No more contemplating separately over the clues. For both our sakes, we need to get him completely behind us."

She nodded. "Thank you, Lucius. I don't know what I would have done without you."

The song ended, and he let out a long sigh as he released her.

"Will you be all right if I leave you? I need to see to Lady Bernadette."

Hating the truth of his words, she nodded. "Of course. You've done enough."

"If you need anything and can't find me, I've asked Lord

Christen to keep an eye on you. I've known him for years. He can protect you."

After he left her, she watched as Lucius walked over to Lady Bernadette. The woman didn't appear to be too pleased with him. A large part of Hannah couldn't bring herself to feel bad for him. Perhaps, he would need to take Lady Bernadette out to the garden and give her another flower, she thought bitterly.

The remainder of the night, Hannah didn't have time to think about her husband because she was too consumed with Lucius's every move. Although she managed to keep a steady conversation with the other guests, particularly with Lord Christen, she knew exactly where Lucius was in the room and with whom he was speaking.

As promised, the following day Lucius sent for her to join him in his study. After everything that occurred yesterday, she wasn't sure she wanted to be alone with him. Too much history and questions surrounded their relationship, and she didn't know what to do about it.

"Close the door," he ordered as soon as she stepped into the room. "Take a seat."

Feeling nervous for some reason, she approached the desk that had belonged to her husband. However, no bad memories surfaced. She'd spent too many good memories with Lucius here to replace the bad. After what she had experienced, it was strange to once again be dependent on a man. This time to erase the pain.

"Why do I get the feeling you want more from me than to solve clues?" She pinned him with a look, hoping to portray a confidence she didn't feel as she perched on the chair before his desk.

"I've been fighting with myself all night, but I think I have to know. What did he do to you on the balcony?"

Her eyes widened and heat blasted her cheeks. She hadn't expected that. "Nothing."

"I was in the garden. I heard your voice. You were terrified. And, you said 'again.' Did he lock you out there regularly? For how long? No one helped you?"

His onslaught of questions made her head spin. She closed her eyes and held her hands up to her temples. How could she tell him? This was his uncle. He shouldn't know the truth. He should be spared the truth of her mistakes and what his uncle had been forced to do.

"Stop. Don't. No one left me on the balcony. Well, except Lisa, but that wasn't on purpose."

"I don't understand." His warm hands took hers off her face and held them in his as he knelt before her on the floor. "Tell me what happened."

"You don't want to know."

"Yes, I do. If you don't tell me, I'll start asking around. It was a long time ago, but I suspect someone remembers."

Horror clutched her heart. "No. Please don't. This is my burden to remember, don't make them do it, too."

"Then, tell me."

Letting out a long sigh, she looked away. "If you must know, I'll tell you, but it's not something you want to hear. During the first month of my marriage I found solace in the garden or on the back of a horse. In truth, I felt the hunting cabin to be more of my home than the manor."

"I find that hard to believe considering I can't get you to set foot outside."

She swallowed. "There's a reason for that. You see, my husband didn't care for my choice of escape. He said it wasn't worthy of his countess to be traversing around the countryside all day. I didn't listen and went for my ride as usual the following morning. When I returned, the doors had been locked and every one must have been instructed not to allow me to come in."

"That bloody bastard. How long did he leave you out there?"

Not wanting to finish the story, a tear slipped down her cheek. Immediately, Lucius stood and pulled her into his arms. She laid her head against his shoulder, knowing that this was wrong. But, why did it have to feel so right?

"It's fine." She pushed out of his arms, knowing she couldn't get used to any of this. "He let me back in the next morning."

Lucius bit out a curse. "You didn't stay outside all night? Tell me you rode to the hunting cabin or into the village for a room."

"As soon as I got back, he sent away my beloved mare, having already sold her. I had nowhere to go." Aching sadness opened up in her chest for what she'd just admitted about his uncle. She couldn't stand herself right now. "Please, excuse me. I don't believe I'm up to working on the code today."

~ ~ ~

Rage, hatred, and loathing swirled through Lucius's mind. After Hannah's confession about the horrors she'd endured, he'd ridden his stallion out hard, then destroyed some unsuspecting brush in the forest to alleviate his rage and exercise his overheated body. Nothing worked. Although physically he was exhausted, his mind still wouldn't leave him alone. *His fault*. He knew exactly where the blame she felt lay.

Pulling the stopper from the second bottle of whisky, he did his best to drown out the voice of his mind. Last night, he had decided it was better to know the truth than to speculate. Now, he wasn't so sure. However, the more he drank, the more clear everything became.

How could he possibly pay for his sins if he didn't know what they were? She needed to tell him everything. Only then could he truly make amends. He had to make this right.

Bitter laughter rose within him and echoed in his study. Months ago, she'd claimed she didn't believe he'd done anything so heinous as to deserve this game his uncle had set up for him. She'd been wrong. If she only knew. She'd hate him.

Knowing what he had to do, he pulled himself to his feet, steadying himself at the edge of his desk before heading to the door. He knew Lady Bernadette and her mother had planned an excursion to the village, but Hannah hadn't joined them. Not that he was surprised. However, he couldn't find her anywhere in the manor. Had he upset her so badly she'd hidden from him?

"Rawlings?" he bellowed, surprised when the man materialized. "Where may I find Lady Rivers?"

"The countess is in the garden. Are you well, my lord? Perhaps you should lie down."

He ignored the man and moved toward the garden. Why on earth would she be outside? Had she lied to him? Nothing added up in his inebriated brain. All he knew was that he had to find Hannah.

When he reached the door, he saw her in the garden with Lisa, the maid. Curious, he slipped outside but kept his distance.

"There, my lady. All is well. I'm not going to leave you."

"And, doors?" Fear etched in Hannah's words.

"Are good and unlocked. And, you can be assured I'll break through the glass to get you inside if I'm wrong."

Hannah nodded. "I used to love it out here. With your help, I think I might be able to love it again. I remember taking long walks with my sister-in-law at Melbourne, but it is different here."

"Of course it's different. You grew up at Melbourne. That was your home for so long."

The sigh Hannah let out was full of pain. "I don't even remember what home felt like. It's been so many years since I experienced it."

That was it. Why he was here. Stepping forward, he approached the women. His eyes were locked on Hannah. The look on her face read embarrassment, but he needed to hear this. To understand.

"My lord, how may I help you?" Hannah's voice was stiff.

He faced Lisa. "You may go. I've got her."

The slurring of his words must not have instilled confidence because the woman narrowed her eyes and opened her mouth.

"I'm fine, Lisa. You may go," Hannah spoke before Lisa could.

Although reluctant, the maid nodded and went back into the manor.

"You're outside," he observed like a fool.

"So, we're stating the obvious. In that case, you've been drinking. A lot from the looks of it. I've tried that, too. Trust me, it doesn't help."

Shocked, he jerked back, nearly losing his footing. "You turned to alcohol?"

"Whisky. I do miss a splash of it in my tea." Her face turned serious. "I'm so sorry, Lucius. I never should have told you."

"On the contrary. I want to know all of it. Right now. Tell me everything he did to you."

Her mouth fell open. "Are you mad? Why would you want to hear such things?"

He clenched his fists against his anger, after all, she hadn't denied that there was more to tell. "It's better to get it all out. You've been silently carrying this burden, and now I'm going to carry it with you."

She shrugged. "I suppose it won't hurt. You already know the worst, and you've been drinking so much, you probably won't remember this tomorrow."

Mentally preparing himself, he planted his feet, but she approached him and took his arm. "What are you doing?"

"Walk with me, and I'll talk. That's better. Now, after that very important lesson he taught me about heeding his warnings, I remained indoors and did my best to obey him."

Lucius felt better with her normal tone of voice combined with how she leaned into him. "I see. Keep going."

"You know your uncle, the man was not a physical fighter unless pushed to the limit. Instead, he had a way with words. He knew exactly what to say to put me in my place."

Recalling exactly how damaging those words could be, Lucius stopped and faced her. The look on her face was full of amusement, but he knew years of verbal abuse took a toll on a person. He'd lived it, after all.

"Is there anything else?" He searched her face to see the true answer.

A glint lit her eyes. "Well, he did subject me to his horrid kisses. However, that is a memory you can help me erase."

Alarm bells went off in his head at the same time his body rose to attention. She'd orchestrated this whole thing. The idea she would do something like this was so intoxicating, lust overtook all other thoughts and feelings within him.

As she took his hand and pulled him into the bushes, he willingly followed her, anticipation making it difficult to see straight. Then, she turned around, and she was in his arms. Unlike their previous kisses, this one was urgent and desperate. He wasted no time and delved his tongue into her mouth as she molded her body to his.

She met his passion, burying her hands in his hair. Thoughts of taking her in this grove assaulted him, but he managed to hold back. Her exuberance spurned him on unlike anything before. This woman would be the death of him, for he was sinking under her spell swiftly, and there was nothing he could do about it.

"We need to go back now," he breathed when he'd had enough control to pull himself away from her.

"Why?" She stuck her bottom lip out in a pout. It took everything in him not to suck that lip into his mouth.

"I've reached my limit."

"Very well." She let out a sigh. "Since you won't remember this tomorrow, I have no problem telling you that you are unlike any man I've ever met. I trust you, and I know you'd never hurt me." She ran her fingers across his lips. "And, your kisses keep me awake at night."

As she sauntered away, he knew he was utterly wrecked. Bloody hell. He certainly hoped he wouldn't remember this tomorrow.

Chapter 7

Hannah closed herself into an unoccupied bedchamber and knelt down by the bed. Slipping her hands under the mattress, she felt around for a key. Nothing. Lifting the mattress as high as she could, she looked under it and didn't see anything. As she moved to the other side, she repeated the process.

This was tiresome. They were only on the third clue, and she was done already. Although they suspected they knew where the key was located, finding it was altogether a different matter.

As she'd anticipated, Lucius had been too drunk yesterday to recall meeting her in the garden. It had been a relief to see him and not suffer the sight of his regret or pity. But, on the other hand, she wished she had the confidence to speak to him candidly when he would remember. However, that would be unfair to him.

She had no future to offer. Another husband was the last thing she wanted. Lucius was pleasant to be around and his kisses made her lose her mind, but she knew there was more to marriage. More that she never wanted to experience again. Barring all that, she couldn't bear children. With no ability to provide an heir, and she was essentially useless.

Pulling herself up, she moved to the next bedchamber and suppressed a shudder as she knocked. She couldn't exactly ask Lady Bernadette for permission to search the room, and the lady certainly wouldn't be pleased if Hannah were found in the room in her absence. With no response,

Hannah quickly entered and closed the door, hoping to have this done as swiftly as possible.

With no luck on the first side, she hastened to the other. At a sweep of her hand, she gasped to touch something. Excitement warmed her face as she lifted the mattress and saw a small key lying just out of reach. With some difficulty, she propped the mattress on her shoulder and grabbed the key.

After allowing the heavy load to fall back into place, she gripped her treasure in her hand, a smile on her lips. Lucius would be pleased. They needed to finish this and allow him to completely claim his inheritance.

The door latch rattled as voices murmured from the hall. Hannah quickly scanned the room. The wardrobe. Slipping inside, she eased the door closed without clicking the latch. Her heart pumped wildly as she prayed it would be a staff member. Her hope vanished at the sound of Lady Bernadette's voice.

"That's not what I'm saying, Mother. It's just that I'm becoming increasingly impatient. I've given that man plenty of opportunities to offer for me, or at the very least to kiss me, but nothing has happened."

"Must I remind you that you knew how slowly the lord moved when you chose him? That man has always shown a reluctance in his affections."

Hannah couldn't believe what she was hearing. Although she knew she shouldn't be pleased, she couldn't stop the feeling from overtaking her. So, Lucius wasn't giving out kisses to both of them. It was certainly a challenge to have him bestow her each one, but his passion made her toes curl at the very memory.

The girl let out an unladylike huff. "I know, but I thought this would be different. After all, he did ask me to come here. That was clear in his letter. I just wish he could be more like Mr. Jeffries."

"I told you never to mention his name," Lady Winslow snapped. "His attentions were inappropriate. You very nearly lost your reputation."

"Then, we won't talk about him. Instead, we need to address the problem of the countess."

Shock jolted Hannah, but she managed to stop herself from banging her head on the back of the wardrobe and alerting the women to her presence. What problem was the lady talking about?

"I think you're making too much of this. I, too, have seen how his eyes follow her, but the girl doesn't have a chance. She may be a nightly activity for him, but it's you he will marry. He needs heirs, not an old, barren wife."

"You're right. I don't like it, but I can send her away once I take her title. Then, I will be the one in his bed."

"Remember that when you talk to her, and you'll be less likely to give in to your unbecoming nature. Now, are you going to collect your shawl? I wish to leave now."

Fear danced across Hannah's skin. If the lady opened the wardrobe, she was done for. The sound of footsteps neared, shoving Hannah's heart into her throat. Then, they stopped.

"Got it."

As the two exited the room, chattering about the shops they planned to visit in the village, Hannah fell hard against the back of the wardrobe. She was safe. Although, the whole conversation she'd overheard made her feel ill. Did everyone believe she had allowed Lucius into her bed? The thought was absurd. No woman would willingly do such a thing.

Bile rose to her throat, the burning sensation making her want to retch. This woman would become her niece. And, when Bernadette wed Lucius, would she be able to convince him to send her away? Where would she be exiled this time? London for a full year? The thought didn't sit well with her.

Forcing herself to her feet, Hannah climbed from the wardrobe and exited the room. This was too much to handle at present. The taste of freedom at the estate had spoiled her, and she didn't relish the idea of her life changing anytime soon. Tears formed in her eyes.

She needed to distract herself. With the key in her hand, she moved toward Lucius's study. They needed to claim his inheritance. Before he did that, she knew he wouldn't marry Lady Bernadette, but she refused to be neglectful in her promise simply to award herself more time.

"Lady Rivers?"

Spinning around, she saw Lord Christen in the hallway behind Mr. Rawlings. "My lord, how nice to see you." She feigned happiness, trying to keep her true emotions hidden.

"I thought it would be nice to pay you a call. Are you available?"

Shocked, she glanced at Mr. Rawlings, but he only appeared slightly perturbed to have his routine altered. It didn't bother her as she hated to stand on ceremony. As she moved her gaze back to the baron, Hannah realized he may be the exact distraction she needed at present.

"I most certainly am, my lord. Would you care to sit in the drawing room?"

He offered his arm. "The weather is pleasant. Do you suppose we could go for a stroll through the garden instead?"

With a nod, she slipped the key into the folds of her gown and took his arm. As she had told Lisa, she should be able to handle it as long as she wasn't alone. Yesterday had been the first time she'd stepped foot in the place since she'd spent the night out there. It had gone well, more so after Lucius had joined her.

"Is this purely a social call, or was there something you needed from me?" she asked once outside, suddenly anxious to have this over with.

He chuckled. "Is it so hard to believe I wish to spend time with you? I enjoyed our conversations at the ball the other night, and I thought to further our relationship."

Warnings went off in her mind. He was exactly like all those other men. They saw a married woman and thought she would fall into their beds. She couldn't believe she had put herself in this position.

She stopped and pulled her arm free of his. "Our relationship? I don't know you."

When she took a step back, he followed her. "That's not what I meant, my lady. I only want to talk. To get to know you. Lord Rivers said you can trust me, remember?"

Recalling how Lucius had appointed the baron as her protector the other night, she nodded. She hated how her husband had installed a complete distrust of all men within her. Taking his arm again, she shyly smiled, intending to make it up to him.

"You're right. I'm sorry, my lord. Come, let's continue."

~ ~ ~

Lucius sat in the drawing room, staring unseeingly at the items Lady Bernadette put in front of his eyes. He was drained. Ultimately and utterly. In so many ways what he was currently dealing with was far worse than anything his uncle had subjected him to. This was something he would be lucky to survive.

"Are you listening?" Lady Bernadette whined. "Honestly, Lucius, sometimes I feel as though you don't care about anything I say."

Making himself focus on the girl, he took in her pouting face. At one point he saw a touch of Hannah when he looked upon her, but not any longer. This girl was much too young and selfish. Did he truly want to spend the rest of his life dealing with her? In his heart, he knew the truth.

When he returned from his ride, he'd seen Hannah walking through the gardens with Ronald. The sight of her pleasure in the man's presence brought out an intense jealousy he'd never experienced before. How could he feel something so strongly for her? True, the woman had put his body in turmoil. But, it had been months since he'd had any relief, and she tested his patience. One night. That was what he needed. One night would keep him sane. Then, the ache would be satisfied, and she would be just another woman.

"No. I'm not listening," he responded to Lady Bernadette at last. "You're right that I have no care to look at baubles. Considering you have felt the need to show me your every purchase from each excursion, my only assumption is that you wish for me to understand that you have a great need for funds, is that correct?"

She sucked in her breath. "Of course not. I only thought you would wish to see the items purchased from your tenants."

"I have visited the shops before and have no need to browse their wares any longer. I thank you for your consideration."

The glare she shot him spoke of a temper he'd not seen from her previously. "Why did you invite me out here? I had thought you were hoping to further our association, but I can see that's not the case."

Lucius let out a sigh as he got to his feet. He felt like an ass. She was right. The point of having her here was ultimately to offer for her, but as he'd gotten to know her, he wasn't sure he wanted that any longer. However, how could he turn her away after he'd taken so much of her time?

"That's exactly what we've been doing," he argued. "Every day we share meals together and have daily walks. What more are you looking for?"

When he turned around to face her, a gleam lit in her eyes. She'd set this up. Her comments had been intentional to get him to ask such a question. He clenched his teeth, not liking her underhanded manner.

She sauntered toward him. "At this point, I don't believe it would be inappropriate of me to request some form of physical connection."

Her eyes zeroed in on his mouth, and he tugged on the collar of his shirt, feeling as though the garment was strangling him. The idea of kissing Lady Bernadette held no appeal to him. This wasn't right. Why did the thought send him into a panic when with Hannah he had quite the opposite reaction?

"I appreciate your honesty regarding your feelings, however, I believe that is a little premature."

"How can you say that?" Her bottom lip jutted and her brows creased. "Honestly, Lucius, if you can't kiss me now, I don't think I can remain here any longer. Are you so set in your belief that you are prepared to lose me over it?"

The agony of making the decision at this very moment tore into him. He shifted his feet. In truth, he felt it may be worth the sacrifice in order to share the short time with Hannah. He couldn't believe he was going to give up his future for a few months with her, but at the moment, that was all he could think about.

"If that's how you feel, then I believe it's time for you to return home."

Her mouth fell open. "You can't be serious. Instead of kissing me, you're sending me away?"

Putting his shoulders back, he felt better about his decision. "Yes. It's becoming very clear that you and I want different things from life. You would be happy with someone who is more willing to move at your speed."

"You'll regret this. Be assured that--"

"I wish you all the best, but you must excuse me before you say something you will regret."

Not wishing to hear another word, he left the room. Luckily he found Mr. Rawlings lurking outside, and he told the man of the new situation. The murderous intent he'd seen in Lady Bernadette's eyes didn't bode well for the breakable items in the room. His butler would certainly ensure the safety of all the estate belongings. In addition, Rawlings had told him Hannah was waiting for him in his study and he didn't want to delay getting to her.

As he moved down the hallway, Lucius took a deep breath. A sense of freedom he hadn't felt in a long time overtook him. For the first time, he was allowed to feel. His desire for Hannah wasn't inappropriate or at an inconvenient time any longer. As such, he fully intended to take advantage of this opportunity.

Once he entered the study and shut the door, she stood and offered him a beautiful smile. She was so glorious it hurt him to simply gaze upon her. The only thing stopping him from collecting her in his arms was a damn promise that he was going to make her absolve him from.

"There you are. I was beginning to despair that you would come at all."

He crossed his arms over his chest. "I believe you know me better than that."

"True. Well, I have something for you."

She moved her hand to her waist and slid her fingers under the folds of her clothing. His mouth dried. When she retrieved a key and held it out to him, it took him a good while to understand the meaning. The thought of her removing her gown emblazoned on his mind, and he wanted nothing else. Then, the significance of the key struck him.

"You found it? Already?" He made no move to retrieve the item from her hand as he knew getting closer to her would only be a mistake, so he floundered for an excuse. "I have yet to locate the corresponding coffer."

Her wink was self-assured. "I'm good for that, too. Are you going to take this from me?"

The small, shining metal taunted him as the words she'd said to him when he'd been drunk overwhelmed his mind.

Did she want to push him? She'd made it clear she enjoyed his kisses. Perhaps she wanted him to kiss her now. Or, she simply wanted to hand the key to him and had no idea about the turmoil writhing inside him.

Giving her an amused smile, he lifted an eyebrow. "You may place it on the desk until we have need of it."

She frowned. "I'd rather you just take it from me."

Her response gave him hope. There was a chance she wanted him as badly as he wanted her. He hoped so, and if she did, he would be happy to oblige. The one night he craved may be more attainable than he'd thought.

"You are playing a dangerous game. Are you sure you know what you're doing?"

~ ~ ~

Hannah's breathing accelerated as Lucius's deep voice washed over her. Did she know what she was doing? Honestly, she didn't know if she could answer that question. All she could say was that the only time she felt safe was with him. And, when they were together, she measured time by when her next opportunity to see him would be.

Her walk with Lord Christen today had been pleasant, but the entire time and in the back of her mind, she'd felt the need to run. Whether it had been the garden or the man, she couldn't say, but the feeling hadn't dissipated. She never felt that way with Lucius. And, soon he would be wed to Lady Bernadette, and Hannah would find herself exiled and would never enjoy the warmth of his embrace or the pleasure of his kiss again. That truth firmed her decision. She would pay whatever consequence to have this fleeting time with him.

"Every move we make is part of a dangerous game." She took a step toward him, but he didn't move. "Some people sit back and pass all their turns, therefore, missing opportunities. I, however, choose to play."

"But, this is me, Lucius Dobson. The man you've spent the better part of ten years despising."

She shook her head. "Not despising. Just not knowing. Now, are you going to take this key from me?"

"Only if you absolve me of my promise to not kiss you, because, if you come any closer, I will break that promise."

The knowledge that he wanted to kiss her as much as she wanted him to shot pleasure through her body. She licked her lips, anticipation rushing across her flesh. This is what she wanted. It was so wrong, but also so right.

"Consider that promise just a memory," she rasped.

His blue eyes darkened to almost black as he closed the distance between them. Instead of taking the key, his arms drew her tight against him as his lips crushed hers. His desperation fueled her passion, and she dropped the key in favor of running her hands into his silken hair. It had become a favorite pastime of hers, and she refused to deny herself the enjoyment.

As she had come to expect from kissing him, her body came alive, craving attention. It was delightful and confusing as she'd never wanted or enjoyed her husband's touch. But, dear God, she wanted Lucius's.

In an effort to relieve her need, she pressed herself further up against him. She moaned at the contact, not having expected such an amazing sensation. Before she could try again, Lucius pulled back, settling a fair distance between them.

"Bloody hell, Hannah, you sure know how to push a man."

Heat rushed up her cheeks. He had no idea how inadequate she was in that area. However, she wasn't inclined to inform him as that wasn't something he needed to know.

"I'm sorry."

He shook his head. "Don't be sorry, but we need to cool down. It's only midday. This certainly isn't the time."

Although she didn't understand what time had to do with kissing, she nodded. "Very well. Then, did you wish to work on the next clue while we're in here?"

With a nod, he glanced at her now empty hand. "Where's the key?"

Rolling her eyes, she retrieved it from the floor. "It's right here."

"Good. Now, let's go open the coffer."

"Wait, you said you didn't know where it was."

He winked at her as he took the key from her hand, lingering a little longer than necessary. "I lied. I found it in the portrait gallery behind the painting my uncle must have commissioned to replace the ghastly one you have hidden in the hunting cabin."

Laughing, she followed him to the gallery where they thankfully found a large sum of funds with another note. Although the search was difficult and time-consuming, it was satisfying to be rewarded for their efforts.

On their way back to the study, she noticed Lucius held her arm a little tighter. As a result, her body brushed up against his with each step. The result had her senses heightened. There was a growing tension between them that would only dissipate with her in his arms, which was a place she wanted to be. However, back in the study, he released her to read the note.

With raised eyebrows, he handed it to her. "My uncle didn't expect the two of us to work together in his little game."

Glancing at her husband's scrawl, she read.

You're doing well, but this won't be quite so easy. Remember the importance of your power. You are the Earl of Rivers. You must act like it. Now, the next clue on the list is missing a vital piece. This is one you must obtain from my dear wife. As I'm sure you've discovered, she's not the most obedient of creatures, so you must be stern with her. Don't let her Stall. Ask her why she never rides. Good luck, for you're going to need it.

"He also didn't want us working together, for I can tell you, had you asked me this months ago, it wouldn't have gone over well."

He crossed the room and caught her hand. "I'm so sorry for everything he did to you. I promise as soon as I have the funds secured, I'll buy you a new mare."

Touched, she ran her hand down his handsome face. "You are so sweet, but it isn't your responsibility to right every wrong he did to me."

A look she didn't understand crossed his face, and he took her hand and placed soft kisses on each finger before settling one on her palm. The tender action set her blood pounding. Something shifted inside her chest.

"Care to take a walk to the stables with me? I found the key yesterday and was confused to not see the coffer nearby considering there wasn't another part of the clue. Now I understand why my uncle warned us to do them in order."

She nodded. "Although, I should be vexed you solved one without me, let's go."

Excited to have another part of the puzzle found, she couldn't contain her smile as he escorted her outside. At the stables, Lucius was brilliant in his methods of distracting the staff with her so he could slip in to visit her mare's old stall.

When he reemerged with a huge grin, she knew he'd found and managed to retrieve the contents of the coffer. The day had gone pleasantly, and she was surprised at the lack of Lady Bernadette's presence each time she and Lucius had emerged from the study. Interestingly enough, Lucius never remarked upon it.

However, when they met for dinner that night, Mr. Rawlings informed them that Lady Bernadette and her mother had packed their belongings and left earlier in the day. Lucius hadn't seemed surprised, but Hannah's head was reeling throughout dinner.

She had no idea what the departure of the lady meant, but Lucius clearly didn't seem bothered. His laid-back manner was flirtatious, and she found concentrating on anything but him rather difficult. And, when it was time to turn in for the night, she found herself disappointed.

Facing him, she was surprised when he grasped her hand and lightly kissed it. "See you soon," he whispered.

Unable to react, she nodded, then made her way to her bedchamber. Suddenly, everything made sense. His insistence that she know what she was doing. The comment about the time of day. His apathy regarding Lady Bernadette's departure. A sick feeling formed in the pit of her stomach.

He was going to join her tonight, and there was nothing she could do to stop him.

Chapter 8

Anticipation raced up Lucius's spine. With all the teasing and the sexual tension today between him and Hannah, he hadn't been sure he was going to make it, but he had. A large part of him had wanted to take her right there in the study, but he knew that wouldn't have been fair to her. At least, not for their first time together.

Considering his uncle hadn't taken the time to kiss her properly, Lucius didn't imagine she'd found much pleasure in the marriage bed either. Her reeducation would begin tonight. His hands clenched as he tossed his jacket and waistcoat in the corner chair in his bedchamber.

Sitting down, he debated removing his boots, but decided against it. Her lack of reaction to his promise to join her disturbed him. He had no desire to frighten her and arriving in such a state of undress could do just that.

Unable to handle waiting any longer, he moved to the door adjoining his room to hers. The conversation they'd shared on her first day on the estate about her not taking the bedchamber returned to him, and he smiled. He'd been wrong and was glad she insisted upon remaining in the room.

When he entered her bedchamber, he blinked, surprised to see the amount of light in the room. Several candles had been set out and Hannah sat perched on the edge of the bed. Either the woman had a fear of the dark or she enjoyed seeing what would happen. His breathing sped. He definitely enjoyed the light, for he didn't want to be blind for any part of tonight.

The sight she presented now with her silken blond tresses cascading around her shoulders, virginal dressing gown, and bare feet set his heart in an erratic pattern. Nothing he had ever seen before could rival her. He had no idea what he had done in his life that was so right for her to desire him, but he welcomed it.

With clear hesitation, she slid to her feet and stood at the foot of the bed, her expression unreadable. This wasn't exactly the reception he'd expected, but he understood her nerves. As such, he would be sure to pace himself.

"Do you know why I'm here?" He had to ask as she made no other move.

She nodded.

"And?" He desperately needed to hear her say the words. To admit she wanted him here as much as he wanted to be there. Or, at the very least, to approve his arrival in her room.

Instead of speaking she lowered her head, then in one move pulled her dressing gown off, dropping it to the floor. His mouth dried as he remained rooted to the spot. Bloody hell, she was more glorious than he'd imagined. And, that was the answer he needed. However, she didn't take a step toward him.

Before he could react, she climbed on the bed. Although confused by her behavior, the sight she presented put his body in a painful state. Unable to stand it any longer, he stalked toward the bed, then froze.

Hannah pulled out ropes that had been tied to her headboard and slid one on her wrist, pulling it tight. Then, after lying on her back, she slipped her other hand in the looped rope on her other side. He stood there, horrified at seeing her tied to the bed. He'd never pictured her as the type to enjoy such a thing and from the distressed look on her face, she didn't appear to be filled with desire.

"What do you think you're doing?" he forced through the cloud of fury threatening to overtake him.

She squeezed her eyes shut so tightly that her face wrinkled before reopening them and pinning him with a pleading look. "I'll be good. I promise. I won't move. Just don't make me tie my legs, too."

Rage unlike anything he'd ever felt exploded within him. His hands shook and he clenched his fists to fight against the urge to trash the room. If his uncle was still alive, he'd kill the man with his bare hands. He spun on his heel and rushed from the room, slamming the door behind him before he did something that would certainly frighten her.

He didn't stop at his bedchamber. Despite the hour, he had to get out. To escape. Anger propelled him forward and all he saw in his vision was Hannah tied to the bed as his uncle violated her.

Tossing open the doors, he set off at a run down the steps and into the night. He pushed his body as hard as he could, until his legs could carry him no more. Falling to the ground, he yelled out his frustration at the evil man he was ashamed to call family.

It was difficult to breathe, but he didn't care. He deserved any amount of discomfort. *His fault.* How could Hannah have told him she hadn't suffered any more at the man's hand? Why had she lied? Then, why go through the charade tonight? Reality hit him, making him sick to his stomach. She didn't know any better. That man had led her to believe being tied to the bed was acceptable.

By the time he dragged himself back to the manor, it was late, but he knew sleep would elude him. Choosing to sit in his chair, his eyes continually moved to the door that would take him to Hannah. Likely, she wouldn't welcome his presence, but they needed to talk. Although he had no idea how he could possibly fix this, he certainly had to try.

The next morning, Lucius awoke from a fitful sleep. His back burned and his neck wasn't much better, but he welcomed the physical pain. It was preferable to think on something other than the events of last night. He groaned. Unlike the aches in his body, that wouldn't go away. He had to talk to Hannah. Checking his watch fob, he imagined she was already up for the day, so he quickly dressed and made his way downstairs.

"Good morning," she greeted him cheerily as he entered the dining room.

He lifted an eyebrow. "Good morning? That's what you have to say to me?"

She froze in the process of refilling her cup and set the teapot down. "You wish to do this right now?"

Someone walked in, and he didn't even turn to see who it was. He pointed to the door. "Out."

"Honestly, Lucius—"

"Don't," he warned. "After last night, I'm not faring too well."

She let out a sigh as her gaze dropped to her plate. "I'm sorry about that, just as I'm sorry you had to find out this way." She looked up at him then, her eyes full of misery. "I know this is the part where I'm supposed to promise to try harder next time, but I don't think that is such a good idea. Why do that again since we both know I'm not good enough."

Had the world gone mad? "Are you seriously apologizing to me right now? You have nothing to be sorry for. I just want to know what happened last night."

Her brow furrowed. "You were there, why make me repeat it?"

"Because I think you and I saw two completely different things."

She shook her head. "I don't think so. I understand your confusion. This may be a new experience for you because you have the benefit of selecting the woman you preferred in the past, but this has happened to me many times before. It's not your fault, it's mine. A man should be enticed before he joins a woman in her bed. I didn't entice you."

Lucius hadn't thought it could get any worse, but he'd been wrong. Gripping the back of the chair in front of him, he fought his emotions. He needed to remain in the room. She had to understand how wrong this was.

"Let me get this straight. The man ties you up—or rather makes you tie yourself up—to ensure you don't move. Then, you must entice him to join you? That's not right, Hannah. It's not right." Lucius stared into her eyes, willing her to understand. "He should worship you with every bit of himself.

"Then, if you find enjoyment in him, in his kisses, in his touch, you invite him to your bed. That doesn't make him worthy—just the luckiest man alive. Once in your bed, if he doesn't make you deliriously happy, you kick him out. That's how it works."

She tilted her head to the side. "I don't think you have that right."

Frustrated, he let out a growl. "Damn it, Hannah. That man was poison. Can't you see everything he did or said was wrong? Trust me, not him."

The pain his unexpected demand brought out was too much. He pushed back from the chair and marched out of the dining room. There was no stomaching breakfast. Besides, he had more pressing matters to attend to at present. He was going to burn that bed.

~ ~ ~

Hannah pulled her shawl around her as she walked through the garden with Lisa. The cooler weather meant winter would be setting upon them soon and for once, she wasn't looking forward to it. Normally, she enjoyed watching the snow from the warmth of the manor while bathing in the heat of the fireplace, but at present, all she could think about was returning to London. She couldn't do this any longer.

The discussion with Lucius this morning hadn't gone well. She was unaccustomed to such lengthy talks about the ongoings of the previous night. On those days her husband had left her room without joining her, he'd yelled and berated her the next day, then accepted her apology and they'd moved on. The times he had joined her though, was nothing like Lucius had described for either her or her husband.

No matter the circumstances, her husband always left her in anger. She was never enough, and always did something wrong. The business between a man and a woman was embarrassing and difficult. However, from Lucius's anger and abrupt departure that morning, he clearly hadn't wanted to give up on the idea. And, considering she hadn't seen him the entire day, she imagined he intended to avoid her now.

"Lisa, can I ask you something highly personal?"

Her friend laughed. "I imagine you're going to ask regardless, so my response doesn't matter. However, if this has anything to do with the earl insisting your bed be removed from your bedchamber, please do."

Stunned, Hannah's mouth fell open. "What? My bed?"

The woman nodded. "This morning he collected a few men and had them disassemble it. He, himself, helped. No explanations. They took it out to the burn pile and set it on fire."

Stumbling toward the nearest bench, Hannah dropped down upon it. "Why? Where will I sleep?"

Lisa's eyes widened. "You didn't know? Perhaps you said something to anger him? I didn't realize the man had such a temper."

Swallowing, Hannah desperately tried to think of an excuse to give. "I-I merely mentioned disliking the piece as it was uncomfortable. The previous earl never allowed me to redecorate. I had no idea Lord Rivers would react in such a way. Dear God, what am I to do?"

The woman patted her on the shoulder. "Don't fret, my lady. From the sound of it, the master did it for your own comfort. It's likely he'll have another bed moved in there for you. Or, I can move you to another room."

She shook her head. What had Lucius been thinking? After this, everyone surely would know he'd gone to her bed last night. But, she didn't want to move to another bedchamber. For some reason, she felt safe knowing he was in the next room. In addition, he truly believed she'd been wronged in that bed and had hoped to fix it for her by removing the reminder. The fact that he would do something like that said so much more than words could.

The remainder of the day, he'd evaded her, even going so far as to not take his meals with her. By the time she retired for the evening, she was filled with nerves of what she would find in her bedchamber.

When she pushed open the door, she saw the bed from the room at the opposite end of the hall. Although smaller than her original one, it was the nicest bed in the secondary rooms and the most difficult to get to. She couldn't help her smile.

Lisa arrived shortly after to help Hannah ready herself for bed. The maid filled her in with the buzz about the house. Lucius had certainly gone through some trouble for her today. Then, why did he hide from her? As soon as Lisa left, Hannah decided to find out.

Marching over to the door adjoining her room to Lucius's, she pushed it open. It was dark inside. A fire crackled in the fireplace, giving off the only light. Seeing Lucius's silhouette in the chair, his hand over his eyes, she shut the door with a loud click. He dropped his hand and quickly stood.

"Hannah? What are you doing in here?"

She took a second to glance around. "I've never been in here before."

"If you have come in for a need to satisfy your curiosity, I give you my permission to do so tomorrow when I'm not present."

Taking a step toward him, she took note how his body tensed. His reaction confused her. From his words earlier, she thought he had wanted to try to join her in bed again. Had she been wrong?

"I'm not here to see your bedchamber. I'm here to see you."

"The bed's gone." His voice held steel.

"I noticed. Do you want to talk about it?"—He shook his head.—"That's fine. I must tell you that is the nicest thing anyone has ever done for me."

He cringed. "I set fire to your bed, and that's the nicest thing anyone has done for you?"

"It's the thought behind it I'm talking about. And, that's why I'm here. I want to try this again if you'd like."

"I'm beginning to believe you don't know what that means." He crossed his arms. "I have no ropes or any restraining implements in my bedchamber."

"Good." She sauntered toward him. "Then, you can teach me what I'm supposed to do."

His eyes watched her warily. "I'm not sure this is a good idea. You need slow and gentle to erase the damage, but that's not me. Not tonight. There's a tempest brewing inside me."

She ran her hands along his arms, pulling them from each other. He was closed off from her and that would never do. "Let it out. I can handle it."

He shook his head but at the same time, he wrapped his arms around her and took her lips. Melting into his demanding kiss, she clutched onto him. This was what she wanted. As long as he kissed her, she would suffer all the rest.

Similar to last night, he only wore a shirt and trousers, so she felt the heat of his skin through the thin layer of her dressing gown, and the feeling taunted to her. Unlike her husband's soft body, Lucius was hard everywhere. She itched to touch him.

Moving her hands down his chest, she lightly grabbed the material of his shirt and tugged it free of his breeches. Obviously as anxious as she, Lucius drew back, then pulled his shirt off and tossed it aside before gathering her back into his embrace and claiming her mouth once again.

Her breath hitched as her hands came in contact with his warm, hard flesh. His muscles jumped under her curious fingers. The power she felt in him struck a chord with her. This was what she needed. A man who made her feel like this and who could protect her. She wondered how different her life would have been had Lucius been interested in her before his uncle had taken notice of her.

Her thoughts dissipated, and she froze as Lucius's hand closed over her breast. As he kneaded her, she found herself relaxing. His attention was pleasurable and when his hand ran across her nipple a shock ran through her centering between her legs. It was curious. This was nothing like the slightly painful mauling she'd endured in the past, and before long, it wasn't enough.

For once in her life, she craved more. Stepping back, she gripped her gown, but Lucius's hand closed over hers. His eyes were blazing, needy. She shivered.

"Allow me." His tight voice was nearly unrecognizable.

As he slowly drew the material off her body, she thought she would die from the torment. She was heated and something inside her demanded a satisfaction she'd never known. By the time the garment hit the floor, she was mad with desire. This whole experience was new to her, and she was loving every moment.

"You are beautiful," he breathed. He slid a hand around to her lower back and tugged her closer as he bent his head down. To her surprise, he caught her nipple in his mouth, and she would have fallen and he not kept hold of her. Spikes of pleasure ripped at her as he lavished attention with his free hand and his mouth.

Painful need assaulted her and, knowing what would happen next, she was desperate for it. Surely, when he pressed himself against the throbbing part of her, she would find the relief she sought. The act she had hated was the one she now craved the most.

She pushed on his shoulders, ignoring the confused look on his face as her hands went to his breeches. "No more, Lucius. I'm ready."

Unfortunately, she couldn't seem to unfasten his clothing.

He chuckled. "Let me help you."

Within seconds, Lucius removed the garment and stood before her, completely nude. She gasped and took a step back. This wasn't right. Having had the lights on each time she'd been with her husband, she certainly would have known if he'd looked like that. He had not.

"Lucius?" She cleared her throat, suddenly frightened. "What's wrong with that?"

~ ~ ~

Lucius simply stared at Hannah, disbelief and hurt overtaking his desire, which consequently only added to his humiliation as his length lessened.

"What do you mean, what's wrong with that?" he snapped, unable to temper his voice.

Her eyes met his and he read fear in their depths. What the hell was going on?

"My husband never looked like that."

Crossing his arms, he kept his gaze fixed on her, refusing to cover himself. He knew he was above average in size, and he tried not to let it bother him to know this was another area his uncle bested him. Unfortunately, the thought had further diminishing powers. He couldn't believe this night had moved from his best to his worst in seconds.

"This isn't going to work if you are going to spend it comparing me to him. Men come in all different sizes."

She nodded and took another step back. "I can see, and I am afraid your size might be a problem."

"Why is that?" he practically growled, furious she would continue to insult him while she eyed him as if he were deformed.

"You're significantly"—she swallowed—"larger. And, rather stiff. If you put that on me, it's going to hurt."

Larger? So, she wasn't insulting him. His anger subsided as his male pride swelled, as well as other parts of him. He grinned. Those were the words he'd rather hear from her lips.

"You are past hurting as the pain only comes the first time. I promise to only bring you pleasure. Not to mention, I'm not stopping at putting it on you. I intend to go all the way."

Her eyes widened, and she took another step back. "This isn't such a good idea. It was different when I thought you were smaller, but—"

He quirked an eyebrow as he moved toward her. "You thought I was small? Not sure how I should take that."

"I didn't mean that like it sounds. I have never thought of your, um, it's just . . ."

"It's just getting worse, is what it is. You should stop." He scooped her up in his arms, loving the feel of her silken skin against his bare flesh. "Time to continue your reeducation. Lesson one, don't insult a man's size when he's preparing to bring you pleasure."

Setting her on the bed, he moved toward his prey, his earlier desire having fully returned. This was what he had wanted for so long now. Although years late, he finally had Hannah in his bed.

"I hadn't meant to insult. I—"

"Next, stop thinking. Just feel." With that, he claimed her lips, cutting off anything else she could say.

As her arms wrapped around his neck, he settled himself between her legs. Although he was ready, he knew all their talk had cooled her down, and he'd be damned if she didn't leave his bed without experiencing absolute bliss.

Moving his kisses down her body, he licked a path to her sensitive breasts. Her small gasp spurned him on and when she began to writhe beneath him, he ran his hand along her heated flesh, wanting to give her the relief she craved.

He slipped a finger into her slick body, taking in her every sound and movement as he worked her. His own body hummed as she neared the edge. He lifted his head to watch her face. To see what he was doing to her. She cried out as her body clenched around his finger. The sound was pure heaven. Not often had he been with a woman so vocal, and he thought he would lose it right there.

"What was that?" she demanded through her heavy breathing. "I've never . . ."

"That was the beginning," he promised, wishing he could come up with something clever to say. But, his body was too tightly wound to be able to come up with anything more.

Beyond ready, he positioned himself at her entrance and locked his eyes on hers. She smiled up at him, clearly no longer concerned over their joining. Inching forward, he hissed. She was tight. So much more than he'd expected. He knew it had been a while for her, but he'd never expected this. The amazing sensation made moving slowly rather difficult.

A little bit more, then Lucius froze. He stared down at Hannah in shock. He'd reached a barrier. One that shouldn't be there. How was this possible? Ten years of marriage didn't leave a virgin. Not a virgin who was accustomed to being tied to the bed.

"Why are you looking at me like that?" Her voice held strain. "This is so different. I don't understand."

He swallowed. "This is going to hurt, but only for a little while."

She opened her mouth to speak, but he was beyond explanations. At the moment, he was doing his best not to maul an innocent. A bloody innocent.

In one thrust, he broke through her barrier, burying himself fully within her. The sensation had his eyes rolling back in his head as he lost the ability to think. Never before had he experienced anything so wondrous.

After giving Hannah time to accustom herself to him, he began to move in short thrusts. When she began to move with him, he kissed her long and hard, wanting to make the night last. But, her tight body, roaming hands, and vocal mouth was sending him close to the precipice.

Unwilling to allow himself to fall without her, he increased his pace until she screamed out. The sound echoed in his mind and combined with her spasms, he lost it. Intense spikes of pleasure shot through his body as his release hit him.

Never in his life had he imagined he would have another chance at such an incredible gift, and he had absolutely no idea what he was supposed to do now.

Chapter 9

Hannah stretched, never having felt so wonderful in her life.

"Did you sleep well?"

The sound of Lucius's voice had her jumping up to a sitting position and clutching the sheets to her chest. Confusion clouded her mind. Glancing around, she could see it was dark and the fire still burned in the fireplace. Dear God, she had allowed Lucius to do those things to her and then had fallen asleep in his bed. Heat burned her cheeks.

"I'm so sorry. I hadn't meant to fall asleep. You probably want your bed back. If you would be so kind as to hand me my night rail, I'll be on my way."

"You're not going anywhere. You and I need to talk."

He was propped up on the pillows, still unclothed but the coverlet was draped over his lap. The sight stirred her desire, and she realized talking was the last thing she wanted to do. Finding pleasure in the act between a man and a woman had been a welcome surprise, and she wanted to experience it again.

Allowing the sheets to fall, she bared her breasts. "I'm not sure I feel much like talking."

Seeing his eyes zero in on her chest, and the speed of his breathing, gave her a great sense of power. Perhaps her husband had been wrong, it wasn't that she was undesirable, for Lucius didn't seem to have any trouble. In addition, he hadn't seemed upset when he collapsed on top of her before she'd fallen asleep.

"Hannah." Her name was a strangled sound. "Please, don't. I won't be able to resist, and we need to talk."

Blowing out a breath, she crossed her arms, knowing that the action would draw his attention. "Very well. Talk. I'm listening."

"I'm not sure how to say this exactly." He ran a hand through his hair. "You mentioned how what we did was different than what you've done before with your husband."

"As I told you, you are much larger, so naturally it felt completely different."

"You also said I was, um, harder."

"Why are we talking about this? You told me not to compare the two of you. Now, you want to hear all of it in excruciating detail?"

"Not really, no. But, I'm trying to understand."

"Understand what?"

He cleared his throat and sat forward. "How your husband could possibly have left you an innocent after ten years of marriage."

Her mouth fell open in shock, then she shook her head. He was wrong. She wasn't an innocent. Too many nights of her marriage when she resided in the same house as her husband, he'd joined her in her bedchamber. He took that part of him and shoved it against her repeatedly. Although it hadn't felt anything like how Lucius had done it, it had been the same thing.

"That's impossible." Feeling uncomfortable sitting here undressed, she pulled the sheet around her. "I may act like an innocent, but I've done that many times before."

"He may have tried, but he never made it inside you. Hannah, a man must be stiff in order to take a woman. I'm beginning to believe my uncle lacked the ability."

"But, you said yourself, all men are different sizes." She stuck out her chin, unwilling to believe that she'd spent her entire life living a lie.

"Arguing about this is pointless." He threw the coverlet back. "Look. In this state, I'm not capable of joining with a woman."

She gasped. "Dear God. What happened to it?"

"This conversation has robbed me of my desire to engage in such an act. What you saw before only happens when that desire is present."

Fascinated, she dropped her arms and leaned forward to inspect the changes. Lucius was still larger than her husband had been, but the difference from before was astounding. Then, to her surprise, it began to grow before her very eyes. Lucius quickly covered himself back up.

"Do you understand now?"

"It moved." Her eyes were focused on the sheet that now had a noticeable bulge beneath it. He could no longer hide that fact from her. Did that mean he desired her? She couldn't contain a smile at the thought.

"How else do you expect me to react when you're staring at me like that? Now, Hannah, I took your innocence tonight. Do you realize that?"

Stated like that, she no longer cared that she'd survived marriage as an innocent. Somehow it seemed special that she could have done something so incredible with Lucius for the first time. She'd meant it when she told him he was different than anyone she'd ever met.

"Does that upset you?"

He reached out and cupped her face. "Upset? Of course not. It's the greatest gift that anyone could ever give me. You can't even imagine how ecstatic I am."

"Then, show me," she breathed.

In one move, he had her underneath him as he claimed her lips. The contact of his skin against hers sizzled as his tongue invaded her mouth. It was much too easy to become swept up in him, and she didn't know if she would ever get enough of the man.

Hours later when she awoke, hearing Lucius's even breathing beside her, she slipped out from under his arm and quietly collected her night clothes. After shrugging on the garment, she returned to her bedchamber.

After spending the majority of the night in Lucius's arms, the empty, cold bed held no appeal, but she had no choice. It wouldn't do for Lisa to arrive in the morning and find her gone and the bed not slept in. Talk would begin, and she would be ruined.

Although she was a widow, she knew Lucius would insist on doing the honorable thing should the truth get out. Then, she would be forced to refuse him. After all, she had spent ten years with one husband, and she wasn't looking for another.

~ ~ ~

Lucius glanced in the drawing room and frowned. He hadn't been happy to wake up alone, having not heard Hannah leave his bed, and her absence at breakfast only further irritated him. Did she already have regrets? With her exuberance last night, he hadn't expected such a reaction this morning, and he had to find out her reasons.

Last night had been the greatest of his life. He could still hardly believe Hannah had been untouched after all this time. Seeing the proof of her virgin's blood on his sheets this morning had struck pride deep in his chest. However, her disappearance had diminished his joy. He had to find her.

"Rawlings," he called out to the butler. "Do you know where I can find the countess?"

"I do believe she has gone out for a ride, my lord."

The unusual response had Lucius staring at the man for a few moments before he could find the words to say. "Lady Rivers has gone for a ride? By herself?"

With a shake of his head, the man's expression didn't change. "No, my lord. Lord Christen called upon her early this morning. I do believe the baron had hoped to take the countess to the village, but she consented to a ride."

Lucius nodded, but he couldn't help the overwhelming jealousy from filling him. Although he knew he didn't own her, after what they shared last night, he hadn't expected her to rush off with another man. And, his friend no less.

"Thank you. When they return, please send the baron to my study."

As he moved toward the room that had become his sanctuary, he couldn't think of anything other than Hannah and Ronald. What were they doing at this moment? Why had the man arrived so early without notice? Or, had Hannah been aware of his intentions?

To make matters worse, Lucius was painfully aware of the fact that Hannah had never wanted to ride with him. She had no problem kissing him in his study or slipping into his bedchamber, but she wanted nothing to do with him in public. He was simply a convenient male. Could he live with that fact simply to have her temporarily?

By the time his friend opened the door, a pleased smile on his lips, Lucius was in a bad state. He silently prayed he could keep his temper and his jealousy under control. Ronald wasn't at fault, but bloody hell, Lucius wanted to punch his friend right in his smug face.

"You seem overly happy today," Lucius observed.

"And, why shouldn't I be? The day is lovely, and that aunt of yours is quite a riding companion."

Gritting his teeth, Lucius raised an eyebrow. "Is that so? How was she any different than your other riding partners?"

Ronald laughed as he took a seat. "Poor me a whisky, and I'll be happy to tell you. I've never seen anyone so attuned to her mount."

After splashing whisky in a glass, Lucius slid it to his friend as he eyed the man. If there was even the slightest chance of anything untoward befalling Hannah, Lucius wouldn't be able to control his reaction. She may no longer be an innocent, but the woman lacked the experience to handle a man like Ronald.

"I understand she enjoys horses," Lucius prompted.

"That's an understatement. The woman was made to ride. Watching her was pure enjoyment and keeping up with her a challenge. I have to admit, she is a puzzle to me."

"Is that why you came at such an early hour? I was quite surprised to learn you had dragged yourself out of who's ever bed you were in to arrive here at such a time."

With a grin and a wink, Ronald took a sip of his whisky. "She intrigues me. Most of my visits, she gives me minimal time, telling me she already has a plan for the day, so I thought arriving early would give me my chance. I'd been right."

"I see. With my uncle being deceased, the responsibility of looking after her belongs to me. So, I must ask after your interest."

The baron set his glass down and crossed his arms. "Come now, Lucius, the lady isn't a debutante who needs her virtue protected. I mean her no harm. She's safe with me."

Swallowing his anger, Lucius focused on breathing in and out. What did Ronald see with Hannah? Did he see her for the treasure she was? Or, was he only seeking a barren widow who would be an easy target to sate his lust?

Barren. Bloody hell. She wasn't barren. He'd taken her last night with the assumption that there would be no consequences. It hadn't occurred to him that her innocence had changed everything. This very moment, she could be carrying his child.

Your nine-month clock shall begin ticking. The words reverberated through his brain. Her plan to use him would fail if he'd given her a child. The very idea reached deep inside him, reviving his long-forgotten plans. In his mind's eye, he'd seen him and Hannah in their home with their children.

He closed his eyes against the sight, but it was too late, he'd already seen it. Putting the image from his mind would be near impossible now. He inwardly cursed. It was a childish dream as she still didn't see him as anything other than convenient man.

"And, what does the countess think about your plans for the two of you?" he forced the question from his dry throat.

"I'm not sure as of yet. The lady is quite skittish. My attempt to kiss her didn't go over well, but I suspect she just prefers to move at a slower pace."

Drawing back his chair, Lucius stood. "Define, 'not go over well.'"

"What's gotten into you? I said I didn't hurt the lady. I arrived in a good mood, remember? Besides, you know me."

Lucius nodded. He did know Ronald. Although the man had jumped from as many beds as Lucius himself had, he was a good sort. This obsession with Hannah had just gone too far. His irrational jealousy had almost caused him to lose a friend. He needed to get himself back under control.

"You're right, of course. I'm sorry. I simply feel protective of her. Don't let her status of widow fool you. My uncle seemed to treat her differently than one would expect. I'm discovering the lady needs to be handled as carefully as a debutante."

"Thank you for the advice. I will make sure to keep that in mind in the future." Ronald tilted his head, giving him a curious look. "Your attentiveness is purely for the lady's best interest, right?"

Lucius swallowed, wishing he could tell him no, that Hannah belonged to him, but he could not. "Absolutely."

"That's good to know. Since you don't share her blood, she is as viable for you as she is for me. Just as we've always done, I have no intention of stepping in the way of your claim."

"I appreciate that, but I don't think the countess could see me as anything to her after looking upon me as a nephew for the past ten years."

The laughter Ronald let out in reply was filled with relief. "I can certainly see that. Women are strange that way. Ten years ago, you were, what? Twenty years old? How she could see you as anything other than a lustful man, I'll never understand."

Another memory of being young and full of dreams struck him. Hannah hadn't remembered how they'd met, but Lucius would never forget. His uncle had been at Melbourne as he'd had dealings with the marquis. In those days, he'd used Lucius as a footman, so Lucius had been outside walking through the garden, kicking rocks and leaves on the path.

Out of nowhere, the seventeen-year-old Hannah had rushed up and grabbed his arm. He'd been speechless as he looked into her molten brown eyes. He'd never seen anyone so beautiful. After she put her finger up to her lips to silence him, she pulled him into the bushes and pointed.

He had followed the direction and saw a bird had made a nest in a nearby tree. The mother was feeding her young who looked to be no older than a day. As he'd looked back at the vibrant young woman, he'd seen the wonderment on her face. She'd brought him there to silence him so the baby birds wouldn't go without food.

In that instant, he'd realized he had wanted to marry her. His life had lacked goodness and selflessness. That's what he had wanted for his future.

Returning to reality, he shook off the bitterness. Shortly after that moment he'd gone and made the worst mistake of his life. One that both he and Hannah had dearly paid for.

~ ~ ~

Hannah did her best to concentrate on her embroidery, but she was finding it near impossible. All she wanted to do was see Lucius, but she knew that was unwise. She knew he needed his space. After all, it was simple to find her in the drawing room, and he had yet to seek her out. That could only mean he didn't wish to see her.

An uncomfortable thought struck her, and she tossed her material to the side, having lost complete interest. Last night she'd been insistent and hadn't given him much of a chance to refuse. Perhaps he was angry with her this morning.

She hoped they could have gone past the awkward stage at breakfast this morning, but Lisa had arrived at her bedchamber explaining how Lord Christen had arrived to take her to the village. She only consented to a short ride in order to pacify him, but he'd been relentless and their outing had taken much too long.

Glancing at the door, she willed Lucius to appear. Was he angry she'd not been at breakfast? Perhaps he'd had his fill of her and was done. Too many possibilities swam in her head, making her sick. She couldn't take it any longer.

Without another thought for her embroidery, she marched out of the room and headed to Lucius's study. Outside the door, she paused. Normally, she would simply walk in, but she didn't know what reception she would receive. This uncertainty was going to end now.

She knocked and let out a sigh of relief when his rough voice granted entrance. As she walked in and closed the door, he stood, watching her warily. This was not good. And, definitely not what she had hoped for after last night.

"May I join you?" She hated the desperation in her voice.

"If you wish." He held his hand out to indicate the chair before his desk.

Anger lit her cheeks. "Obviously you are upset with me. Maybe I shouldn't have gone to your bedchamber last night, but I did, and I'm not sorry."

"I'm not sorry, either." His blue gaze was cold today. "I trust you had a nice ride this morning."

Not sure why he changed the subject, she drew her brows together. "It was fine. Although, I had been surprised by Lord Christen's presence this morning."

Lucius nodded, thoughtfully. "Were you also surprised when he kissed you?"

Her mouth fell open. "How did you know about that?"

Anger flashed through his eyes. "So, he did kiss you. And, from your reaction, I can see you didn't intend for me to find out. I know you are new at this, but this isn't the way I do things. I don't share."

The fury rolling off of him confused her. She'd done nothing wrong. It hadn't been her fault the baron had caught her off guard. Then, suddenly she realized what was going on. Keeping her smile at bay was difficult.

"Are you jealous?"

"No. I'm bloody furious, that's what I am. You jump from my bed to another man's arms before the sheets have cooled."

She crossed the room and rounded the desk to stand next to him. Although he faced her, he made no move toward or away from her. His anger was so palpable, she could practically taste it.

"That's not what happened. I agreed to go for a ride to pacify him so he would leave. He was the one who insisted we rest the horses. When he pulled me from my mare, he drew me up against him and pressed his lips against mine."

"I don't want to hear this," Lucius growled.

"I pushed him away. The only reason why we didn't return at once is because he talked me into remaining for a walk. He seemed so sincere in his apology, I couldn't refuse."

He grabbed her shoulders. "Is that supposed to make me feel better? Do you have any idea the position you put yourself in? Don't ever go anywhere alone with a man again. Do you hear me?"

Nodding, she wasn't sure if she should be upset or thrilled that he cared so much. "Nothing happened and now he knows not to do it again."

"You're wrong. He's going to do it again. He'll keep trying until you want to kiss him back."

Her focus dropped to his lips. "You're the only man I want to kiss."

His jaw clenched. "Don't say things like that."

"Why not? It's the truth."

Before she could say anything more, he gathered her to him and his lips crushed against hers. His kiss was furious and desperate. She met him, feeling much the same as she pressed herself tightly against him. As he devoured her mouth, she clung to him, her desire for him reaching dangerous heights.

He shifted and the hard length of his bulge pressed into her, making her gasp and pull back. She hadn't meant to do that to him. Guilt streaked through her.

"Where are you going?" He reached out for her, but she moved away.

"I'm sorry. I didn't mean to make that happen." She pointed to his breeches, feeling her cheeks heat.

"That isn't exactly something you have any control over. You simply need to walk into the room, and I want you. Does that bother you?"

His voice was curious, but it held a hint of steel. The way he'd said it as if it were a natural fact sent another wave of longing through her. Dear God, she wanted him, too. How would she survive this feeling until tonight? It would've been wise to remain away.

"No. It's actually nice to know you feel that way. I do as well."

Seeing his eyes darken as he advanced, she swallowed. Was he deliberately trying to make this difficult for both of them?

"Then, I don't see a problem." He lightly ran his hands up her arms, leaving tingles in their wake. She nearly groaned as he put his mouth to her neck and placed tender kisses.

"I'm merely respecting your wishes," she breathed. "About the time."

He drew back. "My wishes about the time? I'm not sure I'm following."

"Yesterday, you mentioned it not being the time. I can only assume that means you have specific time requirements when it comes to that activity. I hadn't meant to cause you any distress."

"I see." He pulled her tightly against his hard body. "That was only for the first time. I wanted to make sure you were fully aware of what you were doing. I couldn't have you giving in to a moment's passion and regretting it later." His lips returned to her neck as his hands held her firm.

"And, now?" She could hardly force the words past her lips.

His answering chuckle resounded through her. "I'm fairly confident you know exactly what you're getting into. I suspect you crave it as much as I do."

Shivering in anticipation, she pulled back and headed for the door. She was done waiting. He was driving her crazy and now that she knew he would give in to his passion, she saw no reason to pause.

"I shall go first, just don't take too long to join me."

"Go where? I have no intention of leaving this room." His voice held amusement.

Heat ran up her cheeks. "I'm sorry. I must've misunderstood. I thought you said you would join me in bed."

"You didn't misunderstand. I'm going to join with you, but we don't need a bed."

She bit her lip. "We don't?"

He shook his head and spread out his hands. "We have the sofa, chair, floor, desk, wall. Take your pick. Or, if that's not good enough, I can get creative."

Swallowing, she stared at him. "Wall?"

A slow smile transformed his face. "Good choice."

"Oh, I didn't mean . . . Rather, I'm not sure how that works."

He held out his hand. "Let me show you."

As she looked at his open palm, she wasn't sure she was ready for that. "Another time. I think I'd like to try the desk this time. I've always hated the large opposing piece. I think a new memory with it is in order."

"As you wish."

Excitement tore through her as Lucius stalked toward her. She was afraid she could easily become addicted to him. Then, she didn't know where that would leave her.

Chapter 10

Lucius smiled as he took the offered tankard of ale from Oliver, one of the tenants who had been on the estate for as long as Lucius could remember. The village had come together and repaired damages to the bakery caused by a fire a week earlier.

Although the majority of the men seemed surprised to see the new earl helping in a physical way, they also appeared grateful. The winter would soon be upon them and the baker's family would have nowhere to turn with their home destroyed. So, Lucius hadn't hesitated to give his time.

Over the past week, he and Hannah had managed to solve another clue. Although the sixth one made no sense to either of them, they had retrieved five of the twelve keys. So, he was feeling quite hopeful for his future. In addition, spending the night with Hannah in his bed and the days in her company had filled a missing piece of his life he hadn't realized he'd been lacking.

"We are grateful for your help, my lord," Oliver said as he took a long pull of his own ale. "Saul and Molly would have been lost without everyone today, and you showing up here says quite a lot."

Lucius grinned. "I'm pleased I was able to help. We are all part of this estate, and I believe in us standing together."

The man studied him. "I can see you intend to be a very different kind of earl than your uncle."

Straitening his back, Lucius willed it to be true. "I intend to do everything in my power to ensure the estate thrives under my care. On that note, it has recently been brought to my attention that the tenants no longer take their concerns to the manor, do you know why that is?"

Oliver scratched his head." You don't remember? Well, I suppose during that time Lord Rivers was using you as part of his staff. The lord decided any troubles we experienced were of our own doing and therefore we were to handle them by ourselves."

"As the owner of the estate, the earl has responsibilities to the tenants," Lucius argued. "He couldn't simply turn his back on those."

"Apparently, he could." Oliver shrugged.

Looking out over the men milling about the taproom after a job well done, Lucius wondered how his uncle could be so heartless as to turn these people and their troubles away. The estate was profitable. Judging from the funds he'd already uncovered that his uncle hadn't needed to touch in years, the earl had no reason to deny help. He could easily provide for these people.

"That will change soon. I'm still working on making sense of everything my uncle left behind, but as soon as I do, I intend to right this wrong. You have my word on that."

"I look forward to it." Oliver glanced away, a look of discomfort coming across his features. "My lord, how did you hear about the effort today?"

Judging from the man's tone, Lucius knew his answer would be significant. Not able to fathom why, he shrugged. He had nothing to hide.

"I saw the smoke last week. By the time I arrived, the fire had been extinguished, so I asked that I be informed when restoration would be underway."

"Then, you had no other reason to come to the village today? To speak to the tenants?"

Ill at ease with the man's questions and his sudden change in demeanor, Lucius put his tankard down and squared his shoulders. "You'll find you have much better results with me when you take a direct approach. If you have something you wish to ask, do so."

Oliver winced. "The rent, my lord. Did you wish to speak about it?"

"Is it being paid?" Lucius hated that he had to ask, having no knowledge of anything regarding the tenant's payments due to his uncle's stipulations.

"Of course." The man's back stiffened as if insulted.

"Then, we have nothing to discuss."

Oliver was silent for a time, then he stood. "Please excuse me for a minute."

Stunned by the man's odd behavior, Lucius sat there, wondering what he should do. Thinking over their conversation, it hadn't turned uncomfortable until Oliver wanted to know why Lucius had come. Had his uncle done something similar only to be compensated? Honestly, Lucius couldn't see Uncle Herman doing anything physical for anyone else, regardless of what he would get out of it. With his uncle, it was more about what a person could do *for* him.

When Oliver returned, three men flanked his sides. Lucius recognized them from having worked at the bakery today. As the four men approached him, Lucius eyed them warily. Although he could hold his own in a fight, he knew he couldn't take on four opponents at the same time regardless of their size or age.

He stood. He'd spent the majority of his life fighting. Physically from his father and mentally from his uncle. This was nothing new as the odds were typically stacked against him. Cracking his knuckles, he prepared himself for this. He would bleed, but so would they.

"My lord, we need you to come with us," Oliver spoke for the group.

Nodding, Lucius followed. A fight in the taproom would only harm innocent people as well as property. At least these men had the sense in them to understand that and take precautions.

"You sure this is a good idea?" The youngest man in the group whispered to Oliver, who nodded in response.

Good. Lucius could work with that. It gave him a fighting chance that they were not all comfortable with what they were about to do.

"Gentlemen, if you have a problem with me, let's get this done. Although I can't see how you think to benefit from this, I won't back down from a fight."

Oliver and another man exchanged glances. "We aren't here to fight you. Why would you think we were?"

"You didn't seem pleased by my responses in the taproom, so you left to retrieve reinforcements. I don't see what else I could think you had planned for me." Lucius was still skeptical and refused to lower his guard.

"He's definitely got courage. I admire that," the young man nodded at Oliver. "I see now. I say go ahead and tell him."

To that statement, the group responded with nods of their own.

"Very well." Oliver faced Lucius. "When the previous earl died, the butcher received a letter and a small key. The letter was from Lord Rivers. It said that when you come around asking us to increase our rent, but to pay you directly, we were to give you the key."

Lucius's mouth fell open as the words of the next clue ran through his mind.

Even the mighty fall. Squeeze them, then take your treasure to a faraway place to hide under a bed. That's what she always did.

A sick feeling formed in the pit of Lucius's stomach. Would he truly have been driven to that point? And, how long would he have gone before resorting to something so underhanded? His uncle clearly believed him capable. This was by far the worst clue he could have been forced to deal with.

"So, you've been waiting for me to come to you and increase your rent this entire time?"

Oliver nodded. "But, I can see you're not going to do that. Now, I'm not sure if this key is something I should give you because, knowing that man, he likely didn't mean it for good."

"Thank you for your concern, but I would very much like to have the key."

Once they retrieved the key, Lucius pocketed it, still feeling uncomfortable with the situation. The men seemed to sense it as well, and insisted Lucius meet their wives before returning to the taproom with them until late into the night.

By the time he made it back to bed, he was drunk and it was much too late to call on Hannah. The day had been positive, but he still was filled with questions and left with *what ifs*. Fortunately, or not, they were questions to which he wasn't sure he would ever have an answer.

~ ~ ~

Hannah ate her breakfast in silence. She hadn't seen Lucius since yesterday morning, and the fact bothered her more than she cared to admit. She had no idea when her life had begun to revolve around him, but somehow, it had. Everything she did was with him in mind. She'd also refused visits from Lord Christen on Lucius's words the other day.

The baron was diverting and when he kept his space he provided pleasant company, but she only wanted to be with Lucius. Here at the estate, they had created a fake reality to exist in, and she didn't want to lose that. Visits by other people only proved to her how the outside world would get in and take everything away soon enough.

"Good morning, beautiful." Lucius's raspy voice washed over her, and her gaze shot to the door, desperate to see him.

"Good morning," she replied. "You were out late. I hope everything went well."

He nodded as he slid into his chair, not bothering to fill a plate. "Very well. You are never going to believe what happened."

After reaching into his pocket, he pulled a key out and dropped it on the table. She gasped. The clue had been impossible. They had searched everything that could remotely be squeezed. How had he solved it?

"Where did you get this?"

As he told her what had transpired with the tenants, she could see pain in his cloudy, blue eyes. This was another reason for her to hate her husband. Why would he think of something so horrible to force his heir to do?

"He wanted me to run out of the funds that he'd given me. To give me no other choice than to go to them. Why? To prove I was like him? What kills me is not knowing if I would have taken that option."

She covered his hand with hers. "Stop thinking like this. You're a good man. Remember, we are done trying to figure out how such an evil person thinks, or do I need to show you the painting again?"

Lucius smiled, then immediately, his smile drained from his face. "The painting. You hid it under the bed. He knew about it."

Shaking her head, she didn't want to believe it. "That's impossible."

"A faraway place hidden under a bed. That's what she always did," he quoted. "I suppose he felt honored you wanted to keep his painting, so he let you have it."

Sickened with the idea that her husband had known about the painting, she pushed her plate aside. "Are you saying the coffer is in the hunting cabin under the bed? And you have the key? Why are we still here?"

He grinned. "That's my girl."

The words, unconsciously said, sent a tingle of awareness through her. She certainly didn't want another husband, but belonging to Lucius felt like something different. As they mounted their horses and headed to the cabin, she couldn't shake the uncomfortable feeling his comment brought.

Once inside the cabin, she allowed Lucius's excitement to capture her as he moved to the bed to check for loose floorboards underneath it. As expected, he found the box and retrieved more of his inheritance as well as another letter.

After he scanned the lines, he handed it to her.

Very good, my boy. I know that was a difficult one, but it was necessary. Now, I know that you will do whatever must be done in order to survive. That is an important lesson, and one I hope you will retain.

Your actions have also proven that you are ready for the next part of the puzzle. The remainder of the clues are in London. The city is more difficult than the country, but I'm certain you are now equipped to handle those pitfalls. Keep moving, you're halfway there.

She swallowed. The winter hadn't even set in, and he would be leaving for London. One day without him had been difficult enough. She had no idea how she would stand a lengthy separation.

"So, London?" She handed the letter back to him.

"Yes." He smiled, capturing her around the waist. "We finally made it to London."

The excitement on his face was infectious. "I knew you'd make it."

He kissed her and walked them back toward the bed. Although her body responded, she pushed at him. They couldn't do this. Not here.

"What are you doing?"

"Exactly what it looks like. I missed you last night, so we're going to make up for the lost time." His lips were on her again, and she had trouble stopping him a second time as her need for him increased.

"We can't. Not in here."

"Why ever not?"

"The painting," she explained, desperate for him to understand.

"I don't give a damn about that." He advanced on her again, but she held out her hand to stop him.

"I can't. It's like he's here. Like he's watching."

Lucius groaned, then paced the small space before her. "I respect your wishes, but believe me, he can't see anything. After everything that man has done to me, has done to you, I daresay—where he is, *they* don't let him watch."

Seeing the pain on his face, she changed her mind. She grabbed his hand and halted his movements. He eyed her cautiously as she tugged him toward her.

"I've changed my mind. Let him watch. As a matter of fact, I hope he can see. Recalling all those times he left my bed angry, I now know he was frustrated at his inability to take me. Let him know that you are doing something that he never could."

Apparently not needing to be told twice, Lucius picked her up and put her on the edge of the bed. He pressed her into the mattress while he still had his feet on the floor. Unlike the previous night, he was frantic and desperate. She moaned as his hands roamed over her clothed body. He lifted her skirts, only stepping back to toss her drawers aside, then he pressed himself against her. The sensation of his hardness covered by his breeches drove her mad. She was more than ready for him, filled with a desperation for him to join with her.

It was odd to be fully clothed and be so needy, but it also was somehow sensual. He pressed against her again, and she cried out, trying to rub herself against him, but he was gone. Snapping her gaze up to him, a wicked glint shown in his eyes. Before she could question him, he knelt down and when his mouth touched her, she sucked in her breath.

Surely that was wrong, but as she thrashed on the mattress, overcome by his lavish attentions, she was powerless to deny something so wonderful. When the ray of burning release struck her, she screamed out his name. Her return to reality was slow, but she was sated and drained.

Lucius stood as he watched her with his nearly black eyes and immediately, her body reacted, readying itself for him again. She just couldn't get enough. Luckily, she didn't have long to wait as he freed himself and entered her in one stroke. The position seemed to allow him to reach deeper, and she couldn't contain her moans at the pleasure of having him completely fill her.

His movements were quick as he took her. She reveled in his onslaught, just as desperate. Their fully clothed bodies only added another layer to the act. She never wanted it to end. His intense gaze as he watched her proved he felt similarly. His fingers dug into her hips as he took her, and she shattered once again, swept away by a glimpse of heaven.

She kept her eyes open to watch his face as he, too, was struck with pleasure as he quickly withdrew himself from her. Never once did his intense eyes leave hers. As their breathing settled, they never broke eye contact and it was in that moment Hannah realized she loved him.

It was the best and the worst feeling, for when this ended, and he was married, she would be heartbroken. That pain would hurt far worse than anything his uncle had ever put her through. And, there was nothing she could do to change that fact.

~ ~ ~

Lucius saw the minute when the glow of their lovemaking wore away from Hannah. He hated that moment. He hated reality. And, he hated that he couldn't do anything to stop it from coming.

After retrieving a towel to clean up the mess, he righted his clothing. She sat on the edge of the bed, not speaking. Did she already regret what they'd done? He had wanted to taste her for so long and he hadn't wanted to wait any longer. The sound of his name on her lips and her flavor on his tongue as she lost control would be something he would remember for the rest of his life.

"You are very quiet," he observed, attempting to keep his tone light.

"As are you," she aptly replied.

He wanted to point out that it was only in response to her silence, but he had no desire to argue. If she wanted him to talk, he would talk. This was a time to celebrate. Although his uncle was a bloody bastard, Lucius had managed to master half of the clues, and now he understood why none of the others on the page made any sense. He hadn't as much as put one foot in the London townhouse in a good fifteen years.

"Then, I will be happy to fill the silence. How soon will you be ready to leave for London? I'm anxious to end this soon."

Her eyes snapped to his. "Leaving? I'm not going to London."

Crossing his arms, he tried to temper his reaction. "Why would you think that? There are still six clues on the page. Did you believe I would complete this task without you when I have failed up to this point?"

She moved to the opposite side of the room, facing away from him. "London is very different from here. If you go alone, you can avoid much, but not with me. There would be obligations. Parties we would be forced to attend. Not as many as during the season, but gatherings nonetheless."

There it was again. He clenched his fists. She was content to be with him behind closed doors, but a public appearance was unacceptable. The reminder was a hot knife plunging deep into his chest. She'd gone out with his uncle repeatedly, but *he* wasn't good enough.

He'd known she was using him, and he thought he was content with that fact, but the truth was that he wanted more. So much more that he would forever be denied. He had no idea why he thought this would work.

"Considering you spend the season in the city, I imagine you are not adverse to such activities. As your guardian, it is natural that I would attend with you. I hardly believe this is reason to avoid making the trip."

A look of panic crossed her face. "I simply think it's a little early for all that. You would be better served to make your foray into London society at the start of the season when the selection is better."

Raising an eyebrow, he studied her, desperate to know her thoughts. "Simply because I attend a few gatherings doesn't mean I'm in the market for a wife at this time. I'm certain I don't need to remind you about my uncle's warning. I'm already taking enough of a chance with you, and a wife wouldn't understand my need to withdraw myself."

"I suppose you're right, but think of how much time will be wasted at each of these events. I still think I'd be detrimental."

Furious, Lucius sliced his hand through the air. "I don't want to hear any more excuses. You're going with me, and that's final. I need you and you know it. Not only do you know the townhouse, but you understood him better than I did."

She dropped her gaze. "Yes, my lord."

Clenching his teeth at the sound of his bloody title on her lips, he fought his urge to bellow at her. Or, to beg her to understand. This was further proof of her lack of feelings for him as she could turn so cold after their time together. He only wished he could be as emotionless.

"Much better," he ground out, although it cost him. "You have nothing to fear from me. I have no intention of interfering with your London routine once we arrive. With the exception of solving only six more clues, you can act as though I don't exist. And, choose your bedchamber wisely. I am simply a man after all."

Her mouth fell open as she looked at him. He realized he shouldn't have said that, but he needed her to understand. As long as she slept in a room connected to his, he would carry her into his bed at every opportunity. His obsession with her was too great to be sated in one week.

"Anything else, my lord?"

"Yes. We are leaving tomorrow. Let's return to the manor at once. There is much that needs to be done and arrangements to be made."

She nodded, then proceeded him out the door. As he followed her, he couldn't help but feel empty inside. He didn't know what he had expected, but this certainly wasn't it.

Again, everything went back to his uncle. Had the man not imposed this task upon him or forced this trip to London, he would have had the entire winter with Hannah to himself. As it stood, the man had put an abrupt halt on that before the season could fully set in.

He supposed he should be grateful. After all, in such a short time he'd grown too attached. Hannah's assumption that he was searching for a bride returned. It hadn't worked with Lady Bernadette, but perhaps he should consider beginning to look again. He needed another woman that would be enough to distract him from thoughts of Hannah. He only hoped she existed.

Chapter 11

Hannah rubbed her aching toe as she sat in her favorite room at Lady Constance's House of Reform. She could hardly believe she was back in London. Nothing felt right anymore. Not since that day with Lucius in the hunting cabin.

"Hannah!" Regina rushed into the room, then she stopped and broke out into laughter. "I told you that you would find it."

"It's just that you moved that blasted table to an even more inconvenient place. Honestly, you need to hire someone who has an ability to place furniture and stop trying to do it yourself."

"My, my, someone sounds rather bitter. I take it your brief stay in the country didn't go over well." Regina sat on a chair opposite to Hannah.

"It went as well as could be expected considering you didn't deem it necessary to visit me as I requested."

With her eyes wide, Regina perfected a look of innocence. "You can't blame me. I had planned to make the trip next month. It's not my fault you changed your mind and returned here before I could arrange my schedule."

Forcing a smile, Hannah nodded. "It's nice to know you were going to visit. So, how are the classes going? I'd like to resume checking in daily if you still need me."

"Of course. Your help is always welcome. How long do you intend to remain in London?"

"I'm not certain. The new Lord Rivers was the one who insisted I aid him in the inspection of his London property.

Considering I was recently in town, he believes I can be of assistance."

A calculating glint shone in Regina's eyes. "I'm sure you can be a great help to him. You can also extend him an invitation to come to the House of Reform. I'd imagine a man who has recently inherited in the way the earl has might be in need of navigating the crowds of ladies to find the right bride."

Hannah's back straightened. A sick feeling slithered through her stomach. One day in London and it was already beginning. If Lucius had come without her, the droves of women wouldn't have as much access to him. However, she had obligations, and he would have to attend with her. Like Regina, all the matchmaking mothers would be salivating. Not that it mattered anymore.

Thinking about her cold bedchamber back at the townhouse only upset her further. When they'd arrived in London yesterday, she made herself select a different room when everything inside her rebelled. In addition, she'd chosen one as far away from the earl's chambers as possible as to not tempt herself. Or him.

Not only did she need time to attempt to put distance between them in order to dull the ache she knew she would feel when he left, but his comment had firmed her decision. He felt nothing for her but a means to sate his pleasure. And, when he left the decision up to her, that hadn't been fair. So, she had refused to prove her need by giving in to him.

Forcing her thoughts back to the present, Hannah faced her friend. "I don't believe Lord Rivers is ready for marriage. He is still working on going through everything his uncle left him."

"That's quite all right. We will be here when he is ready."

"Enough about that. Tell me what I have missed in my absence. Any trouble clients that I should keep an eye on?"

"Not that I'm aware. We are moving at the same rate as usual. Constance has put out some additional flyers, I'm hoping to add to the clientele. I have some new ideas to help generate income and more work of the instructors, nothing concrete as of yet. I may need your assistance later."

"You know where to find me."

"Excuse me, my ladies." Marvin bowed from the doorway. "Lord Reston is here to see you, Lady Regina."

"Thank you," Regina replied in a quiet voice.

Hannah watched with amusement as Marvin left and Regina made no move to see to her visitor. "I see nothing has changed in regard to that either."

"I have no idea what you are talking about. Of course I have clients to see to. Why would that change?"

"You can fool everyone else here, but I see more than they do. The marquis has taken a liking to you. I've also noticed he is the only man you go out of your way to not flirt with. That's significant."

Her friend's mouth fell open. "What are you saying? You make me out to be a wanton."

"You know that's not what I mean. You're naturally friendly, except with Lord Reston. I'm just wondering why."

"If we're asking difficult questions, then perhaps you'd like to tell me why you have no desire for Lord Rivers to wed. It seems to me that you of all people should have a concern over the man procuring an heir."

Stunned, Hannah's mouth fell open. She hadn't meant to push her friend, and certainly hadn't expected such a reaction. Clearly, there was something going on between Regina and the marquis. Something the woman didn't want to talk about. Hannah couldn't blame her as she had no desire to divulge her feelings for Lucius. Likely, the two of them were in similar situations.

"You're right, of course. I should be pushing the earl to find a bride. The man made it clear to me he wasn't ready at the moment, but as soon as the season begins, I have no doubt that will change. I'll see to it."

"Is that what you want?" Regina's low voice held remorse. "I didn't mean for that. I just . . . I'm sorry. I have a bit of a temper."

"No apology necessary. I'm not offended. The man should marry. And, I have no doubt he won't need assistance in that regard."

Regina nodded. "That's wonderful for him. Well, I should go see to my client. It's nice to have you back. Tomorrow, we should have tea together."

After her friend left the room, Hannah thought about how nice a glass of tea sounded. The comforting burn of whisky as it welcomed itself into her system. Then, soon after, the numbness would set in. An existence where she didn't have to think or feel like this any longer.

She couldn't believe her London trip had already begun so badly. Who knew the city would drive her to drink?

~ ~ ~

Lucius paced the study of his London townhouse. When put up against the estate, this residence was sorely lacking. So far, everything he encountered in the city paled in comparison. Including his relationship with Hannah. She had chosen a different bloody bedchamber. One that was so far from his, there was little chance that he could fetch her undetected.

The countess's chambers had already been readied, but she denied him. He'd gone as far as having her bed replaced. As far as he knew, she hadn't even opened the door, which meant she would never know the trouble he'd gone through to arrange it from the country. Not that it truly mattered.

He ran his hand through his hair. Where was she? He'd thrown out the idea that she was visiting a lover as she'd been an innocent—until recently. Was she deliberately avoiding him?

Glancing at the papers on his desk, he let out a curse. Six clues and after inspecting every inch of this place, he couldn't solve one. Didn't Hannah know how much he needed her help? Of course she did. That was probably why she wasn't speaking to him.

Suddenly the door to his study crept open and Hannah slipped in, gently closing the door so it didn't make a sound. That was interesting. He crossed his arms and looked at her. When she turned around to face him, she jumped.

"Lord Rivers? Allen said you went out."

"I've returned. So, tell me, my lady, why are you sneaking into my study?"

She put her shoulders back and glared at him. "I have a need for some whisky and my bottle seems to have gone missing."

"I thought you said that was in the past. That drinking didn't help." He didn't like this. Why would she need to go back to the bottle after one day in London? Her reluctance to join him couldn't be the city, as she'd spent the entire season here and intended to continue to do so in the future.

"It doesn't help to remove your problems, but it dulls them for a time. Now, either you return my bottle or I'll take another."

"What makes you believe I've taken it?"

"The bed is gone, too. I imagine that was your doing as well. With that, I can only assume you were in there."

"I destroyed that bed, but I had nothing to do with the bottle. That being said, I also don't intend to allow you to take another."

Her back straightened. "You would rather I do something scandalous like procure my own?"

"Why do you need it?" he demanded, determined to fix this. If it weren't for him, she never would have turned to the drink to begin with. He had an obligation to see she not go back.

"That's none of your concern, my lord. You may be legally allowed to make my decisions for me, but you don't own my thoughts."

He clenched his fists, he wanted those, too. He was a greedy bastard. The idea of owning all of her appealed to him, but she had to want him, which she clearly did not. He was left with one course of action.

Crossing the room, he collected the whisky bottle from the cabinet and two glasses. Unstopping the decanter, he poured one full glass and the other just half. Then, he set the bottle down and faced her.

"You want to drink, fine. If you're going to do it, you are going to do it with me." He lifted his chin, expecting her argument.

"The glasses aren't equal. Afraid you can't hold your liquor, my lord?" She sneered.

"If you want me angry, keep going. You're doing a fine job." He forced his blood to slow. "As a man, my tolerance exceeds yours, therefore, I will be drinking double what you do."

"Why?" Her voice was full of suspicion.

"Because drinking alone when you're upset only compounds your problems. With me to balance you, I can make sure that doesn't happen. I will warn you, however, after a few drinks I suffer a great loss of control."

She dropped her shoulders as defeat streaked across her face. The fact it was the possibility of sleeping with him that changed her mind angered him. What had happened between them? What had London done to her?

"Since I'm here, why don't we look at the clues instead?"

"As you wish." He nodded, then rounded his desk to collect the paper.

She sat in the chair before his desk, not touching the whisky. Part of him wanted to put it away, but he refused to make it look as though he'd won. She needed to discover she didn't need it on her own.

As she read the paper, he studied her face. She appeared tired. The idea of her catching a sickness due to lack of sleep bothered him. He hoped the trouble was due to traveling here and sleeping in strange beds. Again, he wished she would just talk to him. Did she act like this toward her husband, too? He imagined the man never even noticed.

Without looking up, she spoke. "Each one of these, he'd been trying to either teach a lesson or enforce something he'd already taught you. When you read through these, keep that in mind. Remember, he planned for you to do this by yourself, so he must have left you hints within these lines."

Lucius let out a sigh. "He may have or at least thought he had. I've been playing his game, and I'm done. If your knowledge can end this, I want to know."

"*Women are manipulative and deceitful, but we need them regardless. Find her and bring her the jewel you know she wants,*" she read.

"Judging from his problem, I can imagine that he had a mistress, and unless you're an incredible liar, you don't have the key either."

"She's not the key. The jewel is. She's the coffer. Think of the lessons he's given you. What woman had he needed? The answer has to be here."

Rubbing a hand over his face, Lucius tried to remember everything his uncle had ever said about women. "The key might be with the jewels. Perhaps locked with the countess's jewels?"

She nodded with a thoughtful expression. "Possibly. He never felt the need to give the jewels to me, so they aren't in my possession."

In that instant, he solved it. "The key is with the jewels. And, seeing as a wife is the one woman a man needs and that you never received the jewels, you are the coffer. Tell me, did my uncle have a portrait of you commissioned?"

Excitement filled her eyes. That's what she needed. The thrill of the chase. His body hardened at the sight. He was painfully attuned to her every reaction and feeling. It was sickening and wonderful at the same time.

"One. It's in the portrait gallery."

Lucius shook his head. "That's not very inventive. He used that place before. Honestly, I'm disappointed."

"Not that I wish to defend him, but everything he does is for a reason. The last was behind himself with a note about how important the position was. Then, he directed you to force me to tell you something. That was your lesson. I suspect this one is about finding a wife and obtaining an heir." She looked away from him. "It's something you need to think about doing."

The thought of marrying some random woman and using her for children didn't sit well with him. He wanted to marry Hannah, damn it. The realization didn't surprise him. It was what he had wanted for years now and never thought it possible. Now, she was here and available, but just as unattainable for him.

"That's not something I want to think about now, and at clue seven, he'd be a fool to tell me to begin searching now. There are still five more to uncover. It's taken months to get to this point."

"Well, if you are correct about where this clue is taking us, then we shall see." The light of a challenge lit her eyes.

He grinned, knowing this had to be the answer. "The jewel should be locked in my bedchamber. I'll retrieve the key then meet you in the portrait gallery."

She opened her mouth, then closed it and nodded. If she wanted to join him, he wouldn't complain, but she left the room before he could offer. Making quick work of the stairs, he used his signet ring to unlock the drawer with the jewels.

It was empty, save one key placed in the center of the drawer. Not surprised, he took it to the gallery.

"You are right," she conceded. "However, instead of the coffer being behind my portrait like the one at the estate, it's here."

She pointed to a sideboard oddly placed below her portrait. Lucius cast a glance at the painting and frowned. The look on her beautiful face spoke of misery. She hadn't even been able to hide it from the painter.

Looking at the piece of furniture, he pulled open the cabinet and found the coffer where Hannah directed. Sliding in the key, he found the jewels, more of his inheritance, and the expected note.

So, you found my deceptive creature. Know this, my boy, you never know the woman you shall take until after you wed her. Beware. This lesson should resonate with you above the rest. Make your pick thoughtfully and with great care. Don't rush to wed the first skirt you lust after. Keep in mind, she gave me no heir. You would do well to remember that every time you curse my name. Think of it like a sacrifice I took for you.

Beyond furious, he crumbled up the paper and shoved it in his pocket. He'd be damned if he let Hannah see it. That bloody bastard was the reason he had no heir. Why do this? Why put it on her?

"Why did you do that?" Hannah demanded. "What did it say?"

"You're right. He wants me to think about marriage."

With that, he turned and walked away from her. He'd be a damned fool if he ever let her find out the truth. She hated him now, but that would surely make her despise him. He knew that was something he couldn't handle.

~ ~ ~

Hannah stood in her typical place near the back of the room, being generally ignored by all the happy couples dancing around and chatting at Lord Matteson's ball. Being a winter event, the room wasn't as full as she was accustomed, but there were certainly more in attendance than she'd expected.

Not for the first time of the evening, her eyes sought Lucius. The man had yet another dance partner in his arms as he couldn't seem to pause for one minute before another introduction had to be made and obligatory dances offered. Exactly like she'd expected. The sight made her stomach ache.

Then, there was the letter from his uncle. What had it said? Why did he hide it from her? Ever since that day, he'd become distant from her. Although she knew that was exactly what she needed at present, she didn't like it. She wanted to be able to return to how they'd been in the country before all this.

"Enjoying the party?" The slimy voice of Lord Leyson washed over her skin, giving her the desire to go cleanse herself.

"It's a lovely night," she blandly observed, wishing he would leave her alone. Too many times the man had tried to talk his way into getting her to go somewhere alone with him. Unfortunately, tonight she didn't have the threat of her husband to frighten him away.

"More lovely now that you're here and appear to be out of mourning."

She ducked her head in an attempt to appear anything but sickened by his compliment. "When one loses a husband, I'm not sure if you can ever truly be out of mourning."

"I can't imagine your pain, but I'm certain your husband wouldn't have wanted you to be lonely. There's nothing wrong with wanting companionship."

Accustomed to these offerings, she held her head high. "I'm not lonely. As you see, I'm surrounded by friends and acquaintances. Everyone has been so wonderful during this difficult time."

He laughed. "They aren't there for you, but you can say what you will. How about a dance? I'd love to continue our talk over the next set."

The viscount moved in closer to her, and she did her best not to cringe. Men like him enjoyed seeing fear. It gave them the illusion of having power. Regardless of the unwashed stench coming off of him, she stood firm.

"I'd rather not."

His eyes narrowed. "Then, perhaps we can take a turn about the garden. The cool weather would offer a welcome change."

The look in his eyes told her getting away would not be an easy feat. He took her arm, and she tried to gently tug away without causing a scene, but he held firm. Panic crept up her throat. A scandal wouldn't be good. Perhaps a walk would be worth the trouble it would save her.

"I'm comfortable in here," she argued, attempting to keep her feet rooted to the floor.

"Perfect. We can have our little talk in the library. It's just a few steps away."

That was definitely something she couldn't do. Terror clawed at her throat. For the first time in her life, she missed her husband. He'd kept her from this fate by his presence and apparently respect to his memory had helped her through the season. Clearly, she'd run out of that. A ball was no place for a widowed woman who had no protector.

"What's going on here?" Lucius's voice was low, but she heard the menace.

"There's no need for concern. The lady and I were taking a walk."

Lucius crossed his arms. "As her guardian, I don't approve. She doesn't leave this room without me."

With a raised eyebrow, Lord Leyson held her tighter. "She's not an innocent for you to chaperone. The lady can make a decision for herself."

"Actually, she can't. As my ward, she belongs to me. Remove your hand from her or I shall do it for you."

A flutter moved through Hannah's stomach at Lucius's words. He may have kept his distance, but clearly he hadn't abandoned her. She wanted nothing more than to be able to cling to him. To have him protect her always.

The viscount released her, but there was reluctance to his movements. "When you get tired of being told what to do, come see me. I'll show you how a man should treat a woman."

Unable to help herself, she moved to Lucius's side and clutched onto his arm. The comfort she felt was immediate. She was safe.

"Not as long as there is breath in my body," Lucius practically growled, then led her away from the odious man.

"Thank you. Normally, they're not so insistent."

He stiffened. "Normally? This has happened before?"

"I told you, the men who seek me out at balls are looking for trouble. The threat of my husband held the majority of them off, but the earl is gone now."

"But, now you have me." His eyes searched her face, but she fought to keep her expression neutral. "Do you want me to take you home or do you want to dance with me?"

The question caught her off guard. Truthfully, she wanted both if it led to his bed, but she knew it didn't. By her choice, she reminded herself. What had she been thinking? She should move bedchambers at once.

"I'd love to dance, but what about all your ladies? They'll be so disappointed. And, as your uncle reminded you in that letter, you must marry."

"I don't give a damn about any of it if it stands in the way of our dance."

Her heart pounded, and as he drew her into his arms to join the waltz, she nearly melted into him. The rightness of being in his arms was an unfair tease. She'd missed this. Missed him. Her body was on fire as each movement taunted her. Suddenly, the idea of the library didn't sound so bad, but with Lucius this time.

"It is times like this I regret my choice of bedchamber," she admitted, then grinned when he missed a step.

"Then, why did you choose the one you did?" he rasped.

"It seemed like an appropriate response to your threat," she told him.

"That was no threat." He leaned his mouth closer to her ear. "It was a promise."

She shivered. Lust clouded her mind, but she knew this was another bad decision. Falling into his bed would only make things worse for her in the future, but the present would definitely be more pleasant.

"I think I want you to take me home," she whispered, desperation in her voice.

His eyes darkened as his grip tightened. "Stop looking at me like that or we'll never make it there."

Although the idea of his desire drove her mad, she tore her gaze from him. It wouldn't do to have anyone looking at her and having any idea about their conversation. He still needed to find a bride, but he wouldn't tonight. Until the season began, she would allow herself to steal a little more time with him.

Once the dance ended, Lucius led her to retrieve their coats as he called for the carriage. His focus was absolute, and she couldn't deny how much she enjoyed that fact. One word from her and he'd forgotten all the other women. It made her feel special.

As such, she couldn't contain her need. The second the carriage doors closed, she vaulted herself into his arms. He caught her to him, then proceeded to add another location to the list of places in lieu of a bed.

She may regret it later, but she couldn't think about that now.

Chapter 12

Lucius ran a finger down Hannah's arm, enjoying her answering shudder as she stood leaning over his desk. With the feeling that his time with her was limited, he couldn't keep his hands to himself. He would take every opportunity to receive any amount of her he could.

The ball last night had been difficult and wonderful at the same time. He'd spent the entire night doing his best to avoid Hannah as she preferred, but it had been torture to see her standing by, watching and not participating. Then, when the bloody viscount had tried to violate her, Lucius had been ready to rip the man apart.

Still, he hadn't counted on Hannah's reaction. She'd clung to him as if she'd been thrilled to be near him. And, their dance. Memories of the erotic movements brought an ache to his groin even now.

He'd never been so desperate to take a woman in a moving carriage, until last night. Then, when she'd been prepared for the night, he'd taken a chance and snuck into her bedchamber before carrying her to his bed. He had no idea how she managed to escape this morning, but the night had been worth their risk.

"If you keep touching me like that, I'll never be able to concentrate on the clue. I've read it ten times and not retained any of it."

"Then, perhaps you aren't trying hard enough." He moved to stand behind her and ran his lips along her neck. "Is this better?"

Her head leaned to the side, giving him better access as she moaned. "I think we are going about this the wrong way."

"How's that?" he breathed, loving the reedy quality of her voice.

"These are your clues. You should be the one solving with my help, not the other way around."

He chuckled as his hands slid further up her body. "No. You've been pushing me to remember the lessons my uncle taught me. One thing he always said was not to do anything you can have someone else do for you. I'm simply following his teachings as you requested."

When his hands reached her breast, she stopped him. "Lucius, we can't. Not here."

Drawing back, he turned her to face him. "Why not? You had no such reservations about the desk before. Or the sofa, if I recall."

"This is different." She smoothed a piece of her hair behind her ear. "We're in London, not the country. I snuck in here this time, but if anyone were to find out . . ."

Frustrated with her confusing mixed signals, he walked away from her and thrust his hand through his hair. "I don't understand. You know I can lock the door, but you don't even suggest it. You choose the bedchamber far away, then turn around and drive me to distraction at a ball. Which, strangely enough, was the one time you accepted my presence publicly."

"What are you talking about?"

"Your aversion to being seen with me in public."

Her mouth fell open. "Lucius, what we're doing—"

"I'm not suggesting we make our personal dealings known," he shot back before she could say otherwise.

She let out a steadying breath. "London is full of scandal. In the country the staff is loyal to my title, but here, they were his. My husband lived here the entire year, and one word to one person would be detrimental."

"I'm talking public, Hannah. I want to take you to Hyde Park where you will introduce me to your friends. Perhaps walk to the shops and let me buy you something. Surely, these are appropriate things for a guardian to do."

Her mouth formed a tight line. "I don't think you understand what you are asking of me."

Unable to take it any longer, he stormed from the room. He couldn't understand how she could do this to him. Although he wanted her desperately, he wasn't sure he could handle being used in this manner any longer. Never before had he cared after a woman's reasons for joining him in bed, but Hannah was different.

Once outside, he walked down the street with no particular destination in mind. In the past, he'd avoided London as it had been the primary residence of his uncle and Hannah. Seeing them together had never been easy. The tormented look on her face had always affected him, but it was so much more than that.

He kept walking as he allowed his thoughts to continue. It wasn't easy as he had no clear solution. The simple answer was to do as he had tried before and find another woman to replace her, but if last night was any indication, there was no chance of that working. The entire ball, his thoughts and entire being had been consumed by Hannah. He watched her every move while trying his best not to show his preoccupation.

Casting the thought aside, he made his way back to the townhouse. At the door, he learned Hannah had gone out again. He wondered where she disappeared to each day, but knew he had no right to ask her.

Forcing himself to his study, he determined to solve the clue on his own. This had been drawn out long enough. He needed to do as Hannah had suggested and recall every lesson his uncle had taught him. After all, the man must have wanted him to prevail in this task.

Lucius opened the book and set out the papers his uncle had left for him, including all the letters in each coffer. There had to be clues somewhere in all this. He closed his eyes and pictured his uncle in those first days when he'd been young. The man seemed to have an exuberance for life about him that had been lacking in his later years.

Pulling out the clue sheet, he read: *Take to your bed who you choose, just make sure you don't lose sight of where you should be.*

As he and Hannah had suspected, there had to be something in or around his bed, but he couldn't think of the other side. Where should he be? He'd already searched the study to no avail, as well as his chair at the head of the table. Uncle Herman always made it clear a man's place was at the top or in front, so what did he mean by this clue?

Considering Lucius wasn't getting anywhere with this, he made his way up to his bedchamber deciding to search for the part he knew. He felt no key under his mattress nor did he find any loose floorboards. This was ridiculous. The clue was clearly directing him to his bed.

He sat on the mattress, propped himself against the headboard, and closed his eyes. Immediately images of him and Hannah last night filled his mind. With a tortured moan, he cast the thought aside. He had to be missing something. His uncle had already warned him about taking staff members to his bed, so what did this mean?

Turning his head to the side, he noticed an odd depression in the headboard. He moved toward it and couldn't believe he had found it. There was a small key hole disguised to look like a knot in the wood. This wasn't the key. It was the coffer.

Excitement filled him. Now he only had to find the key. So, where should he be? With his uncle, there were so many possibilities. And, one place in particular he wanted to be.

The thought had him bolting upright in his bed. That was it. The one place he should be was in Hannah's bed. Or rather, what his uncle was saying was in his countess's bed. The man had never produced in heir, so he was telling Lucius to complete what he never could.

Jumping out of bed, he moved to the adjoining door, then froze. The countess's bed was gone. He'd destroyed it. Hurrying into the room, he felt along the floor, hoping to find it discarded. Nothing. Beyond frustrated with himself for his thoughtless actions, he slammed his hand down on the bedside table.

A clinking sound caught his notice. Glancing over he saw a small key lying on the table. Someone must have found it and placed it there for the countess. Smiling, he collected it and returned to his chamber to obtain a little more of his inheritance.

~ ~ ~

Hannah threw herself into a chair at the House of Reform and did her best to exercise patience while she waited. The urge to march into Regina's class overwhelmed, but she held herself back. After having already checked on the lessons, Hannah knew it was time for Regina's current class to end.

"I'll be back for my next lesson unless you change your mind," Hannah heard Lord Reston say.

"You can stop offering. I'll never change my mind."

"We shall see."

The sound of footsteps reached Hannah and shortly after, Regina arrived in the doorway. Her friend looked haggard, but perked up as soon as she set eyes on Hannah. That was definitely interesting, but she refused to ask after what was going on. Not after what happened last time.

"I'm so glad to have you back," Regina admitted as she claimed her seat. "Not having to check in on the classes has been nice. It frees up my time."

Hannah studied her friend, but saw no sign of anything other than sincerity. No traces of her encounter with Lord Reston remained. The girl's curly blonde hair and round face gave her an automatic look of innocence, but Hannah wasn't fooled. Something was going on between the two of them. She would have to watch their lessons more closely.

"I'm happy to be back in my routine. It's the only time I feel normal. If I'm being truthful, I have to admit being at the townhouse has been rather difficult."

"Truly? I was under the impression you were freed when your husband passed. Was I wrong?"

"No. You're absolutely right. However, my current problem isn't with the previous Lord Rivers."

Realization dawned on Regina's face. "It's the current one. I understand. I'm not sure why men believe they have a right to women as soon as they become their guardians. I've seen it too many times. You don't have to say a word, we'll have a room readied and—"

"You don't understand. It's not like that. He's not pursuing me or anything like that. I'm afraid it's much worse. I'm in love with him."

Saying the words out loud only made it more real, but Hannah knew them to be the absolute truth. No doubt existed within her. She loved Lucius and there was nothing she could do to stop the pain of it.

Regina watched her with rounded eyes. "Are you quite certain of this?"

With a nod, Hannah allowed her hopelessness to fill her. "I've known for some time now. I've been trying to distance myself, but it doesn't work. Once you love someone, it doesn't just go away."

"Does he know you feel like this?"

"Absolutely not. He enjoys my company and would like me to show him around London and introduce him to people, but he's made it clear the activity is one appropriate for guardian and ward."

"That is unfortunate. What are you going to do?" Regina's voice held pity.

"I don't know. That's why I came to you. This is one of the things the House of Reform does. Fix this for me. Tell me what to do."

Instead of an immediate response, Regina stood and moved about the room. "This is certainly not what I expected to hear from you, of all people. Are you sure this is what you want? I certainly wouldn't recommend it."

Confused, Hannah stared at her friend. "I don't know why you feel that way, but I can't live like this any longer. I want this feeling gone. I need you to fix this for me."

If anyone could break her of her unrequited love, it was Regina. She'd seen the lady help several debutantes put it behind them, and they were able to find husbands and move on with their lives. Hannah wanted that for herself, well, except for the husband part. The only man she would consider putting herself through that again for was Lucius. And, he made it clear he had no interest in her in that way.

"Very well. He wants to be taken through London and to meet your friends? Then, bring him here. He's going to sign up for a class with me."

Hannah swallowed. This was what she wanted, but not. If Lucius married, it would make him unattainable for her, but it would do nothing to dull the ache she had every time she was around him. However, once he wed, surely his bride wouldn't want her about. The woman would likely ensure her husband's residence was the complete opposite of Hannah's. That was good.

"That might work, but how are you going to convince him?"

Regina laughed. "Have you ever known me to not be

able to get a man to do what I wanted? Besides, I will have you to help me."

Nodding, Hannah hoped she could be convincing. After all, she truly didn't want this. After a taste of how perfect her life could be with him, she didn't like the prospect of the lonely existence ahead.

~ ~ ~

Lucius looked around the small room at the House of Reform and frowned. So, this was where Hannah had been spending her days. He wondered what she was taking lessons for. Certainly not to find a husband, and he hadn't seen her using an instrument or attempting a language. It was definitely curious.

Glancing over at her, she seemed nervous. He wanted to comfort her, but decided against it. When she'd arrived back at the townhouse yesterday and told him she'd changed her mind and would like to show him what she'd been doing in London, he had been shocked. She also hadn't appeared pleased to be doing this, so he didn't want to make this harder for her.

"Good afternoon," a petite blonde said from the doorway.

Lucius stood as he took in the lady. She had a soft smile and delicate curls framing her face. Her eyes sparkled when they met his, and he couldn't help but smile back.

"There you are." Hannah's voice held a desperation. "Please allow me to present Lucius Dobson, Earl of Rivers. Lord Rivers, this is Lady Regina."

"A pleasure to meet you," he responded, giving her a bow of his head.

She batted her glittering eyes. "The pleasure is certainly mine, my lord. Please sit and allow us to get to know each other better."

Hesitating, he glanced at Hannah. She had no reaction. The lady's overly flirtatious manner didn't seem to affect her in the least. That bothered him a bit, although he knew it shouldn't. After all, Hannah didn't want him.

"Of course." He held out his hand, allowing her to select a seat before he reclaimed his, thankfully opposite to the flirtatious creature.

"Now, where do we begin?"

At that moment, a gentleman arrived in the doorway, drawing his attention. "Lady Regina? I'm sorry to interrupt, but I'm here for my lessons."

A stricken look crossed the lady's face, but there was something not quite right about it. She stood, causing him and Hannah to do the same. "Oh dear. Lord Reston, I completely forgot you changed the time when we spoke the other day."

The man shook his head. "I'm sorry, but I can't adjust my schedule again."

"I'm so sorry Hannah, but . . . Wait, Hannah, do you suppose you would be able to handle Lord Reston's lessons today? That would give me a chance to know Lord Rivers a little better."

Confusion crossed Hannah's face. "Me? But, I—"

"Don't worry, my dear, you'll do fine." Lady Regina turned back to the man in the doorway. "Lord Reston, my dear friend, Lady Rivers will be an excellent replacement for today."

Hannah obediently moved toward the door.

Lucius clenched his fist as the lord's eyes ran down Hannah and the bastard grinned.

"Perfect. I can't wait to get my arms around her."

Lunging forward, Lucius was ready to strangle the man, but a restraining hand from Lady Regina stopped him as Hannah stiffly walked from the room. This was unacceptable. What kind of place were they running here? And, why would Hannah agree so readily to step in?

"It's a dancing lesson, my lord. The marquis is harmless."

Turning back to her, he caught her smug smile. There was more to this than it seemed. As she reclaimed her seat, he did the same, watching her closely. The lady had a plan, and he vowed to find out what, exactly, was her intention. Was this part of the services? To send Hannah into the path of the marquis so the man would consider her for marriage?

"I assume there will be a chaperone for the lesson."

"All our lessons are done with the door open and someone checking in periodically. That's typically Lady River's duty when she comes here."

Leaning back in his seat, Lucius crossed his arms, not believing what he was hearing. "You are telling me that the lady has sought employment here?"

"Oh, no, my lord. The lady has been quite free with her time."

"I see. Then, can you tell me why you felt the need to dispose of her today? For clearly the ploy you had arranged with the marquis was a setup."

A becoming blush moved up her cheeks. "I can't say that I know what you are talking about, my lord."

He laughed. The woman was a delight. Her sly smile only confirmed the ploy. Yes, she had planned this to get him alone or to put Hannah together with a potential suitor.

"Then, perhaps your plan was to put the countess in the path of Lord Reston. Did she request your services? I can't imagine she did as she's never made an indication to me that she has been searching for another husband. Your efforts, although stemming from a desire to help her, are unnecessary."

"Unnecessary? That's such a strong word. Maybe she just needs a little nudge in the right direction. I'm certain there are men out there who will treat her right if she only looked. I'm helping her look."

Feeling the blood rushing through his veins, Lucius tried to keep his breathing steady. This was not right. All this time and he never considered the possibility of Hannah finding another husband. He couldn't imagine that she would even want another one. After what she had been through, he thought she would be his to take care of. That she would in a small way always belong to him.

"I don't believe the lady needs help," he pressed.

With a shake of her head, the lady's curls bounced. "Why don't we talk about something else? I'm far more interested in knowing where you stand on the subject of marriage. I can help you as well."

"I'm not looking to marry at this time."

She lifted a delicate eyebrow. "So adamant. That can mean one of two things. Either you have serious objections to the majority of the available ladies. Or, you have already decided on the one you want."

Clenching his teeth, Lucius wasn't sure if he should be impressed or disturbed. This woman saw far more than she should, and he didn't like it. Yes, he'd already decided, but his chosen lady was unattainable, which left him with no options.

The note his uncle had left him in the last coffer spoke of the importance of securing a line as the other side of their family was not to be trusted. As they were next to receive the earldom, he needed to be the one to see to the future of the estate.

He would see to his duty, but he would do it on his own time.

When he and Hannah finally left, he was irritated and having trouble hiding it. Lady Regina had kept up her flirtatious manner and had tried to glean information from him either regarding Hannah or his thoughts on marriage. The combination had left him with a rather unpleasant feeling.

"What do you think?" Hannah asked him as they strolled down the street.

"Of what? Quite a lot happened today that I'm not certain to what you are referring."

Her concerned gaze met his. "What do you mean? What happened?"

"Why did you take me there?"

Red crawled up her cheeks. "You claim to want to meet my friends. Lady Regina happens to be my friend. Did you not like her?"

He stopped walking and faced her, searching her gaze. The urge to ask her if she'd set this up for the lady to help him find a bride overwhelmed, but he held his tongue.

"Did you know she planned to talk to me alone?"

"I don't believe she intended that. Lord Reston's arrival surprised her. Had I not been able to step in, you would have missed out on your visit."

Seeing the belief in her friend reflected in her eyes, he smiled and resumed walking. "You're right. Would you care to stop in one of the shops?"

Her eyebrow raised as she looked at him. "You like shopping?"

He laughed. "Not particularly, but for you I'm willing to make an exception."

She bit her lip as her blush deepened. "If I didn't know better, I'd say you were flirting, my lord."

Not sure where her comment had come from, he controlled his reaction. "What if I am? I'm with a beautiful woman and it's a lovely day. I see no harm in it."

"You're wrong. Perhaps I would think it was more than a simple flirtation and fall madly in love with you. Then, where would you be?"

He froze. Her speaking the words he so desperately wanted to hear clogged his throat. How did he even respond to that? How did she want him to respond?

"I believe I'm safe with you. So, where are we going?"

"Perhaps the sweetshop," she suggested in a small voice.

Hating to hear her withdrawal, he decided to change the subject. "I found another clue yesterday when you were out."

Her attention shot to his. "You did? How? I read that clue at least a hundred times. Don't tell me it was in your bed. You've been sleeping there."

"The coffer was in the headboard, but the key had been in your bed."

"Mine?"

He nodded. "Apparently, I shouldn't have disposed of it so soon. Luckily, the staff found the key and placed it on the bedside table. I need to be more careful in the future."

"What was the lesson?" He had to strain to hear her.

"To produce heirs. My current heir is an obscure cousin from my great uncle's line. Apparently, the family has coveted the title and caused problems for my uncle on numerous occasions. He wants me to be aware of them, and ensure they not inherit."

"First marriage. Now heirs. You are getting close to the end. And, it appears you no longer need me."

The sad tone of her voice gave him hope. Perhaps she wasn't as ready to rid herself of him as he thought. This outing was good. If only he could convince her to see him in a different light. Then, everything would work out. Yes. She'd already enjoyed spending time in his bed, so that was half of the challenge.

"You are wrong. I will always need you."

Chapter 13

Nine clues complete. Hannah could hardly believe it. There were only three more. The thought clogged her throat as she followed Lucius into his study after they had located the coffer hidden under the seat in the carriage.

As they moved along, it was becoming more and more apparent to her that her husband had received help with his plan since he'd been in London. Even the key Lucius found placed on the night table seemed suspicious to her. Someone must have known about it. Not to mention how sickly the man had become toward the end. Even his handwriting had deteriorated.

Once the door closed, Lucius faced her. "Well, it is clear my uncle orchestrated this entire thing to ensure I remain to do my duties. That's ridiculous. I don't see how he could believe I would turn my back on the estate."

The disgust in his voice made her feel bad for him. With the lack of faith his own uncle placed in him, she could understand him being upset. And, it seemed the man liked to continually remind Lucius how he didn't remain with him all those years ago. This lesson, it seemed, was more difficult for Lucius to handle.

"May I ask you something personal?"

He spun around to face her, amusement transforming his features. "Would a negative response stop you? It never has before."

With an unapologetic grin, she shook her head as she sat on the sofa. "I suppose not, but you can refuse to answer. That, I'm accustomed to from you."

"We know each other so well. Please, proceed." He propped himself on the edge of his desk, looking at her expectantly.

She took a deep breath, knowing he probably wouldn't want to give her an answer for this. "Why did you run away from him all those years ago? He complained quite a bit at first. Grumbling about you mainly, but I never understood. The two of you seemed so close before."

His bark of laughter held no mirth. "Close? That man was never close to anyone, least of all me. I was a pawn. You may not remember how we met, but I recall our first meeting. My uncle had been using me as a footman, which is what you mistook me for. We spent a lot of time in the garden back then."

"That explains why I'd felt like I'd already known you when we were introduced."

He nodded. "You loved the garden in those days. And, the animals. You took such care of every living creature. I looked forward to when my uncle would take me to Melbourne. I always found you in the garden."

"I never knew." Her face burned with embarrassment. She hadn't even been a nice enough person to ask his name, and he'd anticipated seeing her. She blocked out so much of being a naïve child that she couldn't believe she had forgotten him as well.

"It doesn't matter." He offered her a weak smile. "I hadn't done anything memorable. Simply followed you around and listened to your every word."

She laughed. "Then, I'm no longer surprised you've wanted nothing to do with me these past ten years. I must have been incredibly horrid."

"No. Not at all. You were enchanting. And, I'm sorry you felt I wanted nothing to do with you. My anger these years has been directed at my uncle. Although, I will admit I did partially blame you for not producing an heir and saving me all this. Apparently, I must apologize for that as well."

"You don't need to apologize. Considering how far our relationship has come, you should be able to tell we've gone past that."

"Don't be so quick to give out apologies when you don't even know the full extent of the sins." His blue eyes were intense.

Uncomfortable, she shifted. "Perhaps I'm a forgiving person."

"I'd like to believe that."

That didn't sound good, but she couldn't think of anything he could have done to warrant an apology. That meant he was planning something. She swallowed, attempting to stop her throat from closing. After all, he was planning to wed. Regina had whispered to her how their plan had gone so well.

Obviously, Lucius had told her something he hadn't indicated to Hannah. That could only mean he'd decided to use the services to locate a bride, and he hadn't wanted her to know. Definitely something requiring an apology. She shook off the thought, not wishing to think on the future at the moment. She'd been so affected by the knowledge when they'd gone out shopping that she'd done the unthinkable and mentioned falling in love with him. His lack of a real response was not very encouraging.

"Are you deliberately avoiding my question? Or, do you intend to respond?"

He let out a heavy sigh. "As you know, Uncle Herman was fond of teaching me lessons. Some of them were quite harsh and unforgivable. I will never forgive him for some of the things he put me through. I was furious with him, and as he had a wife, I imagined he would have an heir and there was no need for me to put myself through his torture any longer."

"You weren't upset to be potentially replaced by an heir? That's what he told me. He said that was why you disliked me so much."

"I never wanted this. Hannah, if you could do one thing for me, I ask that you forget every word that man said. He was nothing but lies."

The pain in his voice spoke to her, and she couldn't help but nod. He'd suffered at the man's hand just as she had, but in so many ways, his was so much worse. The desire to comfort him overwhelmed her, but she remained in her spot on the sofa for she knew if she gave in it would turn into so much more.

The next day as she sat in Lord Bowlen's drawing room after a dull dinner party, she regretted her control the previous afternoon. Surely, if she had taken him to her bed, he wouldn't be ignoring her now. She wished she knew what all those women offered him that she couldn't.

"You don't appear to be having a pleasant time, my lady," Lord Reston commented as he appeared beside her. "Mind if I join you?"

"I'd be delighted, my lord," she offered, choosing to not respond to his apt observation.

"I had hoped it wouldn't come to this, but Regina asked me to keep an eye on you. Apparently, you need her help more out here than in the classroom."

Stunned, Hannah looked at the marquis. "What are you talking about?"

He gave her a grin and a conspiratorial wink. "Of course. Just give me a smile and I promise to keep my mouth closed."

"I'm sorry, my lord. I'm truly at a loss."

The marquis leaned toward her and whispered. "I'm to help you and Lord Rivers. Regina told me of the trouble you are having with him. Stick by me tonight, and it will help."

"I don't know how, but I trust Regina." Hannah forced a smile.

She didn't like the thought of Lucius searching for a bride tonight, but it appeared he would be doing that regardless of her interactions. It was likely Regina thought Lucius would be less likely to see to his duty while she remained sitting alone, but her friend had been wrong.

Regardless, she intended to take advantage of the situation. The marquis was an amicable sort, and she would be pleased to spend the evening in his company. If nothing else, she would prove she had the ability to pay attention to something other than Lucius.

~ ~ ~

Irritation stabbed through Lucius as he watched Lord Reston and Hannah stroll along the path of Hyde Park. How had the man even known they would be here? Over the past fortnight, it seemed he could not rid himself of the marquis. His eyes followed Hannah and his constant presence at events—and once even at Lucius's townhouse—grated on his nerves.

A large part of Lucius wanted to grab Hannah up to him and demand she remain with him and deny the marquis, but he couldn't. Handling her rejection would be more than he could bear. Instead, he simply watched in irritation.

"Lord Rivers?"

He turned to see Lady Regina approaching. Good. He needed to have a talk with her.

"Lady Regina, how nice to see you." He offered his arm.

She snuggled close to his side as she took his arm. "It's quite a cold afternoon. This winter has been slow to set in, but it seems to be making up for it now."

"I agree with you, but some people don't seem to notice." He nodded his head toward the pair that had held his attention since the man had stolen her from him.

The lady laughed. "Yes. Isn't it lovely? The two of them

make quite a lovely couple, don't you think? Makes me believe you are wrong about her."

"Taking a walk with the man doesn't mean marriage. Otherwise, you have put yourself in a very similar position to hers at present."

"Why, my lord, I'm quite flattered for you to think of me, but I have the feeling I'm a little more than you can handle. You need someone more like . . . Let me see." She pressed her lips together as she thought. "Goodness, I can't believe I hadn't thought of that before. But, I imagine it's too late now."

"What? What's too late?" Foreboding ran up Lucius's spine.

"It's nothing. I simply thought of a lady that would be ideal for you, but as it turns out, there is another gentleman who has developed an interest in her. I have no reason to disrupt that at present."

Knowing Lady Regina spoke with Hannah, Lucius fought to hide his reaction. So, he had been correct regarding the marquis's interest. But, what of Hannah's? Surely she hadn't decided to marry again so soon. As he studied the pair and took in her beautiful smile, he wasn't so sure.

"What of the lady's interest? Doesn't that come into consideration?"

"That remains to be seen, but I'm not sure why you are concerned. Didn't you tell me you weren't interested in marriage? Have you changed your mind?"

Gritting his teeth, he decided not to respond to her. The lady was trouble, and he knew she was only looking for information from him.

"Of course not. I'm simply wondering after your process. It seems your matchmaking services are rather one-sided."

She bristled and he had to work to contain his smile. "We don't offer matchmaking services, my lord. What I'm doing is not a service we offer. It is something different I have been noticing."

"I see. Perhaps you should speak with the lady in question. Then, you will know if she has any interest in the gentleman you've selected for her."

"If not, are you interested?"

Refusing to respond to her question, Lucius kept his gaze fixed in front of them. The last thing he needed was to make Hannah more uncomfortable by having her friend indicate his interest. She already knew of his desire for her physically, other than that, he was afraid she would withdraw from him further. That he could not allow.

By the time they returned to the townhouse, Lucius was irritated, and overwhelmed with the urge to stake his claim on Hannah. He wanted to tell her to stay away from all other men, but how could he? However, he also couldn't allow her to walk away from him right now. Not with him stuck with the image of her and the bloody marquis in his mind. The walk through Hyde Park was supposed to have been their outing together.

Leading Hannah into the study, he closed the door. She lifted her eyebrow, but didn't argue. They hadn't so much as looked at the clues to solve his uncle's game in weeks, so he hadn't had her alone like this in far too long. After the last clue and talk about heirs, his desire to look any further had diminished.

"It was nice to see Lord Reston today. And, unexpected." She moved with an idle purpose about the room.

He grunted a reply to which she merely looked at him.

"What do you think about the marquis?"

"What do *you* think about him," he shot back, stalking toward her.

"He seems like a nice gentleman. Makes me laugh." Her voice was strained and the closer Lucius got to her, the heavier her breathing became. That was definitely a good sign.

"Nice? Funny? Is that what you are looking for? It seems your friend has the idea that you are deciding to wed the gentleman."

Her eyes widened. "I—"

"You what?" He stopped only inches in front of her. "You want him? Does he make your blood race? Your body shudder? Does the thought of him touching you make your knees weak?"

"Why? Why are you doing this?" Her reedy voice told him so much.

"Because if you are going to consider giving any man that kind of power over you again, you better make damn sure he offers you something in return. That should be your condition. Nothing else."

The sight of her melted chocolate eyes nearly did him in, but when his gaze fell to her parted lips, he was struck. Unable to help himself, he took her mouth as he jerked her body up against his. It had been too long, and his desire for her had reached dangerous heights.

She clung to him, meeting his kiss with a fierceness he thought would kill him. Much sooner than he thought possible, he was ready to take her. Holding himself back was the most difficult thing he'd done to date. She overwhelmed him. Her scent, her lips, her tongue, her hands. This was what he craved. What he needed.

When she pulled her mouth away from his, but didn't withdraw, he continued to kiss along her jaw and down to her neck. She moaned, making all those sounds he dreamed about. The woman was so passionate. He'd never known anyone like her before.

"The wall," she whispered. "Take me, Lucius. I choose the wall."

Not needing any further encouragement, he lifted her and wrapped her legs around him as he carried her to press her back against the wall. He was nearly blind with lust as he secured her with one hand so he could slide a finger inside her. Damn. She was slick and ready for him.

Desperate for more of a connection to her, he kissed her hard as he struggled to free himself. Then, he drew back, wanting to watch her face as he took her. Moving slowly, he inched inside her until he was fully entrenched. He fought to keep his eyes open as her tight warmth encased him.

Hannah moaned and dug her fingers into his shoulders as she threw her head back. Being inside her felt so good, but it wasn't enough. It was never enough. He wanted all of her. Thrusting his hips, he tried to block out the thought. Harder. Faster. Her moans became more desperate, and when she took her pleasure, he covered her mouth with his, taking her cries within him.

To his surprise, she went crazy. Tightening her legs around him as her spasms squeezed him. Her hands fisted in his hair as she frantically kissed him. Unable to stop the torrent of pleasure, he lost control as stars exploded behind his eyes.

He couldn't breathe. He couldn't move. That had been the most intense experience of his life. And, he'd forgotten to withdraw himself first.

~ ~ ~

Hannah couldn't stop her gaze from trailing to the wall of Lucius's study. The very sight of that one wall and her cheeks heated. When she'd demanded he use it yesterday, she'd never expected the experience to be so erotic. The very idea had her cheeks burning even hotter.

They had been in London for over a month now, and she'd managed to stay strong with the exception of a few lapses. However, today her body seemed to be in a horrible state of turmoil. She wanted him again. So much more than before. She knew it was partially because he'd given her hope by acting in a manner that verged on jealousy. Biting her lip, she tried to squelch the emotion. This was bad.

"Is there something you wish to talk about? Something you're not saying?"

Her attention flashed to Lucius. "No. Of course not. Why would you think that?"

"You just seem a little preoccupied with that particular wall today. There's no reason to regret--"

"I don't regret it," she rushed to assure him. "It was just. I didn't know it would really work."

He steepled his fingers on his desk as he leaned forward. "So, your request yesterday was a challenge? You hadn't expected anything to happen?"

A hint of anger in his voice bothered her. Was he angry at her or himself?

"Not at all. It just makes me wonder how many other places have a similar use, and I have never known."

His dark gaze enthralled her. "I can show you if you'd like."

The feral way he locked his eyes on her, as if he would devour her, combined with his raspy voice almost made her give in. Almost. Dear God, what was she doing? It was happening all over again. She was becoming addicted to him. Each day she spent in his company only made it worse. The man was the most thoughtful, kind, compassionate person she'd never known. Not to mention handsome and passionate. She couldn't believe it had taken so many years to discover his true self.

"I don't think that is such a good idea," she forced out. "We have a clue to solve."

He let out a long sigh. "Ah, yes. My delightful uncle's little game must be finished. Three more clues and then I can put it all to rest."

"Yes. And, put him behind you where he belongs. He always had a fear of being alone. Perhaps he felt like you would forget him if he hadn't done something as elaborate as this."

"That is possible. Now, this next damned clue makes as much sense as the others. I searched every inch of my desk, it can't be in my bed again, and every other place that I touch every day would be cleaned or in some way altered by servants. Not left alone for months until I found it."

She shifted in her chair. "If we were on the estate, I'd agree, but remember I told you these people were loyal to him. They did his bidding, and I imagine will continue to do so for long into the future. If he told them to make sure a key was undisturbed, it would be safe in the middle of the entryway floor."

With a nod, Lucius's eyes grew distant. "Then, what is it I touch?"

His words sent a wave tingling over her skin. He'd touched her. If only he would do so every day. Her heart sped as she recalled his hands on her skin. His mouth. His . . .

"Hannah?" His voice pulled her from her inappropriate thoughts. "Are you all right?"

She nodded. "Yes. I'm simply thinking."

Heat moved across her face at his amused grin. "Then, you have no thoughts on my suggestion?"

"Can you repeat it? I was thinking of all the possibilities on the clue."

"Of course." He winked at her, further deepening her blush. "I said that I could go over, in detail, every item that I lay my hands on so that we may inspect it, or we could move on to the second part of the clue."

"I don't know the second part any better," she argued, feeling hopeless.

"*Burn it all. It's not worth your time,*" he read. "I've looked inside every fireplace, stove or anything that could possibly burn something. Honestly, this clue frightens me more than most. What did he burn?"

Running the clues in her mind, she also thought of a fireplace. "What about your lessons? Did he teach you anything about touching or burning?"

Lucius shook his head. "This might be a new one. I'm certain he had a few more to teach me when I left ten years ago."

All this thinking was making her head hurt. "If this isn't worth your time, why is he wasting it?"

"Time? Maybe this isn't about burning. It's about time. There aren't many clues left and I'm certain he knew he hadn't had much time left in the end. A clock, maybe? Over a fireplace?" His eyes danced with pleasure.

"It must be," she muttered, loving the complete happiness on his face.

"Why don't you go look for it?" He stood. "I'll move through my routine and check everything I typically touch. I never imagined it would be anywhere that could possibly be moved, so this opens up a lot of possibilities."

She nodded, then made her way to the drawing room. After close inspection, she didn't find anything. As she continued through each room, inspecting all the clocks, she didn't work to hide her movements like at the estate. As she expected, the staff avoided her and not one so much as gave her an odd look. They knew. Just as they knew she was helping Lucius. She didn't mind that as long as they didn't know the extent of her relationship with him.

Moving into the ballroom, she approached the ornate fireplace. A large clock sat on the mantle. The door had a keyhole like the others, but as she tugged, she discovered this one was locked. So, the coffer was a clock this time.

It was a half an hour later before Lucius sought her. His proud grin told her he had indeed found the key. Anticipation welled up within her, making it difficult to remain still. Two left.

"It was affixed underneath the table. Had I not inspected every inch, I never would have found it. Uncle Herman certainly wanted me to go through trouble for this."

"That definitely was in his nature. Now, see if it fits the clock."

She held her breath as Lucius turned the key, only to release it as the door swung open. Unlike the other clues, this one led to no funds, simply a note. Not bothering to return to the study, Lucius broke open the seal and removed another folded paper before reading the letter.

"Damn it. That bastard wants to ruin me." He handed her the paper then opened the other letter, letting out a string of curses as he read.

Looking down at the paper in her hand, she knew this would not be good.

Interesting thing about time and touch. You can waste both. Burn them all until you have nothing. No time and nothing left to touch. Everything is fleeting. Take nothing for granted. Everything you have amassed is gone. Enclosed you will find a list of all the outstanding debts I have. Pay them off and any others my wife has thought to create in my absence. Once this is done, you'll receive another clue. The lines written on the sheet lead to nothing. Pay the debt. Get the clue. And, stop wasting time.

"Dear God," Hannah breathed. "I have added nothing to the burden. I used the pin money left to me."

"That is good. As it is, I shall be near depleted once this list is fulfilled. I suppose he's right. I have no more time to waste. If I don't solve the last two clues and begin generating income, I'll no longer have the ability to run the estate and the townhouse. My reaction is to cut here, but if you're right, I can't afford to lose the people who know about this scheme. He'd made sure to keep his people protected."

She nodded. “Don’t worry. We will solve this, Lucius. No more parties or trips to Hyde Park. Until this is done, we shall work together.”

With a bow of his head, he turned and left the room. She could feel his frustration rolling off him, even as he moved away from her. She needed to do something to help him, but she didn’t know what.

They were out of money and quickly running out of time. If they had waited any longer it was likely Lucius would have been unable to settle the debt. She didn’t want to think of what would have happened then. It was already too much to bear.

She walked to his study and sat down, waiting for him to return with clue eleven.

Chapter 14

The tailor smiled as Lucius entered the shop, but Lucius couldn't bring himself to return it. He was utterly exhausted. Never in his life had he imagined his uncle could have put so many things on his accounts and from so many different people. It was maddening.

"Lord Rivers, please come in toward the back so we may speak in private."

Like the last three vendors, this man seemed to be expecting his arrival. As it turned out, this was the last on the list as well. Lucius hoped that meant the man had a clue for him, otherwise, he was going to be in a lot of trouble.

The familiar panic moved up his throat, but he forced it down. It wouldn't serve him to think of anything now. First, he had to finish his task, then take an assessment later. Fretting about it in the middle would only bring trouble.

"I take it you were expecting me."

"Of course, my lord. I didn't know when, but your uncle told me that one day you would come to settle all his debts. I must admit, I had a hard time believing him. Heirs tend to spend their inheritance before it comes to that."

Lucius grit his teeth. Had his uncle kept any form of books, he'd have known about the debts long before now. The thought that these vendors were talking about him and doubting his ability to pay grated on his nerves.

After setting a pouch on the table, Lucius crossed his arms. "Well, your debt has been settled. Please count it and ensure everything is in order."

The man did as requested, then stood with the funds. "Everything appears to be here. Please excuse me for one minute, my lord." The tailor disappeared down the hallway.

A feeling of foreboding came over Lucius as he waited. His uncle would not take everything away simply to give it back. No. The man relished kicking a person when they were down. That was all part of this lesson. The urge to fight back, to not compete in this sick game overwhelmed him, but he had no choice. Too many people were relying on him now.

That was a new feeling for him. His mother had remarried when his father hadn't even been gone a month, and she wanted all parts of her previous life erased, including him. As such, he'd been free to see to himself. Although his uncle had been quick to step in and put him to work, no one had ever relied on him. Until now. It was unnerving.

"Here we are, my lord. Your uncle instructed me to hand this missive to you and inform you that another will be sent out to an undisclosed party."

"An undisclosed party?" Lucius didn't like the sound of that.

"Yes. He said you should read the letter for clues and not ask me. That I know nothing and will do as I'm paid to do."

Lucius shook his head. "That sounds like the very words he would've said. It's a surprise you would do something for a man who treated you like that."

"I'm not." The man grinned. "You, my lord, have just paid for my services, and in return, have obtained everything I know."

"He padded the numbers." The thought made Lucius sick.

"No. Added a small fee to mine is all. That's why I was at the bottom. The others were to report to me when they received payment. You've been busy today."

"It hasn't been one of my better days." Lucius slid the letter into his coat pocket and stood. "I thank you for all the help."

"You are quite welcome, my lord. And, because of your kindness, I'll tell you that your uncle did have a contingency plan for you should you be unable to settle all the debts. If that counts for anything, I thought you should know."

Lucius nodded, feeling marginally better as he let himself out of the tailor's shop. The letter in his coat was demanding to be read. The second he closed the door on his carriage, he pulled it from his pocket and read the damning words he knew would come.

Very good. I'm sure it wasn't easy to turn over so much money, but nothing lasts forever. One day you, too, will die. You can no longer live like tomorrow is a guarantee, because it isn't. To make sure you are heeding your lessons, I have sent off a letter providing an incentive for you.

At this very moment, a letter with the next clue is being delivered to your heir. You may not hinder his search. Offer my dear cousin and his greedy wife a room at the townhouse if they require one. Just make sure you solve the clue before him. Otherwise, your heir shall collect quite a sum of money, to your detriment. Since I'd rather this not occur, I'll start you out with a little hint. Trust.

Now, here's the clue: Ride out to her. She's alone. Tell him. He'll take care of it. He always does.

Leaning his head back on the seat, Lucius let out a sigh. So close, and now he would have to fight his second cousin. A loathsome man from a brother his uncle couldn't stand. Why? Why was he doing this?

Frustration clawed at him, and he wished he had his uncle there to express his anger. To have something to punch. Something on which to alleviate his anger. But, there was nothing. His uncle ensured he'd be alone. Had he been in the country, he could visit a friend for sparring match, but he knew no one in London.

An image of Hannah laughing with the marquis flashed through his mind. That would give him a good match. He'd loved to punch that man in his cocky face.

Signaling the driver, Lucius changed his direction. If the marquis had no desire for a sparring match, he may know where Lucius could find one. With his excess anger, he didn't want to go home. Likely, one look at Hannah and his rage would manifest in other ways. Although she'd enjoyed their unexpected experience in the study, she deserved better than him mauling her. Or, losing himself inside her again. The thought of the possibilities never strayed far from his mind.

That was just another problem to add to his lengthy list. It didn't matter. He'd been beaten many times in his life, but he'd never been broken. He intended to keep it that way.

~ ~ ~

Hannah leaned her head back on the sofa after she gave her report to Regina for the classes. Nothing untoward was going on and although Hannah felt she needed to be at home waiting for Lucius, she had made a promise to her friend. In addition, she knew Lucius would be gone all day, and she didn't have the patience to sit and not know what was going on any longer.

"Tell me, how are matters progressing with Lord Rivers?" Regina's eyes sparkled.

"Your plan was an absolute failure. Although, I have to admit Lord Reston is a joy, the earl isn't going to decide to marry simply because he sees me with another man."

With a shake of her head, Regina clicked her tongue. "That's because you don't know men the way I do. Besides, I've talked to Lord Reston. He is convinced this plan is working."

Not understanding why Regina wouldn't accept the truth, Hannah jumped to her feet. "Then, you're both wrong. Lord

Rivers has not so much as looked at a woman since you've been assisting him. How is this helping him get married?"

Regina froze, and her smile melted away. "You wanted me to help him find a bride?"

"Yes." Hannah studied her friend, concern wrinkling her brow. What was wrong with the woman?

"Meaning not you?"

"Of course not me. Why would you--"

Falling back to her seat, realization dawned on Hannah. This whole time Regina had been attempting to make Lucius consider her for a bride. Hannah couldn't breathe. This wasn't good. It would kill her if he rejected her. She couldn't handle that.

"Wait." Hannah sat forward, her heart pounding in her chest. "You think the plan is working? That Lord Rivers wants to marry me?"

"Slow down. I'm not sure we're there yet. But, I'm confused now. Is this what you want or not?"

Knowing she had nothing to hide, Hannah released a long breath. "Of course, it's what I want, but if Lord Rivers doesn't want me, I'll be destroyed."

"He's not worth taking that chance? From my observations, and Lord Reston's, I can say the earl is quite protective of you. I also think he gets jealous when you spend any time with the marquis. That's not the actions of a man who is not interested."

"Then, why has he never said anything?"

"Perhaps he is afraid to push you. I know your husband has almost been gone a year now, but the pain of ten years of marriage can't be erased so easily. I know the earl didn't treat you right, as most men don't treat their wives as they should. However, the new Lord Rivers may turn out to be different and this is the first glimpse of the proof."

Hannah wanted to believe her more than anything. But, did she have the courage to ask Lucius? The idea of him dismissing her and marrying another woman turned her stomach. But, would she rather not know?

By the time Hannah returned to the townhouse, she'd had no better idea of an answer. Learning Lucius hadn't returned home yet, she settled in the drawing room, deciding to wait for him. This would also give her more time to organize her thoughts and come to a conclusion.

"My lady, Mr. Daniel and Laura Dobson have arrived."

Unease moved along Hannah's spine. Her husband's cousin was next in line for the earldom. She'd heard many things said about the man over the years. None of them good. And, upon the two occasions where she'd had the misfortune to see Mr. Dobson, he'd been a lecherous cad. Why had he come? If he had any idea Lucius hadn't fully inherited, the man would pounce and do his best to ensure Lucius fail in his quest.

"Show them in," she forced out in her most patient tone.

"Lady Rivers, it's such a pleasure to see you again," the older man gushed as he took her hand in both of his and then put his clammy lips upon it.

She resisted the urge to cringe. "Yes, and quite wonderful to see your lovely wife as well."

"Can we end this ridiculous formality?" The lady complained as she pushed past her husband. "We're all so happy to see each other. Now, can I sit and get something to drink? This oaf dragged me out of the house as soon as he received the letter. I hadn't had my tea yet."

Hannah tried to hide her grin, admiring the outspoken lady. She, too, hated the strictures of formality. Perhaps the lady was more colorful than Hannah would be herself, but she wouldn't fault the woman since she managed to end the horrid small talk.

"Please, take a seat. I'll call for some tea at once." Hannah signaled the butler, who nodded, obviously having heard the woman's complaint. "Now, tell me about this letter."

Mr. Dobson shot his wife a look of annoyance before he offered Hannah a smile. "It's from my cousin, Herman, your late husband."

Shocked, Hannah sucked in her breath. "You recently received a letter? He's been gone for nearly a year now."

"We were especially surprised as well, but he explained how he longed for us to know the entailed property and the running of it better now since I am Lord River's heir. So, we have come. It's likely my wife and I may look about the place to familiarize ourselves with it, per my dear cousin's wishes."

"I'm not sure I know how to respond. Do you have the letter? Might I see it?"

"Absolutely not." The man paused as the tea was delivered. "That is to say. It's a private message. The two of us shared a bond and with the personal nature of his writings, I'd rather not share."

Realizing the man was lying, Hannah nodded as she finished serving the tea. She had no idea what her husband had planned now, but this was not a good development. If the stories were to be believed, Mr. Dobson had attempted to kill his own cousin more than once. She didn't trust this man I didn't want him here. She simply needed to bide her time until Lucius returned and sent them away.

As luck was on her side, Hannah was saved from this uncomfortable conversation when a commotion came from outside the room. Loud laughter and voices could be heard. It was from Lucius and . . . Lord Reston? That was definitely odd. Why would the two of them be together? And, in such a jovial mood?

She didn't have long to wait for an answer as the two men appeared in the doorway. She sucked in her breath at the sight. Although both men appeared drunk and in good spirits, Lucius's cheek was swollen and red whereas Lord

Reston's lip was split with dried blood caking it. What had happened to the two of them?

"My lords." Hannah jumped to her feet in concern. "Are you well?"

Lucius's laughter was free, something she hadn't heard in quite some time. "Of course, my lady. See, we have guests. My wonderful family has come for a visit. They will stay the night and give us a chance to catch up."

"That is very generous of you," Mr. Dobson said, an overly anxious sparkle in his eyes. "We would appreciate it. At our age, carriage rides are taxing."

Hannah had to work to keep her mouth shut. The couple had a residence in London. There was no need for this. What was Lucius thinking? She needed to talk to him. There was more going on than he realized.

"Now, please excuse me. As I hadn't been made aware of your arrival, I have other arrangements at present." Lucius motioned to Lord Reston and then turned back to his cousin. "I'm certain the countess can see to your comfort."

With that, he and the marquis left the room. Hannah stared after the empty space in shock. At this point, she had no choice but to follow his orders, considering doing anything now would seem suspicious.

In addition, Lucius's appearance with Lord Reston made her decision rather easy to not tell him of her feelings. After all, if Lucius had an interest in her, he certainly wouldn't be talking to the very man who had shown a preference for her. This day couldn't possibly get worse.

~ ~ ~

Lucius stared at his second cousin, keeping his expression open and friendly. The day had gone much better than he'd expected after he had visited Reston and managed to reassemble his priorities. The marquis proved to be an invaluable friend. Although Lucius would hate the man if he claimed Hannah, for now, their friendship stood.

Resisting the urge to rub his aching cheek, Lucius mentally shook his head. The sparring had been helpful, but the severity of his anger had taken matters a little too far. The marquis hadn't seemed to mind as the man appeared to have his own issues to work through.

When Lucius had explained that his heir was attempting to make matters difficult for him, it had been Reston's suggestion to play the part of the drunken, absentee lord. If his cousin believed him to be uncaring, the man wouldn't be as careful in his actions.

"I'm quite glad you decided to visit," Lucius said. "My aunt is always looking for a diversion and a man can get tired of catering to a woman's whim. Your lovely wife will provide Aunt Hannah the distraction from the boredom she is plagued with."

The man nodded. "I must admit, I was surprised to find her here. I understood her habit is to take up residence in the country for the winter."

Lucius shrugged as he took a sip of his port. "You know women. They never know what they want. I was content to enjoy the delights of the country when she insisted that I bring her to London. In truth, I'm glad she did. The diversions are far more plentiful here in the city."

With a chuckle, Daniel sat back in his chair. "The title seems to have been good for you, my boy. I don't remember you embracing life so fully before."

"Well, a title does tend to give you better notice." Lucius winked. "I have no worries. I have someone else taking care of everything for me."

"Everything?" The man's eyebrows shot up.

"Of course. Why would I do something someone else could do for me?"

"Very true." His cousin's face turned thoughtful. "But, surely no one is willing to do anything outside their normal duties. That kind of thing, you must do on your own."

"That's not true." Leaning forward, Lucius pitched his voice low. "It seems my uncle left me a game to play, but I'm not interested. That's why I hire a staff. To do the things I have no desire to engage in."

"A game? Sounds fascinating. Then, you're not participating?"

"Why should I? I'm the Earl of Rivers. I don't have need to dirty my hands with such. When it's done, I'll be notified."

The sparkle in the man's eyes told Lucius everything he needed to know. Apparently he'd played his hand correctly. Now, his cousin's attention wouldn't be on him or Hannah. Then, he would be able to observe the couple without being watched in the process. This was turning out better than he'd thought.

"You're absolutely right. As such, I am willing to offer my help on your game. Perhaps with my knowledge of my cousin, I can be of great assistance."

Lucius laughed, not having to force the action. "Such a fine jest. The thought of my heir dirtying his hands that way is quite comical."

The man's smile was forced. "I assure you, I don't mind a little work. I would be happy to help."

"That's not necessary. Now, we should join the women. My aunt prefers to turn in early. Then, once she's settled for the night, I'm free to return to the club. She doesn't approve, but that's not her decision."

"She retires early, and you go out?"

"Well, not tonight, as I have guests. Unless you would care to join me?" Lucius gave him what he hoped was an eager expression.

Daniel quickly shook his head. "I must pass. Traveling and such. However, I have no desire to force a change of plans on you. My wife and I enjoy sitting by the fire, then we will likely go to bed. I do wish the countess could be convinced to remain longer for my wife, but I understand if her routine is set."

That got Lucius's attention. So, the man believed that Hannah was the woman referred to in the clue. Had they thought the travel referred to the townhouse? Or, had they been expecting her to be alone in the country? That was good. Had Hannah not expressed an ignorance of the scheme, Lucius might have believed the same.

"I'm certain she will be available tomorrow."

After a few more obligatory words, Lucius collected a confused Hannah, citing the same excuse and headed upstairs. Instead of taking her down the damned hallway to her bedchamber, he took her to the countess's rooms.

"Lucius?" she whispered.

"I'll be waiting for you in my bedchamber," he responded under his breath. "Good night, my lady. I shall see you tomorrow at breakfast."

He silently praised her obedience as she replied and disappeared into her room. Moving away from the door, he found the young man he'd made arrangements with earlier. After sending the boy on the task of keeping an eye on Daniel and his wife, Lucius made a charade of leaving before slipping up the servant steps and returning to his bedchamber.

"What is going on?" Hannah demanded the second he closed the door. "I'm beginning to believe you've lost your mind."

"I did, but your friend, Lord Reston, helped me find it again." He handed her the letter from his uncle and waited for her to finish.

"Dear God," she breathed.

"I know. I've been doing my best to show my cousin I'm not interested in seeking out the clues and that you are unaware of the whole situation. At present, he seems content to believe me."

"Then, why are we here? If he's out searching you are going to lose out. You can't let him—"

He put his hands on her shoulders to calm her. "I have it covered. I have someone watching them. Besides, I had your maid switch your rooms because the clue reads like you are the answer and I want you to outwardly show that you are taking every benefit of being the countess. Daniel seems to hope Laura can talk the key out of you. Use that. Make them think you know something."

"I can certainly try."

Reluctantly, he dropped his hands from her, otherwise they would end up in his bed. "Good. Now, I've been thinking all day about the woman my uncle could be referring to. Logically, his wife is the top of the list as is a mistress. However, we've ruled both of those out. Who else would be affected by his passing?"

"He knew you'd be in London, so it has to be someone who lives outside of the city. But, that's not right. He hasn't left London in years."

"Could she have traveled here to see him?"

"During the winter, it's possible. However, we are talking about a platonic relationship when you take into account his problem. I do know he enjoyed company. He would expect me to arrange dinner parties for his guests regularly, but most of the time the guest list changed each time."

With frustration dogging his feet, Lucius paced his bedchamber. Feeling the time closing in on him like a vice, he pulled at his cravat and then tossed it on the chair. Still feeling suffocated, he removed his coat and waistcoat, throwing them to create a pile in his chair.

When Hannah made a strangled sound, he turned to face her. The desire on her face as she stared at him brought his body to attention. Bloody hell, he wanted this woman.

Perhaps changing her bedchamber had been a mistake, for he didn't intend for her to leave this room tonight.

"Don't look at me like that," he forced out. "I already want you too much. And, if you don't stop, I'm going to do something about it."

"You can't blame me. You are the one undressing."

"Not undressing. At least, not yet."

She moaned. "You're such a tease."

With his desire raging, he moved closer to her. "Perhaps, it will be an incentive. Keep naming women and I'll give you what you want."

Liking this plan, he grabbed the tie of her dressing gown and pulled her closer to him. She reached for him, but he stopped her by dodging away. His breathing sped. He liked this game a whole lot.

"Lucius," she complained.

"If you want me here, you must follow the rules. I touch. You don't."

"What if I don't want to play?"

He chuckled and ran his lips over her neck. "You want to play." He pulled her toward the corner of the bed. "Reach back and hold onto the bed post to give your hands something to do. And, name every woman my uncle came in contact with."

As she began listing random names, he realized the flaw in this plan. Not one name meant anything to him. Still, he listened, something had to be there. He had to focus on her words and her body. Concentration was difficult as he slid his hands along her smooth skin, but he had to solve this.

When his hand closed over her breast, she moaned and stopped her list. He silently cursed, pulling his hand away. He didn't want to stop. The slow torture was appealing. Unlike the last time they were together, tonight he had all the time in the world. He didn't want this puzzle to interrupt it.

"Don't stop," he ordered. "There must be more."

She whimpered. "There isn't. This is your clue. Surely you know her. What women do you have in common?"

The edge of his desire dimmed. Again, the clue pointed to Hannah. She was definitely a common factor. But, there was no one else like her. His uncle never visited women.

"Not of note. Cousins, aunts, my mother. There are . . ." Suddenly, the answer hit him, and he grinned. "My grandmother. Now, let's get back to our game. This time you don't have to say a word."

As he lavished attention on Hannah, he felt free. He had won. Without the key, his cousin would have no chance of stealing his inheritance. Before long, this would be over and he could start looking forward once again.

Chapter 15

Hannah sipped her tea and tried to concentrate on Laura's babbling. The woman apparently liked to talk, but Hannah had no patience for it today. Lucius had left so early this morning, she'd still been asleep in his bed when he'd left. Waking to find him gone had been disconcerting, and she felt bad for every time she had done it to him.

His journey would take several days, and the lack of information during that time would prove to be rather difficult. She hoped he was right that the key had somehow been placed around his grandmother's grave. If he was wrong, that only gave his cousin all the more time to find the key on his own.

The coffer was another part, but Lucius was convinced that it being a person, the clue would be unsolvable without the key. She trusted him, and agreed to keep his cousins busy during their stay, however long that proved to be.

"Do you miss him?" Laura's question caught her off guard.

"Why should I miss him? I saw him just last night." Hannah felt heat rush up her cheeks. Had the lady noticed her preoccupation with Lucius?

Laura chuckled. "Not the current earl, dear. The former one."

"Of course. And, yes, I do miss him occasionally." The untrue words nearly caught in her throat. "Since he's gone, I only have those few treasures he gave me in his final days."

"Treasures? He certainly did love you to leave you with something valuable. May I ask what they are?"

Leaning forward, Hannah decided to have a little fun. Lucius wanted her to make them believe she had something special, so she would. And, from the gleam in the woman's eyes, she seemed like she would believe anything at this point. No doubt she was expecting Hannah to have diamonds.

"The first was his favorite handkerchief. I always thought he would want to be buried with that, but instead, he chose to give it to me."

"A handkerchief a treasure? How is that possible?"

Feigning shock, Hannah put her hand on her chest. "It was his favorite. So, of course it's a treasure. He also left me his left smoking slipper."

"The left one? Why not the pair?"

Sucking in a breath in horror, Hannah shook her head slowly. "He would never. The man never cared for the right one. As such, I never wish to accept it as a memento to remember him by."

Their conversation was interrupted when Mr. Dobson arrived at the doorway. "I'm sorry to intrude, my lady, but I can't seem to locate the earl this morning. Do you know his whereabouts? The servants aren't forthcoming today."

"Oh dear, not again." Hannah bit her lip as she looked away.

The man entered the room and claimed the chair beside her, his eyes alight with interest. "What is it? What has happened?"

Letting out an exaggerated sigh, she fiddled with a ruffle on her morning dress. She'd never enjoyed lying, but this was different, and exciting actually. It was as if she were providing a performance. In addition, these people meant to take what was rightfully Lucius's, so she refused to feel bad.

"I've noticed, upon occasion, the earl enjoyed visiting clubs once the house has taken abed. And, once or twice he's been known to not return by morning."

Laura sucked in a breath. "That's scandalous! Such a blatant disregard for discretion will reflect badly on the whole family."

"You misunderstand, my lady," Hannah hastened to assure. "It's nothing like that. The last time he did this, he and two other gentlemen decided to take a trip to one of the lord's country estates. Lord Rivers didn't return for a fortnight."

"How dreadful for you." Mr. Dobson shook his head. "The man shouldn't abandon you like that."

Hannah shrugged. "It does become rather dull without him to escort me around, but I always manage."

"Don't fret. We shall remain with you until he returns," Mr. Dobson promised with a smile.

"Oh, no. I could never ask you to do such a thing. It would be better for you to simply call upon the earl when he returns. Then, the two of you can finish your visit that he so abruptly cut short."

When the man smiled at her, she read genuine friendliness in his eyes. "The young lord may have made quite a few mistakes in his life, but he did do something extraordinarily right."

"Is that so?" Hannah could hardly contain her amusement at the man complementing Lucius.

"I'll never forget when my cousin announced that he was to wed. At his age, the family had been shocked. However, Herman always had a soft spot in his heart for Lucius, and when the boy suggested you for a wife, how could Herman refuse?"

Confused, Hannah studied the man. He appeared happy as if she, too, should be delighted by the news. This wasn't a lie to simply get to her. Dear God. Could this actually be true?

"You are saying it was the earl who told my husband to offer for me? He's the reason why my husband chose me?"

"That's right, so even when he's being difficult, just remember you wouldn't be where you are today had it not been for him."

Hannah felt sick. A white, hot dagger had been plunged into her chest. How could the very man who had condemned her to hell join her in her bed? He'd been using her. From the moment they talked, he'd made it clear he needed her help. Of course he didn't wish to marry her. He was doing whatever it took to ensure he retain her services.

"I'll keep that in mind," she forced out through her clogged throat. "Please excuse me? I have a few matters I must attend this morning."

As she stumbled her way to her bedchamber, she couldn't stop the tears from escaping her eyes. Mystery engulfed her, stealing her ability to see. The second she made it into her room, she threw herself on the bed. She had no idea what she was going to do now, but one thing was certain. She was done helping Lucius obtain his inheritance. After what he'd done to her, he didn't deserve to have it.

~ ~ ~

Lucius couldn't keep the smile from his face. He and Hannah had done it. The key was safely in his pocket and the rest shouldn't be too difficult to figure out. In truth, he suspected he knew where the key should go.

The visit to his grandmother's grave had been tedious, but it had awarded him with a good amount of time to think. At first, he had tried to recall every lesson his uncle had said to him. The main ones that stood out had already been addressed in the eleven clues. He couldn't even fathom the lesson in this next coffer, but he was anxious to find out.

In regard to trust, it seemed Lucius's grandmother had been the only woman his uncle had trusted. It was simple to recall stories about her, and each time the man spoke of her, there was a tenderness in his eyes. He'd clearly not extended the same feeling of trust to his wife. But, Lucius trusted her.

An involuntary smile overtook him as he thought about Hannah. This whole process, she'd been someone he could consistently count on, and he suspected that wouldn't change once the final clue was solved. She was loyal and everything he wanted. Now, more than ever, he was determined to have her.

She may not be keen on marrying him, but he was nothing if not determined. As soon as the final puzzle was solved, he would expend all efforts to convince her to wed him. He would do whatever necessary as he would have her and no one else.

As soon as he arrived back at the townhouse, he was informed that Hannah wished to speak to him directly. Per her request, he made his way to the drawing room to wait for her. This was odd and brought a prickle of unease shooting through him. Had something happened while he was gone? Perhaps his cousin has found the coffer and removed it before he could return. Nerves bit at his heels as he paced the room.

When she arrived in the doorway, her face was pale and dark circles surrounded her eyes. Apparently, she hadn't been sleeping. His heart thundered. This definitely wasn't good.

"What's wrong?" he demanded as he moved toward her.

She threw out her hand, and he froze. "Don't come any closer."

Shock rooted him to the spot, and he shook his head, trying to clear it. "I don't know what happened, but I would never hurt you."

"I have one question for you. I just want a yes or no. I don't want any excuses or lies."

Lucius stared at her as if he'd somehow returned to a different time altogether. This didn't make sense. He hadn't lied to her. He could hardly control his breathing, but he would give her what she wanted. Prove to her she could trust him.

"Ask me anything."

"Is it true you are the reason why the earl married me? That without you, I would have been spared the last ten years of torture?"

There it was, the punch in his chest. "How—"

"No. I want an answer, nothing else. You owe me that much. Yes or no?"

She was right. After what she'd been through because of him, he hadn't earned the right to defend his actions. She would hate him, but one day he would make her listen to him and understand. For now, he would give her what she wanted. What she needed.

"Yes."

At his one word, her face crumbled in pain, then she turned and fled the room. He sank down onto the sofa. The agony inside him was too much to bear. How could such a positive day end so badly? He forced himself to stand. This was all his fault, and he couldn't ignore the consequences any longer.

He made his way to his study and straight to his bottle of whisky. Hannah was right that the liquor wouldn't solve his problems, but it would dull the ache that was threatening to overtake him at the moment.

It was late into the night before he left his study and stumbled to his bed.

The next day as he sat behind his desk twirling the key between his finger and the solid wood, he contemplated his choices. He'd given Hannah space and decided to allow her to move around the house freely without worrying about running into him.

A knock sounded at his door and a brief second of hope speared him as he granted entrance. Unfortunately, it wasn't

Hannah. However, seeing as his butler was there, he decided to end the damned clue that led to Hannah hating him.

"My lord, I'm to inform you that Lady Rivers departed for the country early this morning."

Lucius clenched his fists and closed his eyes for a brief second, trying to regain control of himself. The last thing he needed was for the house to talk about how destroyed the news had made him.

"Thank you for letting me know," he forced out. "Please take a seat. I'd like to talk to you."

The man's eyes widened, but he did as requested. "Of course, my lord. Is there a problem?"

Lucius let out a bitter laugh. "Not with you, no. Tell me, how did my uncle obtain such a high level of loyalty from you and the entire staff for that matter? At the estate, they clearly knew a different man."

The normally stoic butler smiled. "The earl could be difficult at times, but he always meant well. Most people are unable to look past actions to see the truth."

"And, you know the truth?"

"I do. That man saved me and my family from disaster. He provided us all a place here and worked to secure our future."

"Which is why he trusted you. Uncle Herman knew if he told you to do it, you would take care of everything. And, why I'm supposed to give you this." Lucius held out the key to the man.

Without hesitation, the butler took the key and smiled. "The fact that you thought of me so quickly after discovering the key means you trust me as well. As long as you provide for my family, you have earned our loyalty. Please, excuse me."

As soon as the man left the room, Lucius dropped his head back in his chair. Hannah had left him. How could he conjure any happiness for solving the clue without her?

In addition, he didn't like her traveling in the winter or by herself. He silently prayed that she would be safe. He very well couldn't go after her. At least, not yet.

The butler returned with a large envelope, and placed it on the desk. "I just want you to know, your uncle never intended for your heir to claim your birthright. Even if they found the key first, there would have been another clue I was to arrange until you bested them."

Lucius nodded. "I appreciate that knowledge."

With a bow, his butler left. Knowing he couldn't waste any time, Lucius opened the envelope and nearly sagged in relief to see the amount of money inside. This should sustain him for at least a month or two. Then, he pulled out the letter and read.

Bloody hell. He'd been set up to fail from the beginning. He'd almost outsmarted his uncle and won, but that possibility dissolved. It was over. All this work, and he had lost everything.

~ ~ ~

Hannah stared out the window as the first flutters of snow dropped to the ground. The sight brought out no emotion within her. It had been over a week since she'd seen Lucius, and every second broke her heart even more. The image of his face as he admitted what he'd done wouldn't leave her. His steely blue gaze haunted her. And, he hadn't really tried to make her understand his reasons. Simply left her alone to be miserable.

A sob stuck in her throat. It was likely he knew she loved him and was relieved at being able to put an end to their relationship. At this moment, he'd probably solved the last clue and was seeking a bride as he'd claimed his inheritance. A bride who wasn't her.

"Hannah," her brother, Anson, called, gaining her attention. "I've been patient since the day you arrived at

Melbourne in tears, but this has gone on long enough. How can I fix this for you if you don't talk to me?"

The knowledge that her little brother had always looked out for her helped to ease her sadness. Unfortunately, she knew there was nothing that could be done for her. In addition, she imagined there would be no harm in telling him some of the truth. She owed him so much, and hated that the list of his selflessness toward her was growing once again.

"I don't imagine that I'm good at talking presently. I'm broken."

He sat beside her and put his arm around her, drawing her against his chest. The strength of him held her upright and allowed her to let her emotions go without completely falling apart. He whispered to her and rubbed her back as her tears ran their course.

"Do you feel better now? Miranda said women need to let their pain come before they can heal, and I've discovered my wife is a wise woman."

Hannah smiled at the love she heard in her brother's voice. They were quite a pair, having both suffered horrible spouses. At least her brother was able to find happiness the second time around.

"I do feel better. Thank you." She straightened on the chair and dabbed her face with a handkerchief.

"Can you tell me what happened now?"

Letting out a sigh, Hannah closed her eyes. "I made a terrible mistake. I fell in love with the wrong man."

"Why do you believe he's the wrong man? Did he lay a hand on you?" Anson's eyes that were so similar to hers flashed with anger. "He's a dead man."

Fear shot through her at the deadpan sound of his voice. Anson wasn't the type of man to issue idle threats. At least he had no idea to whom she referred. Although Lucius had hurt her, she couldn't bear the thought of anything happening to him.

"No. It's just that he doesn't care for me. He needed my help, so we became close, and I suppose I imagined him having feelings for me that he didn't possess. All of this is my fault."

More tears welled in her eyes. After these days of thinking, she realized Lucius's desire for her had been real, not fabricated, so that at least had been the truth. He had used her help because he needed her, but he'd gone to her bed because he wanted her. At least physically.

Anson was quiet for a good while. "I'm not certain you imagined anything. He may very well feel more for you than you realize."

Her brows furrowed. "Why would you say that? You don't even know who he is."

"This is true, but a missive was delivered for you. I imagine your gentleman is trying to get in contact with you."

Hope speared through her. "He doesn't know where to find me. How could he possibly have written? It's not him. He would have come himself if he cared. Where is the letter?"

"We'll get to that. You see, it was hand delivered by a gentleman who requested to see you. Apparently, the letter had gone to Lord Rivers's estate first in hope of finding you. Someone must have surmised you'd come to me."

"Anson, where is my letter?" she demanded.

"The man wasn't happy when I told him I wouldn't allow him to see you," Anson continued as if she hadn't spoken. "He said he'd try again tomorrow."

"You let him take it?" Her voice rose. "The letter was addressed to me."

"Calm down, and let me finish. In no uncertain terms, I told him he'd be denied every time he returned, but that he was welcome to waste his time. Although, he wasn't happy, he handed me the letter."

Exasperated that her brother was dragging this out, she sighed. "Where is it?"

"He told me he didn't know the contents. That he worried over what you would read inside it. That's why he wanted to be present when you opened it."

Her blood went cold. The twelfth clue. It couldn't be from Lucius. She swallowed.

"Who delivered it?"

"Are you well? You look pale."

"Anson, who delivered the letter?"

"Lucius Dobson, the new Lord Rivers."

She squeezed her eyes shut for a second at hearing his name, then she held her hand out. "Give me the letter now. I know who it's from."

"I don't think—"

Frustrated beyond measure, she burst from the chair. "Stop it. I don't care what you think. I need to do this. To finish this whole ordeal. Give me the damned letter before I bring Miranda into this."

He pulled it from his pocket and placed it in her waiting hand. "I daresay Miranda would agree with me, but I concede. However, I'm not leaving."

"Very well." Glancing down, her hands grew clammy at the sight of her husband's writing addressed to her.

With shaking fingers, she broke the seal and a small key fell into her hand. That certainly explained why Lucius had come. The clue led directly to her this time. Casting aside the thought, she read.

Hannah, you are finally free of me. After ten years of attempts, I was never able to make a full woman of you and claim an heir of my own. Not that I'd expected a different outcome. My body had begun to fail long before our marriage.

My marriage to you was to prove a point since I hadn't anticipated living past that year. Apparently, the Lord had other plans and gave me ten unexpected years. It was never meant for me to be your husband for that long.

As such, I have an offer for you. My nephew, Lucius, has been spending some time deciphering clues to learn the remainder of his lessons. I'm sure he has come to you with questions, and now you know why. I hope he has treated you with respect as he has gone through this process, for you are his one last clue. You have the choice of giving him the enclosed key to allow him to collect his inheritance. Or, you may keep the key for yourself.

If you choose the second option, take the key to my solicitor in London. One third of all my funds, current and future, shall belong to you. One third shall be split among my staff at my London townhouse, and the remainder will go to Lucius to maintain the estate, if he is careful. To get to this point, he's proven he is capable of surviving.

I have also enclosed an annulment for you. Since I never consummated our marriage, you have the choice to drop my name and title as well. It's now in your hands. I have righted the wrong of me outliving the doctor's warnings, and I wish you all the best in the future of your choosing.

Good luck with your decision.

Hannah couldn't think or move as she stared at the paper and reread the contents. He hadn't intended to be married to her for long? It didn't make sense.

Flipping to the annulment, her chest quivered. She may have lost ten years, but she would be able to begin anew. Then, she thought about Lucius. Was she prepared to say goodbye to him forever? She wasn't so sure that was the best option. She stood, ignoring her brother as she headed toward her bedchamber. She had a lot of thinking to do.

Chapter 16

Lucius sat in the garden as the snow lightly fell around him. He imagined that it was cold outside, but he didn't feel it. His ability to feel disappeared the third time he'd tried to see Hannah at Melbourne and been denied. She'd been living with her brother for nearly ten days now, and he was becoming more desperate each day. This had to end. He had hoped returning to his own estate would have helped, but it didn't.

In his life, he'd suffered quite a bit, but nothing had given him this amount of pain. This emptiness. It was as if nothing would ever be right for him again. He wouldn't survive it.

As he pictured Hannah's smiling face, a stabbing pain went through him. Would he never be able to see it again? The thought was devastating. He needed to hold her. To see her. To know she was all right. Otherwise, life was meaningless.

He was in love with her.

He sucked in a deep breath at the knowledge, then slowly released it. The realization wasn't surprising, just painful. He suspected it had begun the day he'd met her in the garden. Then, when she'd married his uncle, he had to force himself to forget her. Now that he had completely fallen for her, there was no forgetting. No respite for his heart.

"Bloody hell, it's cold out here," Ronald exclaimed as he emerged from the manor. "I received word you were not doing well. I hadn't expected you to have gone completely mad."

"Go away. I'm in no mood for your jesting today."

"You're not even going to refute me? You must truly be mad. Mr. Rawlings was right to send for me. Come, let's get you inside. You're worrying the staff." His friend motioned toward the door as if it were that easy.

"You go. I'm comfortable here."

Ronald crossed his arms. "Why?"

"It's safe out here," Lucius admitted. "She's gone. Living with her brother. I've completely lost her, and out here, I can enjoy a few memories of her without being overwhelmed by everything she touched or interacted with."

The very sight of his desk in the study was unbearable. He always saw her sensually upon it, open, waiting for him. If he'd had any idea what the one act upon his desk would have done to him, he wouldn't have done it. No. That wasn't true. The experience had been worth the painful, yet wonderful, memories.

"I see now. Although I'm disappointed in you, if you come inside, I'll help you. There is no productivity in falling apart."

Lucius stood and followed his friend into the manor. If Ronald could see something he could not, he'd be a fool not to listen. There was no forgetting Hannah, which meant he would have to fight for her. That, he would gladly do.

Once settled in the drawing room, Lucius pinned Ronald with a stare. "What are your ideas to help me?"

The man chuckled. "When I asked about the countess's availability, I could tell you were not thrilled by my request. I had no idea how interested you were in her."

"I didn't deny you because I've always wanted what's best for her, and I've been unable to provide that. If she chose you back then, I'd like to think I would have stepped aside. However, now I'm feeling selfish. I want her for myself."

"I can see that. You are her legal guardian, why don't you simply go to her brother and demand her back? Per the law, she belongs to you."

Lifting an eyebrow, Lucius studied his friend to ensure the man hadn't completely lost his mind. "You want me to challenge the Marquis of Melbourne? I don't know if you've met the young lord, but with his power and influence, he'll never let her go."

"Then, you tell him how you feel about the countess. Surely the man is not heartless."

Would that work? Lucius's mind rebelled at the idea of telling her brother his personal feelings for her, but if that was the only way to get to her, how could he refuse? On the other hand, he wasn't sure he wanted Hannah to find out from the man. Lucius needed to have the opportunity to explain himself first. Having her brother simply blurt out his feelings would never do.

"I'm not sure that's the wisest course of action. There must be another way."

"It's all about how badly you want her, and how far you are willing to go. If the marquis doesn't let you see her, I'd imagine the staff isn't going to be keen on allowing you either. That means you must get through to the man."

The thought was highly unappealing, but he was willing to do anything for Hannah. However, there had to be another solution. Regardless if Hannah decided to marry him or not, she belonged here. She was the Countess of Rivers, after all.

"My lord," Mr. Rawlings called from the doorway. "Forgive my intrusion, but you wanted to be notified about any dealings coming from Melbourne."

Discomfort stabbed through Lucius. Has she decided to contact him? If so, why hadn't she come herself? The answer struck through him. Perhaps the news wasn't positive.

"What is it?" Lucius demanded, not caring that Ronald was present.

The butler drew out a letter. "This just arrived for you."

Without wanting to show how eager he was, he accepted the missive and tucked it away into his coat. "Thank you."

As soon as the man left the room, Ronald lifted an eyebrow. "Would you like me to give you some privacy? I'm certain you are anxious to read the contents."

Lucius shook his head as he pulled the letter back out.

Unfolding the paper, he found a single key nestled within it. No writing. No explanation. Nothing but the blasted key. Pulling it out, he inspected the item and for once, didn't find the joy he'd previously experienced by obtaining each one. This was the last. He now possessed all twelve.

The significance wasn't lost on him. The last letter from his uncle indicated that the key was Hannah's. That if she kept it for herself, she would have his fortune, and Lucius would be left with the obligation. The knowledge that everything he'd done to that point amounted to nothing rankled. In addition, the clues hadn't been such that his relationship with Hannah would have improved had he not decided to recruit her help. Had his uncle suspected that he would try to claim her for himself?

Since she was giving him the final key, it meant she was giving him everything. Did this mean she cared for him? Or, that she wanted to completely wash her hands of everything relating to the earldom? That was something he was determined to find out.

~ ~ ~

Hannah found herself smiling as she sat on the floor of the nursery stacking blocks. Her one-year-old nephew, Malcolm, squealed as he swiped his hands, knocking over the stack. The pure joy on the boy's face was infectious and Hannah found herself gravitating more and more to him over the past weeks.

She laughed as he picked up a block in his chubby hands and shoved it in his mouth. A trail of slobber dripped down his arm, but she didn't mind as she plucked the boy from the floor and pulled him into a hug. She loved him dearly.

Would this be what it was like to have her own child? The thought made her stomach churn as she clutched the boy tighter. Malcolm wiggled in her arms until she put him back down. The idea of being a mother terrified her. Her life had been in such disarray lately she hadn't realized how long it had been since her last menses until two days ago.

She was with child. Lucius's child.

The decision not to tell him was simple considering she knew he would be forced to marry her. In addition, he hadn't tried to see her since he'd dropped off the letter. That was the proof she needed to discern his true feelings, or lack thereof.

At present, she wasn't sure how to manage with her child as she had no desire to bring her family to ruin. She knew she could find employment at the House of Reform, but to do so would put both her and her child under the eyes of London.

"Are the two of you enjoying yourself in here?" Hannah's sister-in-law, Miranda, walked into the nursery with a fond smile.

"Of course. Your son is a delight. He makes me happy."

Miranda laughed. "He certainly has that effect on people. I'm glad he's been able to help you settle in better, and I welcome the help with him."

Looking at the small boy, Hannah wondered why anyone would need help with something so precious. Malcolm was a wonderful child. In the time she'd spent here, she hadn't seen him so much as cry more than once.

"I see what you mean," Hannah responded dryly.

"Don't let him fool you. He may be a sweetheart at times, but he is still a man. Just like all of them, he's demanding, impatient, and upon occasion, unreasonable."

At that moment, Malcolm decided to prove Miranda right and let out a terrible cry as he held his hands out toward his mother. Miranda promptly scooped him up and cuddled him, effectively ending his crying fit.

"I suppose you want me to believe you now?"

Her sister-in-law grinned. "Let me put him down for his nap, then we can talk."

As Miranda put her son in his crib and lightly sang him a song, Hannah watched, doing her best to control the emotions welling inside her. Would this be in her future? Putting her son to bed and cuddling him, but doing it all by herself? She couldn't imagine it. If Miranda needed help with the child while having a full staff, how would it be for her?

She supposed it didn't matter. Whatever it took, she would provide for her child. Their life wouldn't be the easiest, but her life to this point hadn't been exactly effortless.

"There we go." Miranda closed the door as the nursemaid entered to keep an eye on the child while he slept. "Now, would you like to go shopping or visit the sweetshop?"

Letting out a sigh, Hannah tried not to let Miranda down. She knew her sister-in-law enjoyed both activities, but her heart wasn't in it anymore. She wasn't even sure when she'd be right again.

"I don't think I have the energy to do either, but don't let that stop you from having your fun. Take Anson. I'll be here should Malcolm awaken and need me."

"That's quite all right. Anson is the one who feels you need to escape the manor for a time. Although I agree with him in this instance, there is another matter we strongly disagree on."

That was definitely not a surprise to Hannah. The two of them had very strong personalities. When she'd lived with them over the winter, she'd heard everything. It was an enlightening experience and had only made her long to have such a love for herself. However, now that she'd felt love, she wished she'd never brought this upon herself.

"I imagine there are a number of subjects for which you and my brother are at odds."

"We've always managed to discover an appropriate and amicable compromise, but not this time. At this moment, I'm more convinced that I'm right, so I will tell you what I know. The man you're in love with, is it Lord Rivers?"

Stunned that Miranda would surmise this when she had not so much as mentioned one detail regarding him, Hannah looked at her sister-in-law in a new light. "Why would you believe it's him?"

"Well, Anson doesn't believe you need to know, but Lord Rivers has tried three times to convince your brother to allow him to see you. If the earl is the man you're pining over, I suspect he's in a bit of turmoil to not be with you as well."

The thought that Lucius had tried to see her made her chest quiver. What if Miranda was right? Could he have been concerned over the key, or did he truly wish to see her?

"When did he do this?" Hannah forced herself to ask, although she was afraid to know.

"I believe it was near the time he brought the letter to you. When Anson was adamant that he not be permitted to see you, the earl said to send word to his estate should you wish to see him."

"And, he hasn't tried since then?" Hannah held her breath.

Sympathy shown on Miranda's face. "I'm sorry. I don't know."

Her hope dissipated. It was the key, then. Now that he had what he needed from her, he'd stopped trying to see her. The knowledge was a stab in her chest. Anson was right, for she wished she hadn't learned the truth. This was so much worse than the ignorance of being unaware.

The warmth of the drawing room was a direct contrast to her soul. The coldness inside her spread out to her limbs, and she couldn't contain her shaking.

"Lady Melbourne," the butler bowed at the door. "Lord Melbourne is requesting your presence at once."

After nodding to the man, Miranda pinned her with a look. "You see what I mean about demanding men? Please, excuse me for a minute. I'll be back soon."

The fondness on Miranda's face when she'd been requested hadn't gone unnoticed by Hannah. The woman could say what she would, but she loved it. Hannah was happy for her brother, but she couldn't help the nagging feeling of jealousy.

Movement at the door caught her attention. Had Miranda returned so quickly? She gasped as her eyes took in Lucius. He didn't appear well. Her heart lurched in her chest. She hated that she cared so much. Stealing herself against her emotions, she focused on his face.

She would not break down.

~ ~ ~

Lucius ached as he took in the sight of Hannah. Obtaining the ability to see her had proven to be much easier than he'd expected. The marquis had needed little to no assurances from him. Lucius had simply indicated that he would not leave until he was allowed to see her. After the man studied his face, he had agreed.

The ease didn't seem like a good sign. After all, Hannah must've been doing particularly badly for her brother to give in so easily. That, or she had told her brother she wanted to see him.

"What are you doing here?" she demanded, destroying that possibility.

"I have something for you." He praised his even voice as he reached into his pocket and pulled out the twelve keys.

He opened his hand and held them out to her.

She gasped. "What is this? You need to turn those in. Claim your inheritance."

With his heart beating erratically, he shook his head. "I can't. None of it means anything without you."

Her body froze at his declaration. "What?"

"If you don't come back with me, then I don't see the point of finishing this journey without you. I am your guardian. I'm to provide for you. If you don't come with me, I won't be able to, so I'm giving you the means to secure your future."

"Why?" she breathed. "It was your recommendation that your uncle marry me. Why would you want me to come back now?"

"I never recommended that he marry you. As I told you, I was against the match to begin with."

Questions swirled through her eyes. "Then, why did you tell me it was your fault?"

"Because it was." He lowered himself down on the sofa beside her. "You see, I knew I wanted to marry you from the moment we met in the garden. Everything about you called out to me and offered me something I've never had before."

Hannah stared at him with wide eyes, as if she didn't believe him.

Not daunted, he continued. "I told my uncle such. I had to go to London to handle some matters for my mother, who'd remarried, but my intent was to return when you reached your eighteenth year and request your hand."

Realization dawned in Hannah's gaze. "He married me to prove a point to you."

"Yes. I'll never forgive him for that. For taking you away from me."

"He hadn't expected to live past that year. Perhaps his intention was for you to claim me when he was gone." She covered her mouth with her hand. "Our marriage was the reason why you left."

He nodded, wishing she had more of an emotional

reaction to his confession. "I couldn't bear to see you with him. It was too painful."

A smile tugged at the corners of her mouth. "I wish I would've known."

"That would have done nothing but cause you pain. I never wanted you hurt."

The fact she was sitting here, smiling at him gave him such hope. Although, he knew she still could reject him, he was ready to put everything out there. To give her all the knowledge to make her decision.

"So, you kept the knowledge as your secret and remained away from me."

"Everything changed when you walked into the manor and demanded I attend you. I fought my desire for you at first, but soon I began to believe this was something special. A second chance for us."

She sucked in her breath. "What are you saying?"

Unable to tolerate not being able to hold her, he took her hand. The fact she allowed him to do so made him inwardly give a sigh of relief. After all, if she was still angry, she wouldn't have allowed him to touch her.

"It's been eleven years, and I stand behind what I told my uncle that day. I told him you are my future, and I planned to marry you. That is, if you'll do me the honor of becoming my wife. I daresay you already know what you're getting into as you have served as Countess Rivers for so long now."

Her eyes were wide with shock. "Lucius, I—"

"Wait," he stopped her, not able to handle her denial of him. Not now. Not when he was so close. "Before you answer, I have one more confession. You made me care about you when you were seventeen, but that is nothing compared to how I feel about you now. I love you, Hannah. After having feelings for you for over a decade, you can count on the fact that my feelings will never change."

"Are you finished?" Her voice shook.

"Yes. Unless you can think of anything else I can say to convince you."

"I think you've covered quite a bit more than I'd expected." The smile that broke out over her face eased every bit of suffering he'd felt over the past weeks. "My answer is yes, Lucius Dobson. I will marry you. You see, as it turns out, I love you, too."

The words he'd never expected sent a shockwave through him. Joy unlike anything he'd ever felt before filled him. Unable to handle the onslaught of such happiness, he cupped her cheek and drew her lips to his. She clung to him as he devoured her mouth, wishing beyond anything that he could be closer to her still.

She would finally be his. Nothing else mattered to him at that moment but her. This was truly the greatest gift he could have been given. Hannah loved him. He could hardly fathom the idea.

When she abruptly pulled back, he reluctantly released her. "The clues! What about your inheritance? Do you know where to find the last clue?"

He smiled, of course she would be concerned for him. "Don't fret, my love. I am to take the keys to my uncle's solicitor in London. According to the last letter, everything should be turned over to me at that time."

She stood. "I don't trust it will be that easy. Not with that man. Let's go to London now. I want to have this matter settled."

Confused, Lucius stood. "Now?"

"Yes. I'll pack my belongings at once."

With her determination, the two of them were settled in the carriage to London within the hour. As usual, it took several days to arrive at their destination, but overall it had been the most pleasant trip he'd ever experienced. With Hannah in his arms, it had seemed like their own private escape.

The second the carriage arrived in the city, Hannah had insisted he be delivered to the solicitor before anything else. He complied, although he didn't understand her concern. In the end, he'd received account ledgers and a detailed accounting of the location of the estate funds. In addition, the hold on the future income had been removed. Everything was as it should be. There was one last letter from his uncle.

Lucius,

It's finally ended. You have passed all my tests far better than I would have thought. Through this final act, I have completed all my duties as the Earl of Rivers, as your uncle, and as her husband. Know that I am proud of you and always knew you would succeed. Reclaim yourself and live the life you wanted from the beginning. Nothing is holding you back. Now, it's time for me to tell you goodbye.

Armed with the knowledge that his uncle hadn't hoped he would fail, Lucius returned home, feeling as if a weight had been lifted off him. Nothing in his life had ever come easy, but he anticipated the future being much brighter. With the riddles and puzzles behind him, and Hannah in front of him, he couldn't ask for more.

"Well, is it done? Or, did he put another clue in your path?" Hannah demanded as soon as he closed the door to his study.

He smiled. "It's done. Everything is claimed and accounted for. No more games."

She squealed and launched herself into his arms. He kissed her hard, not having had enough of her. He suspected he'd never get enough.

When she pulled back, a sparkle shown in her eyes. "I'm so relieved to hear that. With the clock having already begun, I knew our time was limited."

"Clock?" He furrowed his brow as he searched her face. "What are you talking about? He gave me no time limit."

"He did." She gave him a saucy smile. "And, if I recall correctly, it came with a warning. One you most assuredly did not heed."

"I'm afraid I have no idea what you are talking about."

"The clock was set for nine months."

Lucius felt the color drain from his face as the realization of what she was saying overtook him. "It's begun? As in, you're with child?"

She nodded with a wide grin. "I never thought it possible, but I'm going to give you an heir."

Clasping her around the waist, he spun her in a circle as he could barely contain his happiness. His mistake of losing himself in her had made a miracle within her. His heir. As he drew her up against him, he proceeded to show her exactly how happy she had made him.

It may have been years later than he'd expected, but he would marry Hannah. They would go to Gretna Green and he would finally have the wife of his choosing. Never had he expected to have everything he could ever want, but as his uncle so aptly taught him. Life was unexpected. And, this was a lesson he was going to embrace.

Epilogue

Hannah snuggled into her coat as she followed her husband through the forest of their country estate at a sedate pace on her mare. She and Lucius had rushed to Gretna Green to marry a month ago, and she still could hardly believe it. Although she had never intended to marry again, Lucius had effectively dissolved any fear she had of the state and gave her reasons to love him more every day.

Today, however, she didn't understand him. It was much too cold for a ride through the countryside, but he'd been insistent, and she found denying him near impossible. Besides the biting cold, it was a lovely day. The air was crisp and the sun high. She only wished she could enjoy it.

When they arrived at the hunting cabin and Lucius dismounted, she let out a sigh of relief. She hoped he intended to build up a fire and have them remain for a while. The outdoors still wasn't her favorite place to be, and the cold didn't agree with the child growing inside of her.

"I remember the first time you brought me here." Lucius approached her and slid his hands around her waist to help her down. "If I recall correctly, you couldn't wait to get into my arms."

She sucked in a breath as he pulled her off her mare and up against him. "You most certainly do not recall that correctly. That was an accident."

"Come now, you can be honest with me now. I'm your husband after all."

Loving the way he said it, she smiled. "Yes, you are.

However, I'll admit to nothing. I may want to be in your arms now, but I didn't like you back then."

He lifted an eyebrow. "Lie all you want, but you wanted me then, too."

"Do you intend to keep your pregnant wife out here in the cold or can we go inside?"

"As you wish." He bent down and swept her up into his arms then proceeded to carry her into the cabin.

Once inside, he put her on her feet and she looked around the room. It was lovingly bathed in the glow of the fire. Clearly Lucius had come ahead and set the place up for her. Her heart swelled as she approached the fire, enjoying the welcoming heat dancing across her skin.

"This is lovely," she breathed.

"Are you hungry? I have brought provisions for us." He moved in behind her and put his lips to her neck.

She moaned as his hands moved along her sensitive body. "Definitely hungry."

"I have bread, cheese, fruit, and a few of Cook's delicious scones. And, if that's not appealing, I'm sure she snuck in a few more items. What would you like?"

Turning to face him, she wrapped her arms around his neck. "You."

His eyes nearly blackened. "We will get to that, but not now. That will ruin the surprise."

"Surprise?" Excitement ran through her. "What kind of surprise?"

"Wouldn't you prefer to eat first?"

She shook her head. "No. You've got my attention now. I'll take my surprise."

He grumbled, but his smile proved he didn't really mind. With a loving look in his eye, he ran a hand down her face. At that moment, nothing mattered except him. She was caught up in a world where only the two of them remained. It was perfect.

"Come with me." He took her hand and led her into the bedroom. On the bed she saw the atrocious painting she had kept of her first husband. Although confused, a smile broke out across her face to see it. The thing truly was amazing in its amount of ridiculousness.

"This is not a surprise. I've owned that thing for years."

His laughter rumbled deep in his chest. "That's not the surprise. I just thought neither one of us needed it any longer. Perhaps it is time to throw it away."

She nodded, then watched as Lucius broke the frame and wrapped the canvas around the pieces. The fact that he'd been the one to dismantle it seemed significant in a way. Then, he handed the bundle to her. She knew exactly what to do. Marching over to the fireplace, she tossed it in.

As the flames licked at the painting, Lucius put his arm around her. They watched in silence as the portrait was consumed. In that moment, she allowed herself to release any hatred and pain she'd been holding onto. The fire was cleansing.

"You did it, Lucius. You have made it so I no longer dislike hearing the title of Lord Rivers. You have eradicated all the negativity."

"You did it, too." He took her hands. "Hannah, I promise to do my best to deserve you, and I will strive every day to make you happy and to remind you how much you mean to me. However, I am human, and I know I will make a mess of things from time to time."

"You can be assured that I shall inform you of each and every time that happens."

He grinned. "I imagine you will. And, in the event that you need something physical to show you what a mess I am, I had something made for you. It's under the mattress."

Realizing what he had done, her eyes widened. Not wasting any time, she pulled away from him and reached under the mattress, feeling the familiar wooden frame. She couldn't believe this.

When she pulled it out and gazed at the painting of Lucius in the exact uncomfortable pose as his uncle had been in, she couldn't contain her laughter. The rendering was so bad, she wondered if it had been done by the same artist.

"I can't believe you did this for me. To intentionally pose so horrendously." Another round of laughter escaped her lips.

"You have no idea how difficult it was to find a painter with the correct level of ineptness. But, I wanted it to be perfect for you."

Feeling the love for her husband rising up within her, she set the painting down and wrapped her arms around him. It was both the strangest and the sweetest thing anyone had ever given her.

"I love you," she whispered, too overcome to speak any louder.

"I love you forever." With that, he sealed his mouth over hers then proceeded to sate her hunger for him.

In the end, she was proud to admit she was another success story for the House of Reform. So many women walked through the doors and left having found their true happiness. Now, Hannah was pleased to say she was one of them.

Her life had moved from trying, to perfect, in such a short time. And, although it was years later, she finally was able to marry the lord of her choosing.

Keep reading for a glimpse from Book 5 in the Reformed Rake series, *To Catch an Earl*.

Chapter 1

Lady Regina Serra sat forward in her chair as she listened intently to the grand lady sitting before her. The excitement of a new client at Lady Constance's House of Reform always appealed to her. Not to mention, her heart always went out to the people whenever they had a sad story. This lady was no exception.

"So, you understand why he must wed soon." The woman looked at her and Constance with pleading eyes.

"I hardly think being thirty years old is a reason for concern," Constance intoned, her eyes narrowed at the woman.

"Come now, Constance," Regina rushed in. "Can't you see the lady is highly concerned over her son's well-being?"

An amused smile worked at the corners of her friend's mouth. Constance was always willing to give her full opinion. Over the past six years they'd been running the House of Reform together, Regina had learned to never ask the woman a question for which she didn't want an honest answer.

"It's the truth, Lady Constance," Lady Burnham professed. "My son is quite lonely. He needs help to find himself a bride. If you can't help, I don't know who else I can turn to."

"There is no question we can help your son," Constance assured. "My comment was only in regard to your assumption that we understand his predicament has occurred due to his age."

Knowing she needed to solve this, Regina cleared her

throat. “Tell us when your son will be able to come meet with us, and we can arrange an instructor for him.”

The lady shook her head. “You misunderstand. Murphy will not be coming here. As a matter of fact, I don’t expect him to be overly pleased at the idea of accepting assistance. At least, he won’t be pleased at first.”

“Then, our help is impossible. We have never met your son and therefore can’t begin to formulate a plan for him.” Regina wondered if she’d made the wrong decision to side with the lady over her friend. Clearly, Lady Burnham was quite mad.

The countess let out a dainty laugh. “No, my dear. I need an instructor to pay a call to him at his townhouse.”

Regina exchanged a glance with Constance. The new initiative Regina had begun, including distributing flyers among members of the ton, had brought in numerous new clients. They were finally at a point where they could turn people away. However, Regina never backed down from a person in need. Especially, a challenge.

“Our classes are performed here to ensure the safety of our instructors, as well as to ensure the happiness of our clients,” Constance explained. “I’m not sure we have an instructor willing to take on such a chance.”

The countess turned her watery eyes on Regina. “Surely, there is something you can do. My dear son may be too proud to accept help, but he needs it regardless. I’m begging you.”

“I’m sure we will be able to arrange something.” Regina ignored Constance’s concerned look. “We will discuss your options and send word to you.”

The three women stood as the countess shot Regina a grateful smile.

“Thank you so much. My son will thank you as well. I promise.”

As the lady took her leave, Constance stood but remained in place. However, as soon as the woman was gone, her friend turned on her. Regina expected no less.

"What were you thinking? We can't help her."

Regina clicked her tongue. "You're wrong. We can help, and we certainly don't want to be known for turning clients away."

A look of indecision crossed Constance's face. "That may be, but I daresay the woman would have been inclined to understand before you went ahead and gave her hope."

"I couldn't help it," Regina defended herself. "I just feel so bad for them when they're desperate. What if Lord Burnham truly needs help? The poor man is likely too shy to come here. The little dear needs us."

An image of a timid man cowering behind the countess entered Regina's head, and her heart melted. The woman mentioned that her son never attended balls or social events with her, so overcoming his shyness would certainly be an issue. Once that was handled, he would need to be slowly inserted into social settings to give him confidence. Her mind raced as she worked out the details of his lessons for the unknown man. Excitement filled her. It was always this way for her.

"Or, you have it wrong." Constance crossed her arms. "He's not shy. He must be hideous. After being repelled from society, he's sworn off such events."

Regina shook her head, getting into the game. "No. Not this gentleman. He's tall, thin and has a nose that may be a little too large, but he's not hideous."

With a thoughtful nod of her head, Constance tapped her finger against her cheek. "I can see that, but he has gone prematurely bald. With no hair, that big nose and exaggeratedly large ears only stick out more."

Both women laughed.

Regina recovered first. "How can you not take pity on such a creature?"

"Very well. I concede. However, I still don't believe this is a good idea. We can't ask any of our instructors to put themselves in such a position."

"True. That's why we are not going to ask anyone. I'll go."

Constance shook her head. "You can't. I need you here. Someone must be available to check in on the classes."

"Sarah is capable. She's been with us longer than the other girls, so I think it's time for her to take on more responsibilities."

"What about Lord Reston? The man won't accept another instructor, apart from you."

"I know what you're trying to do, but it won't work. The marquis will have to arrange his schedule to accommodate my other clients. You can't convince me otherwise. I've already decided I shall be taking on the Earl of Burnham as a client."

Although she didn't appear pleased, Constance nodded her head in agreement. Regina knew she was the only logical choice. Over the years, she'd handled so many different clients, she could easily draw upon her knowledge to help the earl. If he was reluctant at first, she would handle it. She'd always managed before.

She rubbed her hands together as she itched to begin. The earl could very well count himself betrothed. She had a way with men. They always did her bidding, and Lord Burnham would be no different.

~ ~ ~

"You have done, what?" Murphy Cobb, Earl of Burnham, demanded to his mother as she stood erect before his desk.

"I said I have hired a lady to help you with your problem."

Gritting his teeth, Murphy leaned back in his chair and studied his mother. Her reluctance to sit down was only a ploy to tower over him. Considering her short stature, he couldn't blame her. However, that didn't stop him from wishing she would leave him be. She'd always done everything in her power to control his life, but this was crossing the line.

"And, what problem are you referring to? I was unaware that I was experiencing any difficulties. Please, enlighten me."

"Don't be obtuse. You know I'm referring to your lack of a wife."

His eyebrows shot up. "You are paying someone to wed me?"

She let out an exaggerated breath. "Of course not. The ladies at the House of Reform specialize in helping men find brides, not marrying the gentlemen themselves."

Not believing what he was hearing, Murphy closed his eyes. The woman had badgered him constantly about his unmarried state, but this was too much. He didn't need a matchmaking service. If he wanted a wife, there were several who would gladly volunteer.

"I see. You can inform the ladies I will not be needing their services."

"I can't do that." Shock sounded in her voice. "I've only just hired them."

"Then, you are the lucky one who has retained their services. I am not interested."

The glare she shot him was familiar as he'd seen it many times in his youth. "Why are you being obstinate in regard to this? I'm merely trying to help you."

Murphy let out a sigh as he sat back in his chair. She may think she was helping him, but in truth, she was only making him want to marry even less. After all, one nagging woman in the house was more than enough.

"I'm not interested in receiving your help, or that of anyone else. Tell your matchmaker she doesn't need to waste her time on me."

"This will not require much from you. Please, just talk to her."

Shaking his head, he firmed his resolve. "I've given you my decision. I refuse to go so far as to accept an introduction to her."

Without another word, his mother turned and marched from the room. This was not the first time she'd tried to force him to wed, and he knew it would not be the last. He would eventually marry to procure heirs, but not at present. He saw no need to alter his carefree life. Besides, life was so much more enjoyable with a different woman in his bed each night.

Several days later, he walked into his townhouse after having spent an enjoyable time in the bed of Lord Ashton's widow. The woman had been trying to capture his attention for quite some time now, and he'd finally decided to give her what she wanted. It was always immensely satisfying to see the sensual expression on a woman's face when he finally gave in to her.

He made his way to the study and dropped himself into his chair. This was the part of the day he enjoyed the most. His body was sated and relaxed while the room was quiet and still. Letting out a contented sigh, he let his head fall back against the chair.

A knock sounded at his door, and he let out a curse. It was as if the person could read his thoughts and blatantly disturbed him. At his silence, the knock came again. Although grudgingly, he granted entrance.

He prepared to tell the intruder exactly how he felt about the interruption, but when an unfamiliar woman appeared in the doorway, he stood as his surprise robbed him of the words. She, too, appeared surprised as she halted her steps and her smile fell. Curious. Why had she come to his study if she hadn't expected him to be there?

Taking the opportunity to study the enchanting creature, he allowed his eyes to scan her beauty. Golden-blond curls framed a sweet, round face that gave off an air of innocence. Her petite frame was covered by a gown that had clearly seen quite a few washings. This woman must have come to see his mother about a position. From what he could see, he would be glad to welcome her onto the staff and perhaps into his bed.

"May I help you?" He worked to hide his grin at her open perusal at him.

"Of course, I'm sorry to intrude. But, I'm looking for Lord Burnham."

"Well, you have found him." Murphy grinned.

Her eyes widened. "You are him? You are the Earl of Burnham?"

Having no idea what had happened to his reputation to obtain this level of disbelief, he held out his hands, palms up. "I'm afraid it's true. Now, who might you be?"

She shook her head. "No introductions. I have specific instructions."

Without waiting for him to offer, the woman proceeded into his office and stood before his desk. Her gaze searched his face. It was an unusual thing, and he had no idea what to make of her.

"If I can't know who you are, do you at least intend to tell me why you are here?"

The woman intrigued him. She was far more attractive up close, which he didn't think possible considering her beauty from a distance. The idea of taking this divine being to his bed stirred his no longer sated body. His reaction was unusual and definitely something he would like to pursue.

"May I sit?" She lifted one elegant brow.

"Please." He settled back into his chair as she claimed the one before him.

"Much better. Now, I'm here at the request of your mother. She has asked that I help you in your search for a wife."

As realization dawned, he narrowed his eyes. "Ah, yes. Now, I see why you skipped the introductions. You are the matchmaker."

She laughed. The sound of pure enjoyment struck him. He could listen to her laugh all day. The thought had him clenching his teeth. Many women laughed, so why should he enjoy hers more than others? Likely, his body hadn't gotten past the fact that she would not be hired on his staff, and considering her connection to his mother, she was unattainable.

"My lord, we don't offer matchmaking services. I'm here to guide you through the process of finding a personality that would work for you as a wife, and aiding you after you have selected a lady."

He crossed his arms. "My mother was mistaken. I don't need help to find a bride. If I wanted one, I would have one. Women aren't exactly repelled by me."

Seemingly undaunted, she tilted her head to the side. "I can see that. Then, you will be needing a woman who's more of a challenge. One who is not attracted to you."

It was his turn to laugh. "Women require very little. With my looks, my title, or my money, most women see something they want."

"But, you don't want them. After all, what can they offer you? A successful marriage is so much more than choosing the first woman who pays you any mind."

Although he could appreciate the woman's perseverance, he was in no mood to play games. "You are missing the point. I don't wish to marry at this time. Therefore, I have no need to think on any of this."

The woman nodded slowly, as if she knew something he didn't. "Everything makes so much more sense now. After what your mother said, I had the wrong impression of you. Now, I see that you can't handle a challenge."

A flash of anger shot through him, but he pushed it down. Women never understood a man's need to live at his own pace. They pushed and prodded until everyone around them was miserable. As such, he refused to give in to the insult.

"Perhaps, I can't."

"I greatly admire your courage for admitting such a thing." She stood. "I can see that I'm not needed. Your mother will be greatly disappointed to discover she has lost our bet."

His ears perked up. "Bet? I've never known my mother to engage in such an activity."

"Then, perhaps you don't know her as well as you thought." She turned and headed for the door. "Thank you for your time."

With a groan, he rounded his desk and approached her. "You can't leave after saying something like that. And, I suspect you know that, so go ahead and tell me what you are talking about."

The petite lady had to look up to face him. Bloody hell, she was exquisite. The sparkle in her deep brown eyes only added to her beauty. He silently lamented the fact he wouldn't be able to take her to bed. After all, with this much fight her passion would be undeniable. She would certainly be worth the effort.

"I'm sorry, my lord, but I don't feel inclined to do so. Perhaps another day."

He grinned. "You think it'll be so easy to get me to agree to see you again? You are quite wrong."

She tilted her head to the side as she studied his face. "Since this is to be our last meeting, I'll take pity on you. Your mother bet that you would have me in your bed in less than a week. I accepted her bet, knowing that you didn't have enough charm to so much as temp me to join you. So, good day, my lord."

Stunned, he stood there watching as the lady left his study. Not only was the mere idea that his mother would bet on such a thing unfathomable, but the lady had outright rejected him.

In all his thirty years, that had never happened to him. He wanted to turn and walk away. To wish her far away from him, but he couldn't. Because, whether he liked it or not, he was damned intrigued.

~ ~ ~

Regina leaned back in her chair and let out a sigh. Damien Serra, Marquis of Reston, simply shook his head at her. Rolling her eyes back at him, she looked away. Sometimes he could annoy her with just a look, and she suspected he knew it.

"I don't know why you keep doing this," Damien began. "You know you don't have to. I've made it clear—"

"Don't. It may be exhausting, but I enjoy working here. With Constance and Kaylee, I helped create the House of Reform. I've told you many times, I'm not leaving."

"And, I've reminded you many times that you're the daughter of a marquis. This isn't right."

Irritated, she stood and moved toward the window. "If it bothers you so much, you don't need to come see me anymore."

He laughed. "What would you have me do? Cancel my lessons with you? After this many years, I'll say I'm committed to it."

Unable to help her smile, she turned back around to face him. "That's the truth. More than one person has already remarked upon it. They think you have developed an interest in me."

"Then, let them believe what they will. If you have no desire to disclose our relationship, then I'll play the part." He grinned. "Oh, my dearest love, won't you come home to me?"

Her laughter was easy and helped her ease her thoughts. She could always count on Damien for that. Not only was he her cousin, but he was her best friend as well. She needed him now. After the events of the past three days, she'd been on edge. Ever since her meeting with Lord Burnham, in fact. As she'd left his study, she'd been convinced he would have called her back. She'd dealt with his type of gentleman before and issuing him that challenge should have worked. That was the part that bothered her most.

Over her time working at the House of Reform, she'd learned quite a bit, and she prided herself on her ability to read people and discern what they needed even before they themselves realized it. Had she been so wrong about the earl? It made her question all of her decisions.

"Regina? Where have you gone?" Concern laced Damien's words.

"I'm sorry. I have a new client that it appears I'm not going to be able to help. That doesn't sit well with me."

"Do you want to talk about it?" Damien leaned back in his chair and studied her with those eyes that always saw too much.

"Not particularly. Instead, tell me how matters are progressing with your betrothed? When do you see her again?"

The tight line of his mouth told her much. "I'll be making the trip to the country next week. I only have another few months until she's reached her eighteenth year, so I imagine it shall be one of my last visits."

"I wish you wouldn't have done this. I can help you find a wife who would suit you. Not a child that you hardly know."

"That description is not apt. I won't have her until she reaches marriageable age. Besides, this is the right thing to do. I set this up years ago and I'll see it through to the end."

Realizing the similarities between her cousin and Lord Burnham, she tilted her head and studied Damien. The man was quite a catch for any lady. Exactly like the earl, her cousin could boast the same qualities. Yet, Damien chose to go the simple route of deciding who he would marry by claiming the daughter of a man that Regina's own father, the previous Marquis of Reston, had been feuding with. She knew part of it was Damien's way of ending the trouble, but the rest of it was the ease of having the business of a wife over with.

"Why is this choice of bride preferable to selecting one on your own?"

Damien chuckled. "Is that a jest? Do you truly think I'd want to subject myself to the marriage mart? I'd be eaten alive."

Shaking her head, she ignored his comment. "I'm serious. You can have any woman you want, either as a wife or in your bed, but you don't even try."

"I don't have to. When I'm in need of a companion, they come to me. As far as a wife, it doesn't matter who I choose. They are all exactly the same."

She lifted an eyebrow, thoroughly insulted. "Am I as indistinguishable as the rest?"

"Of course not. I raised you to be different." He winked at her.

"Raised me? Hardly. I was twelve when I moved in with you."

"And eighteen when she took you back. Those are critical years for a young woman, and you were with me."

To her answering snort, he let out another peel of laughter. In truth, she couldn't exactly argue with him. He had in so many ways been responsible for her and a lot of her thoughts and desires were due to what she'd learned from him. The fact had been a trial for her mother when the woman had finally decided she wanted a daughter.

"Which is exactly why my unorthodox education makes me such a success at the House of Reform. But, still, I'm at a loss when it comes to your decision. From my professional experience, I'll be the first to tell you that you need someone you can chase, not the other way around."

His sigh was heavy. "Do we really need to do this? I already told you my decision is final."

"Please, Damien. It's actually helping me understand one of my clients better."

"Very well. Now, if I didn't have my bride already picked out, what would I want?" He squinted his eyes as he looked beyond her. "I suppose I would want someone who isn't exactly like the rest. I want someone who would give me something different. And, I suppose you're right. Having a lady who doesn't automatically throw herself in my bed would be a welcome change."

"That's exactly what I thought. Then, why didn't it work with him? The man reminds me a little of you. He should have taken my challenge without as much as a second of hesitation."

As she thought back over her conversation with Lord Burnham, she couldn't think of anything she could have done differently. It should have been enough. She wanted to return to his townhouse and demand he tell her why he hadn't given in already. The man would probably laugh at her. How could she pride herself in her abilities if she'd failed him?

"So, this is the client that you spoke of a moment ago? Regina, you can't help everyone. Don't stress about him."

Movement at the door caught her eye. To her surprise, Marvin, the butler, stood in the doorway. She frowned. The man was never selected to check in on the lessons. In part for his age, and the other part to keep the staff out of the ongoing lessons and allow their clients the ease of knowing their lessons were private.

"I'm so sorry to intrude, Lady Regina, but there is a gentleman here who is needing help. He is quite insistent, and Lady Constance has stepped out."

Exactly what she needed, she thought sarcastically. "May I inquire after his name?"

"Yes, my lady. He's Murphy Cobb, the Earl of Burnham."

At the sound of his name, the corners of her lips twitched against a hint of a grin. She had succeeded. Now, it was time to begin the earl's lessons.

Also from **Jenn Langston** and **Soul Mate Publishing**:

THE PERFECT SERIES
by Jenn Langston

HIS PERFECT BRIDE

Richard Carrack received the title of Marquis of Stonemede upon his father's death six months ago. Knowing of the duties associated with the title, he decides to marry and spend the remainder of his days tending to the estate. His requirements for his bride are simple; he wishes her to be obedient and calm-spirited. When circumstances place him in the path of Lady Brianna Denton, whose wild ways make her an unsuitable candidate, he lies about his identity to discourage her from pursuing him for his title.

Brianna Denton knows what she wants out of life. She wishes to marry an untitled lord and live the remainder of her days in the country with no obligations. Only then can she spend her free time painting. When she meets Mr. Richard, she decides he would make the perfect husband. Little does she know, her boldness puts her in a position where she must decide between what she always thought she wanted and what her heart is telling her.

Available now on Amazon: HIS PERFECT BRIDE

HIS PERFECT GAME

Greyson Thorpe, Viscount Merrick, wants respectability above all else. Knowing the fastest way to achieve that state comes through marriage, he challenges Hammond Everett, the Duke of Donetic, to a card game. After winning the match, the duke agrees to exchange his daughter's hand in marriage for the forgiveness of his debts.

Willimena Abigail Everett had no desire to marry after experiencing the violent nature of men at her father's hand. When Viscount Merrick arrives, she has no choice other than to obey her father and marry him. Will she be able to set aside her previous beliefs about men and judge her husband by his own merits?

After obtaining good social standing, Greyson sends his bride to the country; however, he finds himself missing her. Following her to the estate, he discovers she had been living a double life. Will he discover her secrets and control his burning desire for her at the same time?

Available now on Amazon: **HIS PERFECT GAME**

HIS PERFECT LADY

Notorious rake Jonathan Alastair, Viscount Linwood, has spent six years proving he has moved on after being cast off by the only woman he ever cared for. When their paths cross again, his desire for her re-ignites. Intending to pursue her for one night of pleasure, he discovers he wants more from the one woman who got away. But can he overlook her previous rejection in order to forge a new relationship?

Mrs. Catherine Gates is cursed as evident by the swift deaths of two husbands, both on their wedding nights. Brought to London at the insistence of her uncle to remarry, seeing Jonathan again makes her body ache, however she must maintain her distance to save him from the curse. Unable to fight her building passion, can Catherine find a way to break the curse that threatens his life and her everlasting happiness?

Available now on Amazon: **HIS PERFECT LADY**

CATCHING THE BARON

Kenneth Rawson, Baron Berwick, needs to marry an heiress, but when he discovers his new stable boy, Sam, is actually a woman, he finds himself intrigued. Knowing his choice of a bride must be based on more than blinding passion, he makes his stance on not marrying her very clear.

Samantha Jenkins disguises herself as a boy after the tragic loss of her parents in order to escape a landlord who claimed she owed a debt. After spending time with Baron Berwick, she finds herself falling in love. However, a telling conversation with him makes her realize he only meant to remain with her until he weds.

Will Kenneth realize he is lost without her and beg for forgiveness? Will Samantha forgive him?

Available now on Amazon: CATCHING THE BARON

WINNING THE DUKE

Grace Denton's first Season solidifies her decision to never marry. How can she? The London gentlemen are boorish and unappealing. When reunited with the handsome, yet brooding Braiden Everett, his hidden charm captivates her. If she marries him, she could obtain her dream of having a child of her own and a husband she can stand to be around. Despite his contentions to a union, she is confident their connection will help him as well. She has already seen how her proximity begins to heal his pain. Faced with his indifference, will she be able to control her building passion for him?

Discovering women's heartless nature, Braiden Everett, Duke of Donetic, has sworn off the foolish idea of love. Upon reentering his life, the sweet and spirited Grace illuminates the only light left in his dark world. He agrees her marriage of convenience proposal has some merit. But is it wise? He's intrigued by her mind and tempted by her body. However, he refuses to lose his heart again. Besides, she deserves more than he can give. After all, he's forgotten how to love, hasn't he?

Available now on Amazon: **WINNING THE DUKE**

REDEEMING THE EARL

Rebecca Doutree has a secret. A big secret. She is the author of the famous Unscandal Sheet. The anonymity provides her a unique position to discover the legitimacy behind local gossip and to aid the wrongly accused in her publication. When she meets the Earl of Dunmore, the facts hidden underneath the rumors surrounding him beckon her to unveil them. However, as she spends time with him to secretly uncover the truth, she discovers concentrating on her mission to be much harder than she anticipated. What is it about him that affects her so?

Charles Edwards, the Earl of Dunmore, only wants one thing: an heir. Yet, as a four-time widower, he is surrounded by scandal. Knowing of his duty to the earldom, he ventures to London to clear his name and obtain wife number five. Coming across the husky-voiced Miss Doutree, he turns his attention to her. To his surprise, he finds himself tempted by her like never before. The new feeling is discomforting, and he isn't sure he likes it. Can he marry her and still remain the same man? Or, more importantly, will she survive the endeavor?

Available now on Amazon: **REDEEMING THE EARL**

TOUCHED BY FIRE SERIES
by Jenn Langston

EMBRACING THE KNIGHT
(TOUCHED BY FIRE BOOK 1)

Miss Claire Ashford knows exactly what she wants out of life — to marry for love. When she finds herself alone in the woods with none other than notorious rake Ian Michael Caldwell, Viscount Knightly, her chances of a proper match are ruined. He is willing to sacrifice himself for the sake of her reputation, but she is determined not to marry anyone out of obligation.

For years, Ian has wanted nothing more than to, one day, marry Miss Claire Ashford. When fate forces them into a compromising situation, he vows to do just that. In spite of every effort, she refuses his suit. Not one to easily give up, Ian drafts assistance from an unlikely source.

As her first season continues, Claire finds it increasingly difficult to keep her distance from Ian. His charm, and ability to stir feelings inside of her she didn't know existed, makes it hard to remember why she refused him in the first place. With his relentless pursuit and her weakening resolve, she desperately wants to give in to him. However, after seeing he hasn't changed his rakish ways, how can she trust him not to break her heart, again?

Available now on Amazon: **EMBRACING THE KNIGHT**

ENSLAVING THE DAY
(TOUCHED BY FIRE BOOK 2)

One night's mistake finds Lady Annalise Hera in a very compromising situation. Pregnant, unmarried, and on her way to Gretna Green. Although Baron Dailey put her in this position, she belatedly realizes she can't marry him and will do anything to get him to release her. Even lie. After all, life would be better as a disgraced, unwed mother than the wife of a cocky, irritating man she can barely tolerate.

Gordon Ashford, Baron Dailey, never thought much about his friend's younger sister. That was, until she grew into a beautiful woman. Now, after one drunken night when he took her innocence, he can't seem to get her out of his head. With her constant refusal of him, and perpetual need to argue, he should give her up. But he can't, even though she's told him she's not carrying his child.

Convincing her to accept him proves to be near impossible, but he's not one to easily give up.

Available now on Amazon: **ENSLAVING THE DAY**

ENSNARING LORD STARSEN (TOUCHED BY FIRE BOOK 3)

Tethered to a restrictive life on her half-brother's estate, Lady Isabella Rossland tries her best to find her own happiness. With the dreary gentlemen nearby not appealing to her restless spirit, she's left with few escape options. Then, a man she's known for years catches her attention, and she's intrigued. What could make a man so aloof act so unexpectedly? It seems there is more to Lord Starsen than the person he presents to society.

Marcus Hera, Earl of Starsen, vows to lead a calm existence, due to a fiery tragedy during his reckless youth where he suffered permanent injuries. As such, he wants a dutiful wife to complement his life. When his path crosses unexpectedly with the impetuous Lady Isabella, he's shocked to find himself drawn to her. He resists his undeniable attraction to her, choosing duty over the confusing emotions she's wrought in him.

Realizing Marcus has a spirit that matches her own, Isabella makes her intentions known, only to discover he has made a promise to another. Not one to easily give up, Isabella must convince him she is the right woman for him. With his impending betrothal approaching, time is running out. Has she pierced his barriers and won his heart, or is she too late?

Available now on Amazon: **ENSNARING LORD STARSEN**

ENCHANTING THE DUKE OF DEMOON (TOUCHED BY FIRE BOOK 4)

Miss Carolyn Ashford wants one thing from marriage: love. After spending one informative season in London, she discovers the rarity of the emotion. Resigning herself to a life of spinsterhood, she leans on her brother's charity. When she stumbles upon a secret garden on the Duke of Demoon's property, she sets to restore it. As the garden comes to life, so does her spirit, as though she's finally found her place.

Edmund Marsham, Duke of Demoon, for over a decade hasn't shown his scarred face—the only outward sign of surviving a devastating fire in his youth—to anyone outside of Moonlight Castle. Seeking sanctuary from his callous mother, he rides off to his grandmother's secret garden. Once there, he is surprised to find a young woman has brought life back into the neglected place. Although he keeps his identity from her, they form an unexpected friendship. Before long, Edmund begins to want impossible things. Things he knows he can't have.

Carolyn knows her time with Edmund is limited considering he has no desire for a wife or child. With another man vying for her attention, she knows with him she will have everything that Edmund denies her. She attempts to distance herself from Edmund, but her traitorous body has other plans. Will her heart survive a temporary romance with Edmund, and will those memories be enough to satisfy a lifetime without him?

Available now on Amazon: **ENCHANTING THE DUKE OF DEMOON**

REFORMED RAKES SERIES
By Jenn Langston

TO LOVE A MARQUIS
(REFORMED RAKES BOOK 1)

Miranda Jayne Whittier flees to London, escaping marriage to the Marquis of Melbourne, a man she's never met who is surrounded in rumors she can't overlook. With the last of her pin money spent, she accepts employment at Lady Constance's House of Reform. Assigned to Viscount Harken, a handsome but difficult man who doesn't make their association easy, she is determined to help him and, in the process, solidify her position. She soon discovers he deserves better than he believes.

Anson Greenleaf, Marquis of Melbourne, thought collecting his betrothed would be a simple matter, but he'd been wrong. Miss Whittier has taken on a position in the city, which presents him with a unique opportunity. Using one of his lesser known titles, he poses as a client. Instead of learning why she ran from him, he finds himself drawn to her and is determined to charm her. Before long, he forms an intense desire for her. One he must fight.

When Miranda discovers the Marquis of Melbourne followed her to London, she fights against the need to leave the position she loves and the man she's come to care for. As her life falls apart, she's forced to give up the viscount. When she learns of the Marquis's deception, she realizes she can't marry him. After all, she knows exactly what he wants in a bride. And, she knows it's not her.

Available now on Amazon: **TO LOVE A MARQUIS**

TO TAME A VISCOUNT (REFORMED RAKES BOOK 2)

Kaylee Shepherd knew there was much more to life than marriage when she'd left her stepbrother's house to begin Lady Constance's House of Reform three years ago. Now, more than ever, she is determined to experience everything she is able before she is too old to enjoy it. When Simon Highgate, Viscount Washburne, makes his interest in her known, she seizes the opportunity. One night with him is more than she could imagine and one she will never forget.

Once Simon reached his twenty-fifth year, a special stipulation in his father's will was revealed to him. Regardless of his desires, he must wed a maiden of proper breeding whose behavior is above reproach, or his birthright will pass to his cousin. Duty-bound, he engages the House of Reform to aid his search for a bride. Unfortunately, the more time he spends with the enchanting woman assigned to the task, Miss Shepherd, the more he wishes Kaylee fit the requirements. Instinctively, he knows Kaylee would make him a perfect wife. If it weren't for his sisters, he would go against his father's wishes and claim Kaylee, regardless of her social standing. With his hands tied, he plans to make the most of the time they have together until he must wed another.

As Simon's attention toward Kaylee increases, she finds denying him more difficult. Although marriage isn't what she wants, she can see the merit in sharing stolen moments with him. However, each instance she gives in to him makes it more difficult to control the building passion she feels for him. Worse yet, she's beginning to wonder if she will be able to handle watching him wed another and leave her to live out her life alone.

TO TEACH A GENTLEMAN (REFORMED RAKES BOOK 3)

Genevieve Jubal is desperate for marriage to escape her abusive father, but she is cripplingly shy and has failed during two different Seasons. As such, her controlling mother makes arrangements for her to attend Lady Constance's House of Reform. Alone in a classroom, a gentleman mistakes Genevieve for an instructor and demands she speak to him in French. She complies, then realizes he hasn't a clue what she is saying. This knowledge makes conversing flow with an ease she's never known. With that truth, Genevieve accepts a position to teach French to the Earl of Andel, and in the process, grow confident while speaking in English with potential suitors as well.

Christopher Valentine, Earl of Andel, has one purpose for his trip to London: learn French to marry his chosen bride, then return to the comfort of his country estate. With the instructor he stumbled upon at the House of Reform, he knows this task shall be a simple feat, but he's discovering concentration with Miss Jubal nearby to be quite difficult. The more time he spends with her, the more he questions his decision to marry a woman he doesn't know. However, when his French bride of choice arrives in London, he is torn between his duty to her and his desire for a woman he's come to appreciate.

Realizing Christopher is destined for another didn't stop Genevieve from developing a desire for a future with him. He is exactly the kind of husband she wants although she knows she can't have him. She resolves to help him with his chosen lady, but she is determined to enjoy a few stolen kisses before he's lost to her forever.